Secrets

Valerie Holmes

Friends and Foes - Book 2

Other books by Valerie Holmes include

Friends and Foes series:

Betrayal

Yorkshire Saga Series: (stand-alone novels)

To Love Honour and Obey
For Richer, For Poorer
To Have and To Hold
In Sickness and In Health

North Riding Novellas

The Baronets Prize
Hannah of Harpham Hall
Discovering Ellie

Regency ~ Friends and Foes
Book 2

"No person is your friend who demands your silence, or denies your right to grow."

-Alice Walker

"In the End, we will remember not the words of our enemies, but the silence of our friends."

-Martin Luther King, Jr.

"Do nothing secretly, for Time

sees and hears all things,

and discloses all."

Sophocles

The Battle of Talavera, Spain, 1809

Lord Oscar Farrington awoke gripping his side, wet with his own blood. Following the night's battle, he had been riding towards Lieutenant-General Wellesley's staff, when in the early morning light, a stray bullet hit.

The recommenced battle noise resounded in his throbbing head. Mud spattered the air as each cannon blast ricocheted around him. He hastily balled his clean neckerchief, soaked it in brandy from his pocket flask and pressed it to the wound. The fallen were not so fortunate; a blur of horses, mangled men, and confusion reigned. Try as he might Oscar could not fathom which direction would lead him to friends and which to Britain's foes.

Thankfully, his message satchel with despatches still inside remained slung across his body; he struggled to rise but its weight pulled him back down into the bloodied mud. Again and again, he slipped helplessly back. Oblivion hit as a body fell atop him.

Silence had an eerie quality as the cold seeped through to Oscar's bones, yet he was grateful that he felt it – he actually felt something – he lived, yet all was quiet and cold.

Slowly and painfully, he turned his head and opened his eyes as a dead weight was lifted off him. Blurred figures moved like spectres amongst the fallen. Thieves, he thought, plundering the dead, or were they the enemy? Had Wellesley won or lost? A figure stooped over him, and strong younger arms lifted him up.

He flinched, his side burned, the pain so intense.

"Lord Farrington, you are safe now," the voice said.

"Were we victorious…?" his words were no more than a whisper even to his own ears.

"There is a temporary cessation of hostilities to allow both sides to collect their wounded… We will be victorious, sir." The voice spoke with calm authority.

Oscar felt his back rest against a farm cart. The sickly-sweet smell of death, mingled with gunpowder in the air but, as wheels turned, his body was jerked; his battle had ended here, and he was being taken away.

After what seemed like an agonising age, but could have been minutes, the cart stopped, and the face of an angel appeared as he was pulled up into a sitting position. Oscar breathed deeply; he would not scream like an injured child.

"I know you…" he muttered, "You are…" his voice drifted off as the soldier lifted him over his shoulders. Oscar knew the man; the golden hair was not the glow of an angel, it was human, possibly his saviour. He could not lose his life here, not now. "Lieutenant Arrow…"

"Yes, sir, Micah Arrow at your service, and now I have you. You shall have to forgive my humble quarters, sir, but I can get you cleaned up as we wait for the surgeon."

"No butcher, Arrow! You clean me up and find a trained medic and I will reward you, my good man. You must see that these despatches are taken to Wellesley post haste. Only to him!" He gasped with desperation.

"Yes, sir."

"Good man, and Arrow…" Lord Farrington coughed.

"Yes, sir?"

"I always repay my debts."

"I'll do my best, sir," Micah said.

"No one can do more," Oscar whispered and sighed as he slipped back into the bliss of oblivion.

Chapter 1

April 1816, North Yorkshire, England

Micah scraped his boots outside Dibbledale's vicarage door and was not surprised when it quickly opened.

"There you are, Micah!" The welcoming voice of his mother sounded relieved to see him safely back from his morning ride.

"Good morning, Mother. Was there something specifically you wanted of me?"

"Yes. I worry. So many years have passed since you and your father stepped up in that buggy to whisk you off to join your regiment. When I think of the horror those innocent eyes must have seen," she said, and shook her head.

"Mother, I am no innocent, and I only went for a ride!"

"You do not realise how hard it was for me; the endless days of worry for your safe return – our only son. You only came home once in all that time."

"I am safely returned now."

"I awaited your correspondence … there was so little…" her voice drifted off with more than a hint of reprimand.

"Mother, I was at war! Often nowhere near my regiment and…" Micah silenced, realising his work as an Exploring Officer was far more dangerous than his mother could possibly comprehend as he had ventured behind enemy lines. It was also highly confidential.

His mother waved her hand to dismiss his words. "Never mind your preoccupation with your fellow officers and the adventures you partook. I can well imagine the horror of poor food and cold nights under thin blankets, surrounded by foreigners and the common folk." She sniffed.

Micah did not comment for he could add lice, bedbugs, when they had beds, war, and mutilation, but those words were not for her delicate ears.

"However, your father and I have some excellent news for you." Her smile, as always, was infectious even if her manner bordered crotchety.

Her overly enthusiastic words did nothing to allay Micah's fears that the 'news' may well be regarding some matchmaking scheme. Since he had returned only two weeks since, he had struggled to settle into the once calm water that was the village of Dibbledale. For the past blood-spilling years, he had longed to return to the lovely village of his childhood, no more camping out in the rain, hiding, watching over his shoulder as he ventured into enemy land.

He would soon meet up with Lord Farrington and conclude their business, then life for the Arrows and Dibbledale would definitely improve. His mother would be in her element, and he would make her truly proud and hope that her pride did not become her undoing.

He had heard a threat rumoured locally that could well upset this haven of peace and normality. Micah had learnt that there was a plan that could upset the villagers' way of life which angered him. He had seen workers struggle to survive in the developing mill towns as he made his way northeast and did not want that to happen here. Micah was far from convinced there was a need for the tanning workplace he had heard whispers about.

Micah's own plan for the village was to protect its tranquil setting, for it to grow in a way that was harmonious to its rural way of life. If industry was to come here then he wanted it to be where the workers had a basic education and were fed well; poverty and grime must not become Dibbledale's future. This was his vision. His mother fussed over him to cast off his riding coat as if that act alone would prevent him leaving again.

"Do tell me your news, before you burst. You need not fuss over me – I am a man grown." He placed a protective hand on her shoulder that she instantly shrugged away. Her heart poured love over him, her only surviving child, expressed in every gesture and word, from organising his meals, his clothes – she had offered to fill his diary for him, but he had declined. Yet the day had not arrived when she could open her arms and hug him close to her; it was something she never did, not even when he was a child.

"Sir Benedict Adams has invited us to dine with him and his family. Lady Adams will send an invitation soon!" Her light blue eyes sparkled like cut gems.

Micah saw that sin of pride exude from her face but made no quip about it. "Really, how lovely for you and Father," he said, hoping to slide out of the reference to the collective 'we'. "I am sure that the gratitude you both have for this invitation will warm your hearts for weeks." Why invite the local vicar's family to dinner? It would hardly be a socially balanced table, Micah wondered. "You are included – specifically, Micah! You must not offend Sir Benedict as he has relatives in high places. Bring news to him of your brave exploits in foreign places. We are depending upon you to entertain them with your first-hand account. But remember you are a gentleman. No soldier's talk when ladies are present. The dinner is to honour you and all those brave officers you represent." She nodded her head to stress this point.

"Mother, I do know how to behave in the presence of my 'betters'." He let the last word slip out slowly. She knew her place in God's scheme of things and never challenged it. Micah thought of all the returnees desperate for work. Every man had given so much for their country. The reality was missed on many a mother who saw their young sons filled with national pride and dreams of being heroes go to war, but when they returned – if they returned, even if their mortal beings were still whole, their souls had learned to kill, felt fear, witnessed all manner of cruelty against men, women and children. How could they return the same people as they were when they left? No, the strong and the lucky survived, but some were haunted by the visions of nightmares. "What about all those brave soldiers in the rank and file, Mother? So many did not return, so many men have been injured, unable to provide for themselves or their families."

"There are provisions for the poor and the good Lord provides, does he not when asked?"

Micah did not reply. His ship had docked at Plymouth where the sights that greeted his return shocked him, despite his wartime experiences. The number of men that did not have employment was striking, the able bodied along with those who had lost limbs.

From the south coast he had travelled via London to Norwich to fulfil an obligation. A promise made to a fallen officer on his death bed, to visit his family, relate a heroic account and return a few personal belongings. Pressed to stay a few days, Micah had realised that the numbers of unemployed ex-soldiers were many, their pre-war jobs taken by others. Whilst sitting in an inn he had overheard talk of discontent. The kind of threats that, if he had heard in Spain, he would have fed back to his superiors, but these were his fellow countrymen and he found he sympathised with them. So, he had left unobserved and gave thanks for his better fortune. He swore that he would find a way to help a few of the returnees and protect his rural home from becoming a desperate place like the ones he had passed through. His path was clear, and he had a plan.

Micah calmed his indignation that his mother's ignorance of the situations many faced was so openly revealed. She was a gentle lady, cosseted within a comfortable house, who rarely mixed with the congregation his father so dutifully served. There was no point in rebuking her, but he would make her see the world as it was outside the village, if he could.

"Their skills can still be used if they are given instruction and a chance. They may be poor but are still valuable and needed. No man should feel useless or helpless."

"A real man would not live so. A man should always know his worth." She waved a dismissive hand before Micah could form a rebuke. "Yes, yes, of course, I understand. However, our brave officers represent all of them." She entered the dining room. "Your words would complement any sermon, Micah."

Micah stifled an impulse to laugh at her waspish retort. He had unintentionally taken the conversation away from the topic, she wanted him to show enthusiasm for and to the harsh realities of life.

Mrs. Ruth Arrow had little knowledge of 'lords and ladies' but always tried to put on the appearance of being well informed, who was proud of her husband and their position at the heart of the community. She only ventured into the village when required. Her domain comprised of the church, its church hall and the vicarage which were all organised with efficiency.

"Very well, Mother, I shall attend if the invitation has been extended to our family because of my return. It will be my privilege and duty to escort my parents. I am sure that Sir Benedict's dinners lack for nothing, unlike those of some of his tenants." He raised a defiant eyebrow.

Ruth tut-tutted at him. "You will not talk like that! You know he married well to Lady Ashley Donaldson; the family are influential in the horse world. The family goes back generations, so, they both deserve our respect."

Micah was tempted to say that even the night soil man in the village had a family that went back generations, or he simply would not exist, but he understood what she meant.

"Besides, their beautiful niece is visiting, fresh out into the world. It is well-known that she is exquisite, simply breath-taking in looks, and Sir Benedict dotes on her."

How easily her mother had made the fine lady sound like one of the family's own mares – excellent blood stock!

"You will be on your absolute best behaviour, Micah, and do not let any of your soldier's language slip out. I know you will have heard enough of it from the rank and file!"

Micah sighed. "I apologise if you found my comment offensive, Mother. However, I am not seeking a wife; I have just been set free from the service… believe me the last thing on my mind is to tie myself down. I will spend my life with a special person of my choosing." His circumstances had changed. They did not know yet by how much. Micah did not need to grovel and curry favour of his 'betters'.

"Young man do not flatter yourself that you would stand a chance of consideration in Sir Benedict's eyes. How many people of standing marry partners of their own choosing anyway? Surely, need and sensible matches are opportune, love grows in time once you know each other. You may have done well for yourself as a lieutenant, but Miss Donaldson is beyond your reach. However, if your father had been a more ambitious man and made bishop, you may have had a place in the running for her," she said and sniffed. "Perhaps though, they may know someone who is more disposed to marrying a young war-hero of learning with charm – and has held an officer's rank."

"Mother, be grateful you have a loving husband who dotes on you. Father likes to be amongst his villagers, not hovering above them, somewhere beyond their reach." Micah folded his arms.

"Yes, he does, I have to have his clothes laundered by Betsy over at Mrs. Weeks' establishment – mind you, she does such a good job. Honestly, the places he goes to I am surprised we have not succumbed to an ague! You sound as though you have missed your vocation, Micah. Perhaps you too could take up the cloth and preach!" she huffed.

"No, for my sins are too great." He laughed at her amazed expression, but guilt gnawed at his heart for he had killed men in battles and injured others. He had done so through the need to save his or his men's life, but it was still the taking of lives and that was breaking the Lord's commandment. How to be a soldier then and survive in this hostile world where sin ran rife and keep a clear conscience?

Ruth shook her head and bid him to follow her further into the dining room. Now, she was in her element. Micah understood that for all the years he was away fighting she had worried herself grey that he would fall or be captured; he had tried not to dwell on the prospect when out there. When on a mission he was so alert that he had never felt so alive, despite the dangers.

Relenting, Micah allowed her to fuss over him, but after this initial month was up, Micah would explain all to them, once Lord Farrington confirmed everything was signed, sealed and delivered. Their lives would change for ever. Then his plan could be put into fruition.

In Dibbledale, Wilfred Underwood, the blacksmith, clearly understood that you needed to offer something more than the bog-standard services to gain a reputation and attract custom from further afield. Instantly, an image of Underwood's wilful daughter, Imogen, came to mind. Micah wondered who the lucky man was who had captured that beautiful spirit, for certain she would have wed by now. If only he had not gone to war, he would have courted her, but there was no point in pondering what might have been. Yet her image had stayed with him through many a long night, until the day he married.

Micah had already been in contact with Jamie, an unfortunate young soldier who had lost his right leg from the knee down. Jamie could carve a fallen log into a work of art. He would arrive soon, and Micah saw him as the first worker in his new venture. He intended to get Underwood onside too.

The blacksmith was one man who had the foresight to be an active participant. Micah had the foresight and the means, but not the skills. However, those he could easily acquire.

He realised that the hum in his ears was his mother berating him for talking of sins in a frivolous way. Micah let her words drift on the air as she piled food onto his plate, enough to keep him fuelled for the entire day. The pheasant pie was filling, but unnecessary, but he ate, lost in thought, not realising how hungry he was.

"Micah!" his mother's sharp word caught him out. "Do you not listen to me?" She was clearly exasperated with him.

"No, I do not. Sorry, Mother," he said and lifted a fork full of food. 'This is delicious.'

Chapter 2

Dust filled shafts appeared as Miss Imogen Underwood opened the cottage door letting bright Spring sunshine flood the interior. She listened as her mother sang a Gaelic tale of faeries and battles; Imogen appreciated the enticing smell of warmed oats, lovingly stirred by her mother.

"Morning, Mama."

Pickles, her mother's motley adopted hound, wagged its tail as Imogen crossed the threshold and entered the small, secluded cottage that her father and mother still lived in, within the forest. Once greeted, Pickles laid down lazily in the warmth of the sun.

"Aye, it is that. What are you doing up here, Imogen? I thought you would be working with your pa today. Mrs. Weeks is good to let you sleep in her spare room, better than a cot bed by my fire again."

"She is a good person. I will be with Papa later. Since he showed my pieces of jewellery to folk at the Gorebeck market I have been busy making more. They seem to think he is a jeweller as well as a blacksmith. With his large hands!" She laughed and leaned over to scratch Pickles' ear.

Mary glanced at her. "Hmm. Are you still finding time to teach some classes at the school?" Her petite mother sounded unimpressed as she picked up her chopping board and began to prepare the stew that would cook for hours over the fire for her husband's return from the village. "We are not desperate for extra coin, Imogen, like some poor souls. If you are working too hard, we shall

pay your room rent. You are a young lady. I did not want
you ruining your hands, until they are tough and hard like mine. You know your letters and numbers; I want better for you. Being in the village will see you have it."

"I have two wonderful parents who I adore and who spoil me. I will not have you pay for me, Mama, when I can pay my way. It was you who taught me my letters and numbers, yet you settle for such labour here?" Imogen was torn. She loved the cottage, but as she had grown, just like her married sisters before her, she had now moved out. There had been an eight-year gap before Imogen arrived and so she hardly knew her siblings as they had moved away and rarely visited.

"I labour out of love!" Mary exclaimed, then softened her manner. "No, lass, I want you to have a life that is easier than ours. Now enough chatter and let me get on with my chores. Your destiny is not in the woods, like us. In Dibbledale Mrs. Weeks can introduce you to folk. You can keep an eye on Wilfie for me. See he does not need anything," Mary continued.

Imogen smiled at her mother's affectionate shortening of her husband's name and tucked a stray auburn curl behind her ear. "Why don't you come with me, Mama? It would do you good to see folk. There is a cottage coming vacant at the end of Church Lane; it has two separate bedrooms. We could live together again…"

Dark eyes cast her a knowing stare. "I don't need anything to do me good. I am feeling fine. Now off you go. If you see wild garlic on the way back, select two handfuls of young leaves for me, and pass them back to your pa, he can bring them home later."

"I know you love the woods, but couldn't you come in with me?" Imogen persisted willing her mother to agree

– just once. She loved her mother dearly but could not understand why living in the village scared her so. Imogen sensed Mary's fear whenever the topic was raised, then she turned away from her, the subject changed.

"Oh, and if you see any gorse flowers, eat a few by all means, but give him some of them to bring back too. Now I must get the dandelions collected before Old Amy comes by for some of my tea leaves; she gets dropsy you know. Never mind. Now you best be on your way."

Imogen took a deep breath, infuriated at her mother's total disregard for her question. She watched her as she dropped the chopped vegetables into the pot and bent to pick up her favourite gathering basket before walking out into the light of day. Imogen stood a head taller than her mother. Pickles followed his mistress outside. He was a scruffy ungainly, rough-haired hound, but gentle as a summer's breeze and as light in spirit.

After cleaning her bowl and cup, Imogen fastened her bonnet and pulled on her comfortable riding boots that she always left by the door. They had been a present from her father the previous Spring. Imogen picked up her own basket and hurried outside latching the door behind her. The path from the cottage crossed the narrow Church Lane that cut through the woodland and led straight into the village of Dibbledale.

Water droplets glistened on the grass and ferns, like the 'faerie jewels' her mother had told her of in such tales as a child. The air was fresh, so she held her shawl close and breathed in deeply, her peaked bonnet shielding her eyes from the still low sun. Tempting as it was to cast it aside and run across open fields with her thick auburn hair flying wild behind her, she knew that she should behave more as a young lady. Her wild curls were neatly restrained in a bun.

Her mother was surrounded by her beloved wildlife – the source of so many of her remedies, dyes and 'nature's blessings' as she called the food that she would collect, dry, Pickles, preserve or store so they had a ready supply of nourishing food to keep them through the long dark winters.

Locals often made the trek to their door, drawn by her the remedies, nature gave readily, but she would accept a gift of a fresh baked loaf, a slice of ham, wool, and fabric; whatever they offered she accepted with good grace. Here in the forested outskirts of the village, life was tranquil, but things were changing.

Imogen suspected that the daily trek her father made from the woodland cottage to his forge in Dibbledale was becoming burdensome to him on top of his daily toil. What could she do about it if her mother would not move and her father did not insist upon it? Parents could be so stubborn.

Chapter 3

Micah strode out of the vicarage into the sunshine and smiled, admiring the peace and beauty that stretched out before him. His old home, where his father had been the incumbent for more years than he cared to remember, had hardly changed since he left. Now he valued the simple village life he had taken for granted before his world spun in the chaos of war. How proud he had been when his officer rank in the Light Dragoons Regiment was purchased for him. Yet nine years in service to his king had passed by so quickly.

He glanced back at the vicarage and saw the slight figure of his doting mother waving to him. Micah raised his hand in acknowledgement. How much her fussing had annoyed his younger self and yet, whilst away at war, he had realised how much that love had been missed.

The trees were finally showing their new leaves. The yellow broom made a colourful bank in the lane's hedgerow that dipped towards Dibbledale. Saint Cuthbert's parish church and the vicarage were on a small hill just outside the village. Micah stopped to admire the newly bloomed clumps of primrose nestling amongst the grass. He was home and at peace.

Micah's boyhood was spent climbing trees, hiding from invisible foes and holding up spectral carriages as an imagined highwayman. All before fourteen. The rekindled child in him took over and he ventured off Church Lane and into the edge of the Bagby Estate; Church Lane was a boundary separating Bagby and Denton woodland.

Picking his way through the grass, he admired the budding bluebells pushing their way upward. Spring was a time of revival and that is what he planned for Dibbledale.

Micah needed time to consider. When was it opportune to explain to his mother and father about his initial ill-fortune and the ultimate good fortune in the last year? How would they take his news? Micah's mother would no doubt be filled with horror when she was first told that he had married a foreign lady, but then when he explained his current circumstances, would she forgive all? He thought she might.

Micah swung a leg over a fallen tree trunk, but then, as the metal's edge caught his eye, he froze. Keen eyes saw the danger and the notion of his peaceful village suddenly dispersed – man traps, never before had he seen such things around Dibbledale. The woodland had always been open to all. The food it provided was free, the fallen wood taken as needed by the villagers for repairs – so what had changed?

He placed his feet down carefully and looked around for a fallen branch. Readying to thrust it into the jaws of the metal teeth, his attention was caught by a sound.

Dropping the branch, he stepped behind a stout elm. He had learnt at a very young age to avoid Jethro Kell the Bagby's gamekeeper; he waited to see if the man appeared.

The figure that emerged was light of foot and small. A lad was making his way toward the lane; he was obviously taking a short cut to Dibbledale but seemed totally unaware of the hidden danger.

If Micah shouted to warn him, he might run as, like himself, he was trespassing, so Micah skirted the trees carefully ready to cut him off as he neared. With one swift move he grabbed the lad by the scruff and pulled him close.

"Be still!" Micah ordered. The lad squirmed and tried to kick out, but Micah had him.

"Still," he ordered.

"Get off me! Let go… please!" the lad pleaded, but Micah needed him to be calm so that he could explain about the traps. If there was a gamekeeper about, they could be both shot as trespassers. Where was his peace now?

As Imogen returned to the village, to her left were the wild woods that were thick and rose up the bank to the moor road. To her right was the woodland belonging to Thurley Manor, recently bought up by Sir Benedict Adams.

"Get off me! Let go… please! I weren't stealing owt!" The pitiful screams of a young lad resounded through the trees.

Imogen's grip on her shawl released as she ran for the cover of a tree. Listening to the sounds carefully, she closed her eyes and visualised where they carried from. Sound could be deceptive but the trees, if you knew them well enough, would guide her. Imogen lifted her skirts slightly, so they did not catch on the undergrowth, and began to move silently towards the desperate pleas.

"You fool! Sir Benedict Adams has no pity for those who trespass upon his land." A man's fraught voice delivered its stark warning.

Imogen released her skirt's fabric, bent down, and grabbed hold of a hefty fallen branch. Stealthily she covered the last few yards as nimble as a deer in flight and dipped low amongst the undergrowth lest she be seen. Pickles had not followed her, which was a blessing, as he would have charged through and given her away.

Imogen was not certain, but thought it was Dan the stable lad from the Hare and Rabbit over in Gorebeck; the boy would get a thrashing for sure if his father, a tenant farmer, knew where he had been caught. Sir Benedict had made it known he did not want the villagers on his land.

She edged behind the wide trunk of an oak and peered into the clearing. A well-dressed tall gentleman wearing a tailored riding coat was holding Dan firmly by his collar in one hand. Clearly, he was no common man. Imogen approached carefully from behind.

Imogen stepped into the clearing surrounded by newly leafed hazel and ash. "Put him down... now! Or I'll..." Imogen raised her makeshift club to defend Dan against this bully.

The man's head shot around. She had taken him by surprise. Dark eyes glared at her from over a high collar, thick golden locks framed a strangely familiar face. She had thrown away her chance to attack him, to shock him into obedience instead.

"Do not move one step further, miss. I entreat you! Retrace your steps carefully and go back the way you came. Keep to the path and then remain on the lane!" His voice barked out his orders.

"How dare you tell me what to do, sir! Release him this minute." Imogen took a step forward, her makeshift club still raised.

"Stop!" He spun Dan around so that his feet landed firmly on the ground.

Recognition swept over her. Micah Arrow! He was no longer the appealing stripling she would discreetly stare at when he was in the church with his reverend father. This was a mature Micah, full-grown, strong, bold, and here. Reverend Ezekiel Arrow's son had returned from the wars. Her heart quickened, he had survived and was even more appealing than his attractive younger self. His complexion, no longer pale, showed the hue of a man used to facing the sun and the world openly. His bearing, straight-backed and proud, exuded confidence.

Imogen's will to strike him dissipated. However, she could not leave Dan to face any man's wrath alone. Had the wars changed Micah so much?

"Let him go!" What a hero, Imogen thought, picking on a boy of no more than nine summers. "Please, put Dan down and he will return to his home. I can vouch that he is of good character." She phrased her request politely but there was no softening in his strikingly direct eyes. Imogen was glad of the shadow cast upon her face by her bonnet.

"Listen to me carefully as there are man traps here. Turn around – retrace the steps you took to get here and walk safely back to the path to the village." He loosened his grip on Dan's neckline somewhat; the boy had stilled his frantic wriggling since Imogen appeared.

Imogen took another step closer. "You are so brave, sir, taking on a boy and woman!"

His head shook briefly, regretfully. "You have no more sense than a donkey." He leaned forward and grabbed the branch from her hand.

Imogen gasped when he thrust it hard downwards not two feet from her skirts. Her scream followed the iron jaws that rose from the earth snapping shut, mangling the branch. Imogen swallowed imagining sinews of flesh instead of splinters of bark she was seeing – that could have been her leg! The colour drained from her face.

"Man traps!" Dan's voice mirrored the shock she felt.

"Yes, lad, man – or woman – traps. If you walk off the path onto Sir Benedict Adams' land you may well fall victim to them. Everyone in Dibbledale should have already been warned about them.

Imogen thought of her mother. She could not know. Mama would have warned her daughter, they regularly strayed from the path. Did her father know of them? He had not said anything. For years it had been known as Bagby Hall estate, but when the Bagbys fell foul of their own greed and the law, the name had changed to rid it of their stigma, but now a new owner had brought even more danger to them.

"I come from over Gorebeck Moor," said Dan and looked to Imogen whose hands were shaking.

"And you?" Micah asked.

"We have a cottage through the woods on Denton land," Imogen said and felt shy of admitting it to him. Micah had undoubtedly moved on in life, whereas she was still a daughter of the local blacksmith who still lived in a woodland cottage.

"Then your man should have more sense than to let his woman run around wild in the woods alone, threatening all and sundry."

He did not even recognise her. "I have no 'man' as you so crudely put it. My father, Mr. Wilfred Underwood, is the village blacksmith. I was taking a message to him for my mother when I heard Dan's cries for help."

His expression softened when she mentioned who her father was, but he made no apology. "Well, Miss Imogen Underwood, if I had not been so 'cowardly' as to grab hold of this little fool, his screams would have had a gut churning quality to them and he would have spent the rest of his life, if he survived, a cripple begging in the streets. So, go now and retrace your exact steps. I shall take young Dan back to a place of safety. Spread the word to everyone that these man traps have been placed throughout this stretch of land."

Imogen's cheeks burned. The image of the iron teeth snapping shut made her stomach churn. How she hated being made to look so foolish, but how near she had come to becoming that cripple herself.

She owed Mr. Micah Arrow a debt, but could not mouth the words, 'Thank you', so she turned slowly and carefully made her way to the lane, pausing only to retrieve her fallen shawl, letting her senses guide her feet safely as they had so successfully into the clearing.

Chapter 4

Imogen returned to the safety of the village. The warmth of the day helped to mask the glow colouring her cheeks – Micah Arrow had returned! He was a man, full grown and more handsome for it.

Her surprise was over-shadowed by the manner of their first meeting. She twisted a wayward strand of auburn hair around her finger as she stifled the inner joy his return brought her.

Micah had saved the boy from being mutilated. A hero through and through, and Sir Benedict was wicked to have had the traps set there. Even the treacherous Bagbys had let people take what nature provided from the woodland at will.

Micah's eyes had burned into hers leaving a lingering impression, but then it was only on the mention of her father that he had used her name. Had Micah forgotten her whilst away?

Brazenly fronting him was hardly the way to impress a man. Imogen had not even voiced her thanks for saving her from danger.

Pride before a fall, Imogen thought and bit her lip. How devastating an injury she could have sustained, but thank God she had been as surefooted and guided as always.

It was five long years since she had glimpsed Micah, briefly noticing his tired face as he prayed in church, on one rare visit home. Imogen had wished she could have prevented his return to what had seemed to be the endless wars. He looked so fine in his uniform. The blue jacket suited him well. Her infatuation had ended, she thought, when he went back to war. Now those same stirrings filled her with the yearning that had taken so long to dissipate. Imogen shook her head, a sinner for sure, for her thoughts betrayed her. Far from being cured of infatuation, it appeared her body had merely awaited his return.

Imogen had calmed by the time she reached the first cottages of Dibbledale.

A portly built man was passing by with two other riders. She stepped aside, unnoticed or acknowledged as they talked. Imogen recognised one of them immediately, Mr. Jethro Skaggs. His stout figure, and hideously ornate waistcoat was unmistakable.

Her eyes followed Mr. Skaggs as he glanced back. Light grey eyes met Imogen's blue ones and locked for a second.

"You that Underwood lass?" Mr. Skaggs asked.

"I am Miss Imogen Underwood," she answered politely.

"You turn out well for someone who was brought up in a woodland hut." He leered, eyes looking her up and down, but then he realised his friends had walked their horses on. "This may well be your lucky day. I think you'll soon be saved from trekking back and fore to that hovel."

"I do not understand, sir? It is no chore to visit my parents," she replied.

"Got a tongue on you. I like that." Before she could respond or rebuke the hateful man, he re-joined his associates and continued with their conversation.

How dare he refer to her family's home as a hovel! It may not have the comforts of the townhouses, but it was clean and loved. It was just in the wrong place. Imogen felt a shiver run through her, which was strange as the day was warm. That man meant no good, she sensed it, but would say nothing to her papa about Skaggs' loathsome comments. She would never persuade her mama to move to Dibbledale, if Mary heard such remarks made to her daughter by one of the newly local 'gentlemen'. Imogen loathed his greedy eyes, bulging belly and gaudy clothes. He would never be a true gentleman, even if his wealth grew. An image of Micah, handsome, tall, brave and fair, filled her mind and she sighed – Micah was a natural gentleman and somehow, one day, he would be hers. They were destined to be together; she just knew it.

Wrapped tightly in her shawl and with her bonnet shadowing her face, she hoped her discomposure was not apparent. Mr. Micah Arrow's high-handedness gnawed at her. In her heart she was glad she had not simpered in response. Imogen shook her head; he had referred to 'her man'. Micah was a man she wholeheartedly wanted to impress, but she had thrown that first introduction away by galivanting around the woodland like a banshee! Oh well, she would try harder when next they met.

Micah appeared to be strong, not in a bulky muscular way like her father, but lean and lithe. He had lifted Dan clean off his feet with one hand. Imogen swallowed realising just how aware of Micah's bearing she had been.

Passing the church of Saint Cuthbert's, Imogen was pleased that Micah's parents were nowhere to be seen. She entered the main street with its ramshackle cluster of small cruck-built cottages.

Imogen crossed the small stone bridge over the river that meandered through the centre dividing the village in two. After heavy rains, the water poured down from Gorebeck moor. The far side of Dibbledale had a new road with a firm surface. Behind her was the woodland, the farms, and smallholdings; her home nestled in the woodland on the slopes of the dale as they climbed towards Gorebeck moor.

The village baker was leaning against the wall of her home, chatting to Mrs. Emily Weeks who Imogen boarded with. Mrs. Weeks had made quite a living taking in the linen from nearby halls and houses, hiring local girls and women to set up her laundry. Some of the wealthier incomers to the new houses in the growing towns of Beckton and Gorebeck had given her their business, impressed with her work and to help their own reduced staff – war came at a high price. She had set up new laundries there.

Mrs. Weeks who had held a position as housekeeper before she married Mr. Weeks, was sadly suddenly widowed when her husband died in the service of his King and Country. Rather than fade away in mourning, she started a business using her own muscle initially and then giving work to others. Imogen smiled at the ladies. How she wished she had that opportunity to become an owner of something worthwhile.

"Imogen, are you well, you look a bit flustered?" Amy, the baker's wife, waved at her. "What did Skaggs want of thee? I hope he remembered his manners, lass."

"I've been rushing about, that's all," Imogen answered cheerily. "Mr. Skaggs was merely passing the time of day. I must dash, Papa's expecting me." Imogen kept going before she was pulled into their gossip. Whatever Mr. Skaggs was about Imogen did not want to become involved with it, and she certainly did not want anyone to link her name with his. The man made Imogen cringe, she had loathed him on sight. Her mother would say that if they were back-chatting about her then they were leaving someone else alone. But that did not make

Imogen feel any better; she loved her mother dearly but, for someone who was supposed to be able to use her second sight, Mary did not see how easily she could upset people by keeping her distance, adding to her mystique. It was not that her mother thought herself better than them, even if she could read and write. For some unspoken reason she shied away from the villagers.

Need created tolerance, but ignorance of her ways created wariness. Wilfred was widely respected, a mountain of a man who towered over her small frame, yet, when his wife berated him, he was as mild as a chastened puppy.

Imogen had made haste as she passed by the Pheasant and Duck Inn, the general store and bakery, and kept walking until she saw Wilfred's shining head as he bent over his work. Mary said it glowed like a moonstone – he was Mary's own precious gem. She had such a vivid imagination that everything that could be taken as ordinary by most folk was turned into something, with a special meaning to her.

The noise from the forge up ahead told Imogen that her father was in fine spirits and happily at his work. He sang a sea shanty along with the beat of his hammer. Sometimes it was hymns, at other tales of old folklore and even army marching songs, or he would simply hum, but he was rarely quiet. Music was in his soul.

"Papa!" she called, as she approached. Her heart lifted as his head shot up and he winked back.

"Mama asks you to bring in some flour from the miller when you return home, and can you take this wild garlic back with you…" Imogen lingered at the edge of the street. She knew better than to get too close to the actual fire without some protection for her clothes.

"If we lived in the village, Imogen. I'd not have to cart stuff back and fore like a pack animal. I can afford a cottage in town." He repeated their oft stated refrain as he placed a piece of hot metal into cool water and Imogen watched, still fascinated as it hissed and spat like a wild thing when the heat met the cold. "So, what've you been up to?" he asked, without taking his eyes off his task.

"Up to?" she queried, and hesitated. Should she be honest and tell him how her leg could have been forfeit to a mantrap because she nosed into another man's business instead of standing aside? Imogen watched his bear-like biceps, formed through years of hard labour. How did he know something had happened? "I thought I would finish that necklace…"

"Aye, up to?" Now he gave her a more searching look. "You can't keep nothing from me, lass. I know you too well. I did just mean what had you been doing, but I see clearly, you're hiding summat. Your ma might be able to read them tea leaves, but I can read you like a book – or would do if I could read one," he chuckled, as he cared nothing for the scribbled markings on a page. His wife and daughter could read, write, and recite the fables of old by rote, but Wilfred was a man who worked with his hands and as far as he cared he heard all the news first-hand from travellers or when he drank in the inn. He laughed at his own joke before placing his long tongs down carefully and removing his thick gloves. Then he stepped outside into the sunshine and folded his arms across his muscular chest. His eyes settled on hers, eyebrows rose. "Well, you know you are bursting to tell me."

"Papa, I made a slight error of judgement on my way here," she began and placed her tongue between her teeth whilst she thought of the best way to explain. Imogen needed to tell him about the man traps so she may as well state all.

He scoffed at her, knowing her words would be an understatement. His head tilted on one side. "Carry on… you have a way, girl, of misjudging your slight errors! Like when you let Pickles run over Mrs. Weeks newly washed and drying sheets. Once he had wrestled one to the ground and brought down the line of them, I am surprised she still agreed to take you in."

"That was a simple accident. Pickles saw a cat and…" Imogen gave up defending herself and the dog. The cat belonged to the laundry as it kept the rodents at bay. Pickles knocked the line-prop, and the sheets touched the ground. He had then turned tail and run back over the fallen linens. But that was last month. She decided to carry on with her explanation. "Mrs. Weeks did not hold a grudge and beside she had a spare room that could earn her coin, whilst I give her companionship. It is pleasant though. I may have made a bit of a fool of myself earlier," she said. "But for the best of reasons," she quickly added.

"Oh, that'll be alright then. Explain…" he said and sat down on an upturned tree trunk that he used as a stool. His hands rested on his knees.

Imogen loved this man dearly. Even when busy he always had time for her. Mary had inherited some of her own mother's second sight, it rarely skipped a generation. Imogen often sensed things. But surely, she reasoned, that was just intuition. However, Wilfred could understand Imogen's mood, and her need for a confidant.

"Papa, I…" Imogen began her tale and explained as best she could; even the way she had foolishly threatened a stranger harm, leaving herself vulnerable and alone.

"Man traps have been set?" He looked at her more concerned about this than her behaviour. That was typical of her father, he always cared first for their safety. Yet his reaction made it clear he had no knowledge of them.

"Yes, they have! I would not have thought to run through the woods, but I just heard a cry for help. I knew I'd be safe, though… I mean I felt safe and took great care…" Imogen explained what had happened.

His attention was caught when she voiced the word 'knew'.

"Did you, 'just know' mmm?" He stared at her.

"I 'thought' I would be safe, I mean," she corrected.

He shook his head and sighed. "Imogen, you will carry on as if this had not happened. Unless Mr. Micah Arrow reports you to his father or, God forbid, Sir Benedict Adams. You will act as if you two never met." He nodded at her for her agreement.

"Yes, Papa," she said.

"I'll spread the word about the traps, just make sure one of us tells yer ma. I'll bring the flour and you try to manage to stay out of trouble for the rest of the day. Tomorrow you can do some of your fine work and finish that piece you were working on, but today I will be at the fire all day and I need the place to myself, without distraction." He winked at her.

"Yes, Papa," she said, and stepped forward to hug him, but he retreated a step.

"I'm dirty, love, you take care about what you say you know, lass. Folks get wary and can change like the wind. Your ma always 'knows' too much, yet sometimes we do not see what is right under our noses, do we not?" He stared down at her and she bit her bottom lip. "Go teach some letters and earn your keep woman!"

"You may not be a man of written words, but you certainly have a way with the spoken ones." She laughed at his expression, but he had called her 'woman' not lass and that filled her with pride. She had felt more so since moving in with Mrs. Weeks.

"Flattery will not get you everywhere. Each to their own… Now, I have work to do. Be gone! And no more errors of judgement. You are a fine young lady now, not a child gallivanting around with a wayward puppy."

Imogen laughed. As she walked off, she heard him pounding the next piece of metal, perhaps with more vigour than he had previously.

Imogen saw the rider entering the village before she could divert down an alley. Mr. Micah Arrow was a fine figure of a man, unlike Jethro Skaggs who looked like a brandy barrel balanced atop a horse, but as Micah's eyes settled upon her, they cut like a knife to her heart. Ignored, Imogen watched as he rode directly toward the forge.

Chapter 5

Micah was still feeling shaken by earlier events. Two innocents had nearly lost limbs in the man traps. The headstrong beauty, Miss Imogen Underwood could have been maimed before his eyes. He shivered as he was no stranger to unsightly wounds. This, though, was too much.

"Good day, Mr. Underwood," Micah greeted Wilfred, as he dismounted and tied the reins loosely over a hook outside the forge. The heat from the place was oppressive but the large-framed man carried on pumping the bellows effortlessly. His attention never wavered from his task until the final blow resounded around the small building.

Once satisfied, Wilfred put down what he was working on and came forward rubbing his hands on an old cloth. "Good day, Mr. Arrow. It is grand to see you returned and looking so well. What can I be doing for you?" he asked.

"You are very kind. I am blessed to have come through the war unscathed," Micah spoke honestly.

"Aye, lad, but some scars are not visible, are they?" Wilfred remarked.

Micah nodded slightly in acknowledgment of the sensitive comment but was not going to follow that thread of conversation. His internal wounds were his to deal with in his own time and no one else's.

He smiled. What he wanted to ask was not going to be easy, but he would know the honest answer as he needed to trust Wilfred. "Could you tell me if you were the source of man traps laid recently on the Bagby lands to the west of Church Lane?" Micah realised Wilfred had to make a living but hoped he was not involved in the manufacture or providing them.

"You are behind the times. The Bagbys were arrested two years ago – smuggling, selling out their country – bad business. Their estate was sold to the highest bidder to repay debts, the name deliberately lost. Thurley Manor Estate it is now, only God knows why." Wilfred shrugged.

"The Bagbys were arrested?" Micah was surprised that Lord Farrington had not mentioned this. Then again, a man of Farrington's experience in national security would not feel the need to pass on local gossip to him. Micah knew Farrington had dealt with treachery from Unionists and those stirring up seditious behaviour from France.

"Yes, traitors they were. Mind they didn't get the justice they fully deserved," Wilfred added.

"How so?" Micah asked. His memory of Lady Bagby was of a fine-looking woman with elegant posture and immaculate dress sense who in his younger naive days when she and her rather austere lord had visited Saint Cuthbert's one Michaelmas, Micah had been enthralled.

"Lord Bagby's heart gave out in debtor's goal before he was taken to Newgate prison in London for his final sentence to be carried out and she, well, she is locked away in some place for mad women... Malmesby Hall, I think was mentioned. Lucky not to have been thrown into the local asylum with the key tossed away. Anyway, neither of them hanged... Traitors!" Wilfred barked out the last word in an uncharacteristic way before he looked back towards his work, and instantly calmed.

Micah stared at the man, trying to judge his reaction in those grey, speckled eyes. Underwood had diverted the conversation to the shame of the Bagbys, but not answered the initial question. Lord Farrington would no doubt relate the detail about the Bagbys' demise when they met next if Micah requested it.

Wilfred's daughter had not apparently inherited the man's ability to regain her calm.

"Sorry, I have been away too long it seems. And the man traps?" It had taken Micah a few moments to realise who the little wood nymph was, her face had been shadowed by her bonnet and her hair pinned up, but when she named her father, he realised it was Imogen the fiery haired girl he used to avoid staring at in church – well at least when she could see him, for she had captured his young heart. Striking blue eyes flecked with a hint of hazel – so unique and her boundless energy mesmerising. Her fresh face a joy to behold. There was something delightfully wild about her, symbolised by the way her auburn hair was constantly determined to escape her braid. Back then Micah's mother had forbidden him to ever go near the Underwoods, the 'wise woman' who used plants to heal. They were considered ungodly ways, yet nature, he reasoned, was surely a blessing from God.

"No. I try to use my skills in a more humane way." Wilfred folded his muscular arms. "May I ask why you should want such things? Are you having trespassers at the vicarage? Does your mother fear that the church silver may be stolen by the good people of Dibbledale?" The man's voice had more than a hint of sarcasm dripping from it, which Micah knew was unexpected, as his father respected Wilfred greatly.

If there was offence meant through his words, it was thinly masked. Micah knew the family was not particularly well churched, especially Mary, Wilfred's Irish wife, but his father mentioned the attractive daughter appeared there occasionally.

"No, nothing to do with my father, Mr. Underwood. They have been recently laid in the woodland belonging to Sir Benedict Adams to discourage poachers and trespassers, and I fear word has not spread far enough. A young lad from Gorebeck nearly fell into one. Fortunately, he was unhurt."

Wilfred shook his head and his tone tempered as he continued, "They're wicked things. You sound like you do not hold with them, either."

"I do not. A fence would be ample deterrent in my estimation, although would require more labour and cost." Micah glanced up the main street of the village. There was no more sign of Miss Underwood, perhaps she had already discussed the morning's events with her father. Or she was too shame faced to see him again so soon.

"Why stop folk who have grown up around it from enjoying nature's bounty?" Wilfred began to return to his work hefting the hammer in readiness to bring it smashing down.

"It has been bought and…"

"And one greedy man wants it all to himself, and claims every beast that runs onto it, whilst poor families forage elsewhere. Many men died in them wars with France, sir. He would do well to remember that when he sits in judgement of them from his comfortable chair as the local magistrate." Wilfred slapped his bald head and shrugged his shoulders. "Aye, well, I best not say more, or you'll have me down as a revolutionary. I'll keep me thoughts to myself. Sorry, man, not your fault, I know." He laughed. "Do you reckon I could have made a good preacher?" The hammer was again relaxed at his side, it appeared to weigh nothing in this man's grip.

"You have a good heart and that is always an advantage," Micah said.

"Aye, well, we each have our own opinion. Now was there something else you wanted to ask, or tell me, sir?" he asked.

"Your words are safe with me. I do not hold with greed either. Just please spread the word that these traps have been put there. The church gate is rusted, and Father was asking for a quote for it to be replaced, or fixed. Could you pop over one morning and take a look at it and let him know your estimate? We would appreciate it." Micah relaxed his stance.

"Aye, that I can do. Good day, sir," he said and turned back to his job in hand.

Imogen watched as Micah mounted and walked his horse slowly along the main street seemingly pondering Wilfred's words.

"Could you not wait to tell my father that I had attacked you?" Imogen addressed him from a small alleyway between the baker's and the inn, as he made his way past the narrow snicket. She was standing slightly back in the shadows.

"Is your opinion of me so low, Miss Underwood? That I would run to your father as soon as I was able to tell him of his daughter's recent antics? Does he not know already what an errant waif he has reared?" He stared down at her from his horse.

"How dare you!" Imogen felt so small, and he elevated - so high and mighty, it was a perspective she did not care for. Never had she behaved so carelessly in front of anyone.

"Oh, I dare. You come at me in the woods with a

makeshift club in hand like a primitive Pict from beyond Hadrian's Wall – thank God you were not daubed in woad, wielding an axe!"

He stared at her, and she wondered if he dared to envisage her naked and daubed with woad! "They used swords and spears," she said, not knowing why, but a vision of a wild warrior flashed in her mind.

Micah blinked then ignored her comment. "Now you throw accusations at me whilst standing under the sign of an inn. Where next will you pop up?" His voice was low so it would not draw attention and he looked casually around as he answered her. "Do I have to look over my shoulder to see if you are lurking there ready to pounce?"

Imogen's cheeks burned, her fists balled, as she fought back the urge to launch at him. His eyes boring down at her, a broad smile aimed at her folly. She was standing on her own by an inn throwing insults at this man. Why did she not think ahead? Did she wish Micah had never returned? Was he being just an arrogant gentleman? Then there was Mr. Jethro Skaggs and talk of him setting up a mill of some sort; the village was already changing from the quiet and peaceful place it had been when they settled there to one that was becoming uneasy and tense with rumours rife. What was the man's plan?

"You mock me. Yet you do not know me. I was only trying to rescue the lad..." Imogen's voice softened as she felt the weight of her most recent error.

"So, miss, was I." Micah casually stroked the neck of his horse.

"I did not know that. My father is a good man, I am not so scared of him that I would not tell him the truth myself," Imogen replied undaunted.

"I am delighted to hear it. So will you apologise to me now for judging my character so ill?" Micah challenged her, she shifted uneasily as his words had their impact.

"You have insulted me also," she said, pride bristling, aware that the longer she stood by the inn talking to this returnee, the more likely she was to be seen. Imogen wanted to walk away, but only after he had ridden off first.

"I really must go, miss. I do not wish to damage my reputation by being seen talking to a young woman loitering next to an ale house. Good day," he said in a way that clearly mocked her further and walked his horse on leaving Imogen with an internal raging fire burning like the heart of her father's forge.

Chapter 6

The morning bloomed bright once more as Micah rode through Dibbledale, taking the well-worn road up to Gorebeck Moor. The ruts were dry and deep, it was time the road was surfaced he noted. Progress had stopped still for the village in many respects since he left in the summer of 1807. Micah had such plans for Dibbledale, and he could not wait to meet Lord Farrington and share them with him.

Reflecting on the previous day's events, he recalled the spark in Imogen's eyes. He loved her spirit, but she needed to learn to think before she reacted. She was a brilliant flame and he a simple moth – but he would not be burned. Her embarrassment at his words, humoured him and brought the smile back to his face.

Micah needed time to settle back into what was considered normal life. Sometimes the dreams that visited him turned into nightmares. He would wake up in a cold sweat and have to go for a walk, or read a book, anything to avoid going straight back to sleep. The images were not far-fetched, they were from the events he witnessed. Men turned to drink to drown away those same images, dull their senses but he did not wish to do that. Instead, he would learn to live as he wished too; how and with whom he was not entirely sure, yet. Micah instantly envisaged the picture of Imogen, a rare beauty, he would have to explain about his Spanish wife at some time. Once she knew him well enough, he was sure she would understand. He wanted to harness Imogen's energy and their mutual love of life, not restrict, or tame it.

Micah galloped along the open road, in awe of the wild moor that surrounded him. He wanted to see Farrington – his friend, a lord! How fortunes change. Who would have ever thought that the son of moderately humble parish origins could have met Wellesley, now the Duke of Wellington he corrected himself, and count one of his highest intelligence officers as a friend? When his father had received patronage from a wealthy dowager, Ezekiel had used the money to purchase his son's commission in the Light Dragoons' Regiment, much to his mother's chagrin, and unwittingly changed the course of all their lives. Micah would need to sit down with his father and explain just how much, but first he must see Lord Farrington.

Once on the open moor road he let the horse have its head and covered a few miles with ease. The low cruck-built inn came into view. He headed for the stables behind and left his horse with the stable hand to be tended whilst he entered through the back door of The Bleaky Inn.

He paused inside, children were laughing and being hushed by their mother in a small room immediately to the left as he entered. This had a ramshackle assortment of wooden chairs where a family with three children waited in the chill for the coach to Harrogate to arrive. An untended fire dwindled low in the hearth. He nodded politely at the father before turning towards the more boisterous room.

Micah passed through a low doorway to his right. Here men gathered around upturned barrels used as tables in the middle of the small tap room. The stone surfaces of floors, walls and ceiling seemed to amplify their noise. Micah peered through the smoky fug of the air, to find a well-dressed tall figure seated on a settle by an open range.

Micah joined him, noticing heads had turned as he entered, but soon the local's attention was back on drinks and the food they needed before returning to work.

"Arrow, sit, I have ordered some sustenance, which I hope will be sufficient. The fare here is basic, but they do know how to cook a good piece of mutton."

Micah took off his tall hat and slipped into the other end of the settle behind the wooden table. He was soon greeted by a young serving maid who put a jug of porter and a pewter tankard onto the table.

Micah nodded his thanks and the girl blushed before disappearing behind the serving hatch again. They were waited on; others fetched their own victuals.

"I wonder how long she will stay so innocent," Micah commented, as he poured his drink and refilled Lord Farrington's.

"Do not be fooled by the pretty face of a serving maid." Lord Farrington laughed at Micah's expression, who clearly did not consider himself stupid enough to be duped by the young woman's appearance.

Micah coloured slightly and looked away."How go the arrangements?" he asked. He was eager to know that funds had finally been received and a transfer agreed.

"Do you doubt me, Arrow?" Farrington's hand froze in mid-air as he lifted his tankard.

"Never!" Micah replied immediately, realising that his slow reaction had been misinterpreted. "I am so humbled by your help. That you would go to so much trouble for me, it is generous in the extreme and I would gladly give you a..."

"Do not insult me with the offer of a share of your newly found fortune – I am not your agent and will take no commission. I am your friend so do not offend me."

Micah swallowed and nodded politely, not wishing to reveal how much emotion he was holding back.

Farrington laughed. "Well, man, for all my training and the scrapes you pulled yourself through, you have not learned one universal truth." He drank but replaced the tankard as if it offended him. "Personally, I prefer port."

"What universal truth is that?" Micah asked, glad to let the conversation move on. He had no wish to give insult, but neither had he wanted to appear to be unappreciative. He had no knowledge of dealing with large sums of money across country borders, but Lord Farrington had and was familiar with the international laws.

"Never trust anyone." Lord Farrington looked straight into Micah's eyes, without flinching.

"I disagree, sir. I trust you and my father wholeheartedly. Am I wrong to?" He sipped the drink which, though wet, lacked flavour.

"You saved me at Talavera. The debt I owe you guarantees my patronage and trust. We are the exception perhaps to that rule. If you ever betray me, I will kill you. As for your father, I have never met the Reverend Mr. Ezekiel Arrow, but I hear he is a genuine sort."

Micah raised his eyebrows. He was surprised that he would have made enquiries; he did not know why Farrington had.

"What happened to Lord and Lady Bagby? You never mentioned that their lands had changed hands under such dramatic circumstances." Micah saw Lord Farrington's posture change slightly. He sat back on the settle and folded his arms across his riding coat somewhat defensively.

"The man was a cad and a rogue. He swindled his government selling information and goods, amongst other crimes, and was not man enough to face trial. He died in prison before the justice of the courts could be upheld." Lord Farrington added, "He is in the company of his smuggling minion Amos Kell who also died. I hope they rot in Hell together."

Micah was taken aback by the venom expressed by Lord Farrington, a man who was usually reserved with his words

"I remember their game-keeper, he was a brute of a man."

"Yes, and a murdering bastard."

Again, the venom, Micah thought.

The serving maid arrived with their food and Farrington welcomed her with his usual charm, complementing the two pewter dishes that held the best cut of mutton that they could provide, along with a fresh loaf sitting on another platter.

Micah sensed that Farrington was keen to change subject, but Micah persisted. "What happened to Lady Bagby? Was she involved? Is she serving a sentence too?" he asked.

"She lost her mind when her husband passed. She was to face a court but instead is incarcerated in Malmsbury Hall, which is run by nuns on the border of Yorkshire and Lancashire. She is serving a quite different sentence to that in rotting in gaol; it is austere and pious. If she should regain her clear thinking she may be taken in by the order or serve her sentence in gaol. Now enough of the past gossip. You focus on the here and now. Eat, man!" Farrington sat forward picked up his spoon and began to eat his food.

Micah did likewise. "What do you know of the man who bought Bagby…Thurley Manor? He is littering the woodland near the village with man traps." Micah ate.

"Sir Benedict Adams does not own the land or the Hall. He merely rents it. I think he is an interesting character. I met him briefly. He has invited me to dine with him in the near future. Other than man traps what else irks you about him?"

Micah smiled as Lord Farrington could read him well enough. "I understand that he may have ideas on developing the land. But there are rumours and little substance. Could you possibly find out more?"

Farrington thought for a moment. "He seems to be associated with a slippery character called Jethro Skaggs. That man hails from Manchester, son of a weaver who has made good via London's shoe trade. I would not trust him either in my sight or out. He is vulgar, ambitious and seeks to climb higher."

"Is ambition something to be frowned upon, or does he seek to rise above his God-given station in life?" Micah asked and saw sharp eyes target his.

"Arrow, save preaching for your father. There are ways of attaining rank as we all know, but his ways are unworthy and if I can prove them illegal, I swear I will bring him down, like the Bagbys!" Lord Farrington's words were quiet but emphatic.

"You brought them low?" Micah reiterated.

"No, they did that themselves. I merely applied the law."

"So, you are not retired – totally?" Micah asked.

"I was semi-retired then. Now I have my wife, daughter and a son who is … well, I have a son." He chuckled and finished his food.

"Lord Farrington, I want to use some of the money to develop Dibbledale as a centre for craftsmen, a place where returned soldiers can find a living and take pride in learned skills." Micah stopped as he saw Farrington look surprised, an expression he had not ever seen on his face.

"Well, a noble gesture and I wish you well with it, but I suggest that you consult me again once our dealings are finalised. I know a doctor who would be interested in such a scheme. That for another time though. If we meet elsewhere, Micah, we shall appear newly acquainted, and will keep our friendship to ourselves until our business is concluded and my enquiries are satisfied. I must look to protect my family and so will ensure any rot I cross paths with is doused in flames. You look well. I will send word when I have secured all your funds."

Micah stood. "Thank you, sir!" he said.

Lord Farrington patted his arm as he stood up and then discreetly dropped a package into Micah's hat as he walked off.

Micah picked his hat up and peeked into the corner of it, realising it held some bank notes. Micah swallowed; he had never held so much money in his hands before. It was a payment on account of what was to follow. He quickly slipped them into his pocket, keeping his hand firmly on it as he left the inn.

He must return to the vicarage and consider how to explain to his family his new circumstances, but where was he to begin?

Chapter 7

"Would that be you, Imogen, or has a thunderclap disturbed my day?" Mary Underwood was sitting at the square table before the small open range and cottage fire. Fading auburn curls were escaping from the edges of her cloth cap, but Imogen thought that she was still a good-looking woman with a clear skin and a kind heart that made her eyes shine with life. Ripples of steam escaped the kettle, and her teapot was ready to receive the water, to make a fresh brew.

"Are you expecting someone, Mama?" Imogen asked, the table had a fresh piece of linen spread upon it, set with two cups standing on mismatched saucers. She walked over and gave her mother a hug. Instantly her inner storm calmed, the world outside this cottage could be in turmoil, but where her mother was Imogen always felt at peace.

"Aye, that I am…but it is you, Immi, I am waiting for, no one else." She chuckled as Imogen shook her head.

"Mama, you knew I'd be calling in. There may be times when your gifts shine, but this is not one of them. Anyway, here are the bits you asked for. Papa mentioned again how he wishes we could live in town. The weather has been so bad this winter, Papa has worked so hard. It would be easier on him…" Imogen was trying to reprimand her mother knowing the woman was far from selfish, on anything - except this one issue.

"Sit yourself down, Imogen, and remember it is me who is the mother here." Mary brushed her off with a gentle reprimand as was her way when she did not wish to answer. What was not to like about the cottage in Spring and Summer - but in Winter it was cold. Mary only seemed to see the man's strength and not his weaknesses, but Imogen saw how tired he sometimes looked at the forge.

Reaching for the cloth pad that was kept near the fire Mary wrapped it around the kettle's handle and poured the boiling water into the treasured teapot before carefully placing into the centre of the table.

Her mother was shy of five feet in height, but despite her small frame her character was volatile when roused, like a storm. It was her mother's colouring that Imogen had inherited and the fiery nature that traditionally went with it. She could gently stir, caress all about her or, like a whirlwind, knock an opponent down with a lashing of her tongue. Imogen loved her dearly but recognised her faults. For all the woman's wisdom, she failed to see that keeping distance from the villagers made her a stranger to them.

Mary was proud of both her parents; between them they had taught her so much and allowed her to live an independent life under the watch of Mrs. Weeks. It suited both women, one a widow, the other a young woman establishing herself in the world. Mrs. Weeks wanted her young laundry maids to have a basic knowledge of letters and numbers and so had Imogen instruct them for a few hours each week in her own school in the back room of her house.

Wilfred's forge meant that the people of Dibbledale did not have to trek over the moors to Gorebeck to have their tools and wheels mended. His work was skilful and could be decorative when commissioned.

"What have you been up to?" Mary asked, as she placed a loaf under her arm. With the bread knife she cut a slice off the top end of it and placed that down on a plate. This she put on the table next to Imogen with a bowl of honey and a knife. She put the loaf back and then carefully poured out the tea.

"Why do you cut bread like that instead of putting it down on a board? You risk slicing yourself," Imogen asked. Mary had so many quirks.

"It's a good cut, isn't it?" Mary smiled.

"Yes, but…"

"Then why not?"

"It's what people do, use a board," Imogen said, "I don't want you hurt." She took a refreshing bite of the bread dripping with a spoonful of runny honey. "Nectar…" she mouthed appreciatively.

"Well, this person does not choose to." She smiled. "You like nature, you breathe it in, Imogen, don't pretend it does not speak to you also." Mary tilted her head on the side.

"Why not be like other people, to be accepted. Make life easier for Papa?" Imogen saw both of her mother's eyebrows rise. She braced herself for a tongue-lashing but was surprised when it did not come.

"I have everything I need here. So, is there a reason you would like me to be nearer to those people? Other than to please your papa and stop you getting your finer skirt hems mucky coming to see me?"

"Mama, you know me better than that. Besides, Mrs. Weeks is very generous and includes my dresses with hers when they are taken to the laundry. She has even given me two second hand ones that she came across in good repair. I wear them when I am taking the girls for their lessons. I also sit with Mrs. Entwistle's girls when she visits and give them instruction in embroidery – you taught me well, Mama."

"Good. So, is there a person in particular that you would like to be closer to, Imogen?" Mary pushed the cup to her daughter. "Drink it down but leave a little at the bottom."

Imogen sighed. "I don't need a reading today."

"Drink," Mary ordered.

Imogen finished every crumb of her bread, licked the honey that had dripped on her fingers and then drank as she had been instructed. Sometimes it felt like she would never be more than a child in her mother's eyes.

"That was not so difficult, was it?" Mary took her near empty cup in her left hand and swirled it three times slowly then upturned it onto the saucer. Set back on the table she carefully rotated the cup a further three full rotations never letting her eyes stray from it, then righting the cup in front of her on the table. She stared into the vessel.

Her nut-brown eyes lifted until they met Imogen's. Mary sat back. "You have met someone, Imogen. I see it, clear as the day is long, this person will shadow your days."

Imogen thought instantly of Micah. Her skin warmed, hopefully her cheeks glowing was because the range put out such warmth.

Mary continued, "However, I see a rising star, that is over-shadowed by the shape of a cross? The latter is not a good omen, Imogen. Tell me what happened to you recently that sets events apart from the usual."

"I met Micah Arrow, Reverend Arrow's son. How you knew I do not know, but I assure you he will not shadow my days! I also found out that Sir Benedict Adams has had man traps put on his land. Papa's told you, hasn't he?"

Imogen got up and moved her plate to the stone sink, before stretching her arm out to snatch up the cup, but her mother held her arm, ignoring Imogen's comment about the man traps.

"Believe, Imogen, this man will stay in your life. Do not expect an easy path, his mother does not like me and will never accept you." Her eyes were pleading with Imogen, which was upsetting her. The day was becoming stranger by the minute.

"Enough, Mama, I only stumbled upon Micah by chance in the woods. Our paths crossed, that is all. I am going out to get some kindling," Imogen said as she wrapped her shawl tight, flicked her tawny braid down her back and picked up the basket.

Mary's gaze returned to the leaves in her own cup, but she waited until Imogen left before she asked them where her own future lay.

Chapter 8

Micah was a troubled man. He had asked Lord Farrington to investigate Sir Benedict Adams' activities, but the connection to this man Jethro Skaggs gave him cause for concern. What had happened to the Bagbys to turn them against their own people, and the crown? How naïve he had been in his younger years, looking up to such people. Micah had learned the hard way that appearance and position could hide a myriad of flaws, and beauty could mask a dark soul.

Lord Farrington said that he owed Micah, but with his patronage and friendship Micah felt that the debt was his, for he would never have had the funds to raise legal objection to those who would challenge his rights. Without Lord Farrington's intervention the foundation on which his plans were based would not exist.

An image of Miss Underwood stepping into that man trap haunted him. Her spirit called out to his, she was bold, not brash, had a spark to her that he admired, but to see her hurt in anyway made his guts churn. He had seen too many mangled bodies on the field of battle.

Her striking image, branch in hand, played before his eyes. He had even dreamed of her, although admittedly not accurately. What spirit! She would be a driving force for his plan if the woman would only listen to him.

"Good, so where did you venture to today?" Ruth Arrow asked, as she rested on the window seat.

"I rode for a while then dropped back into the village. I met with Wilfred Underwood. The gate he was working on was quite ornate. His daughter was there although we did not converse, but no sign of his wife. I suppose she would be in their cottage. I remember, she was always a homely sort. By the way, which one is it?" he asked innocently enough and ate with enthusiasm to appease his mother.

Micah looked up when there a silence ensued. He saw her face pale and he recalled instantly that she still disapproved of them.

"Stay away from Mary Underwood. She dabbles in things she ought not to. They live in their woodland hovel!" Her words were snapped out. "That daughter of theirs may dress like a young lady, but her nature is as wild as that hair of hers."

Micah had to stifle a laugh as thinking of Imogen Underwood he could see her as a 'wild woman'. However, his mother's response was concerning for superstition and whispers could be dangerous things when such words were used inappropriately.

"Wilfred Underwood is a large bear of a man, but hardly qualifies as a 'wild man'." Micah scoffed.

"His wife chooses to live with the animals and uses her spells and potions to encourage people away from their God given path. I have hope for the girl, her nature may yet be calmed, as she does come into church, but they are a family tainted by the devil's ways." The finger waved – pointed the warning at him and he realised for the first time how age had gnarled her once graceful hand.

"Mother! I accept that you do not approve of Mary Underwood and her remedies, but she only uses nature as God intended, to heal, doesn't she? Where is the harm in that?" He stood up. "I am somewhat perplexed by your damning comments."

"Micah, how can you be a man of this world and be so blinkered to things? You mark my word, no good will come to them. You stay away, for your and our good name will not be tainted by the likes of the Underwoods." She too stood.

"Mother! Please be more charitable in your assumptions and do not wish ill on other people. You may not mean to directly, but the woman keeps to her own home, as you do yours. Try not to judge her from afar. You may cause danger for them without meaning to." He sincerely hoped it was not her wish to do so, surely; she could not be so wicked.

Ruth looked away. "You may come to me before you retire this day and apologise to me for your harsh words. I will excuse them because you have just returned from the grim life of a soldier. You have obviously been badly influenced by the uncouth." She scurried out of the room calling for the maid to come to her.

"Do not wait up," he muttered and turned away. It was not as he would wish things to be between them, but her tongue was sharp and her wits foolish at times. Micah felt sorry for their maid of all work, Ellie, because his mother would oversee her tidy a cupboard of linen or some other chore that did not need doing until her upset calmed and she regained control of her thoughts and her cupboard once more. However, Micah had a plan, a dream to realise and no amount of superstition was going to stand in his way – whether that came from his mother or not. He wanted to build a friendship with Imogen and that was clearly going to cause some degree of upset.

So be it. He had helped win a war, now he must fight his own battles, but hopefully time would show him a way to broker peace and bring harmony to Dibbledale and the Arrow household.

Chapter 9

Imogen had stayed over at the cottage. She missed it, waking to sounds of birdsong and the noise of Mary humming as she prepared for their day.

The divine smell of her mother's porridge warmed her spirit as much as she knew the oats would her stomach. Whenever she had honey Mary added it, stirring some in to make a swirl pattern, adding the top of the milk provided by Sam from a local dairy farm over on the Kingsley Estate. In return Mary gave him her balm for his mother's chest.

Wilfred started his day with fried eggs, honeyed ham and freshly made oatcakes. Whatever was in season or to hand her mother could turn into a small feast.

"Has Papa left already?" Imogen asked.

Mary shook her head. "Does the cock crow each morning and the sun rise?" she chuckled at her daughter.

"I had hoped to go with him as he said he was going to look at the church gate first thing." Imogen licked the sweetness off her spoon, winking at her mother who laughed at her.

"Well, he did, but his first thing and yours may be a few hours apart."

"The cock has only just crowed!" Imogen said. "She needed to return to Dibbledale as she had to present herself before a small class of younger girls by midday.

"Well either you did not hear the first crow, or perhaps it too likes to sleep in? If you finish that quickly you might be able to catch up with him but take care because you know that Mrs. Arrow does not look upon us kindly."

"Mama, what type of talk is that? She just does not understand our ways. Perhaps she has had something happen to her in the past which has scared her. Mama, she does not venture out of the vicarage or church much. Oh! Now, who do I know who is like that?" Imogen gulped the last spoonful quickly and ducked as a washcloth came hurtling from her mother's hand and whizzed past her head as intended.

Imogen ran out before her mother's tongue engaged. She ran past their one cow and four laying hens. Pickles followed her; she ruffled his ear as he lolloped along by her side along the track toward the church. With each step she was reassuring herself that she was only going to make sure Wilfred was fine and that seeing Micah Arrow again was in no way the reason for her urgency. However, when she arrived at the gate it was still hanging off its hinges and there was no sign of her father.

She waved at Reverend Arrow as he entered the church from the vicarage. He waved back, always a nod and a smile from him. Pickles entered the churchyard.

"Pickles, come back!" Imogen shouted, and he returned to her. It was no place for a dog.

Imogen was about to make her way to the village when Micah saw her. Walking tall and proud he strode purposefully toward her from the vicarage.

He cut a fine figure, she thought. Imogen would rather run away than have another unkind exchange of words with him. Her head told her heart she needed to stand her ground and face him. If she was going to capture his interest, she had to let him see who she was.

"Good morning, Miss Underwood," he said and took off his hat revealing freshly washed hair – the colour of golden corn, in all its wispy wavy glory. How she would love to run her fingers through it.

"Good morning, Mr. Arrow," she remarked, keeping her voice calm and her manner and poise controlled.

Pickles rubbed his head against Micah's hand, and he dutifully fondled his ear. "Were you coming into church?" he asked.

"No, sir, I was just trying to find my father, but it seems he has been and gone." She gestured to the rickety gate that hung precariously on its hinges. I will return to the village and leave you in peace. Pickles come!" She turned, annoyed that the dog lingered, but straight away Micah said the words she secretly wanted to hear.

"Then allow me to escort you as I am heading that way too." Micah had a determined expression upon his face, which told Imogen he would not be easily dissuaded.

"There really is no need… Pickles is a good enough bodyguard." Imogen watched the dog leave Micah as she stressed his name. It clearly liked him too, but it was never a good idea to be obvious as her ma would say and openly 'set your cap at a man'.

"Yes, there is need, for we both behaved badly, and I would begin our reunion again, if you will allow it."

His smile seemed genuine. She looked up into his face, at least a head height taller than her, Micah's eyes showed sincerity.

Imogen glanced around her as if considering it and casually ruffled Pickles ear before relenting. "Very well, thank you," she said and stepped away from the open gateway so that they could walk along with a clear stride of space between them. Far from being an escort Pickles decided to run back into the woods. He would return to Mary, deserting Imogen. Typical! The dog was fickle, but adorable – a free spirit like her mother.

Micah chuckled. "Your guard dog has a mind of his own."

Imogen did not reply, Pickles obviously considered she was in no threat, or he would never have abandoned her. "Are you waiting for me to apologise first, Miss Underwood?" he asked with feigned humility.

"Yes, now that you suggest it, I can confirm that your presumption is correct," she answered politely.

"You have a quick wit, only matched by the speed of that tongue." He stared down at her, his laughing eyes seeming to enjoy the taunt.

How often her father had said that of her. Far from being bored with her predictable routine Micah had injected an element of risk and excitement into her day. Yet she had not realised that it had been missing from her erstwhile contented life, until he reappeared and turned it upside down.

"Is that a compliment? It certainly isn't an apology!" Imogen glanced up at him, meeting his honey-coloured gaze.

"Very well, I apologise for being very abrupt yesterday and a little insulting to you in the village." He folded his arms as if bracing himself for her retort.

"A little!" she said loudly, but when he widened his eyes at her, she stopped. He had baited her, and she had predictably responded. "I apologise for calling you a brute and wishing you would fall off your horse after you insulted me outside the inn. Although you deserved more for such an open insult."

There was a short pause before they both laughed. "Imogen, you are a breath of fresh air, but how you would offend everyone in a gathering at the assembly rooms with your blatant honesty." He shook his head. Then his smile dropped as he could so easily have offended her again.

"Well, I shall not be invited to your soirees, Mr. Arrow, so you need not worry." She walked on. "I would hate to offend your friends and family."

"I do not worry, I admire your candour, and would be delighted to see you in a fine dress at any soiree, with that mass of hair moderately tamed, but the character not. So shall we be friends?" he asked. "I do not worry for my family, and I choose my own friends, Imogen. However, I have no need of foes and I would be saddened if you decline my offer of friendship."

"I would rather have friends than enemies, wouldn't you?" Imogen smiled as she responded. His manner was so different, he kept his pace quite slow. They ambled along, both drawing every step out.

"I applaud your sentiment." His jovial air became serious for a moment. "I sincerely meant no offence."

"I'm sorry, that was an ill-thought-out comment. You must have seen life and humanity at their worst. I only meant…"

"I know what you meant, and I agree wholeheartedly with the sentiment. Now, tell me how does your family fare?" he asked and seemed genuinely interested.

Imogen was confused. Had Micah not been back long enough to hear his mother's concerns for their souls. Mrs. Arrow's maid had told her man, who had not wasted anytime passing the comments on to Wilfred about her mistress's distrust of the Underwoods. They said women gossiped! When Wilfred foolishly relayed this to Mary, the Gaelic outpouring of words had come thick and fast until her angst was vented. Then, in typical Mary fashion, she folded her arms, sat down, and said, "Foolish woman, to speak so." However, since that day her mother would not hear a kind word said about Mrs. Ruth Arrow without her lips clenching. Instead of her venom lessening it seemed to have become more intense, simmering inside like a pot of her broth.

"Well..." she paused then added, "Why would you ask that?"

"I was being polite but also, I would like to help your father and wondered if he was in good spirits this morning?"

"You are becoming a regular visitor, Mr. Arrow. How could you help my father? You may get your lovely coat dirty!" She deliberately goaded him, but from the light sparkling in his eyes as he glanced at her, he was not so easy to bait.

There are more ways to help someone than with brawn," he remarked. "If I may give you some advice, Miss Underwood, do not judge a person purely on the clothes they wear. I have served, worked hard, travelled far, killed, been injured, and spared. I have slept in the mud, drank with thieves, and dined with lords. I am not so shallow that I can be judged by the quality of the coat I choose to wear for a walk to town."

His manner which had become very sincere changed in a trice when he laughed. "Besides, Mother had it made for me and as I am to see her cousin, I thought I would please her for she has worried these past years, but soon I shall cease to be so obediently predictable."

Imogen was surprised at how open he was being. He had delivered a very powerful message and then dismissed it in a trice as he returned to light banter. But in amongst his words there was a confession, Micah had killed! How it must sit ill with him, for whatever else Micah was, he was a sensitive soul. "I ask your forgiveness and realise that you do not judge me unfairly, I looked wild as I came to Dan's 'rescue' and today, in my primrose day dress and straw hat, I hope I present a very different image." She was fishing for a compliment and he duly obliged.

"Yes, Miss Underwood, your hair the colour of flame dancing in sunlight suits your choice well. You have the most striking eyes. In the shadow of the woods and the inn I had not reminded myself of their beauty, but today they shine like the purest gems. I confess to be quite taken by you and your appearance." He raised one eyebrow and added, "Have I made up for my insults now, Miss Underwood?"

"Thank you, Mr. Arrow." Imogen paused to allow the welcome flattery to sink in, even if it had been exaggerated. "Why would you want to help father? Why should he need help, Micah?" she asked, curiosity overflowing.

He tilted his head on one side and faced her as she spoke his given name without realising at first. It had seemed a natural enough thing to do.

"Well, Imogen, we are to be good friends - I have a proposition, but I would like to talk to him alone first. Tell me…"

Imogen's mind took flight. Had he said he was going to run a proposition by her father? Surely, he was not seeking a wife! He had just returned. No, surely not. She would press him further for an answer.

"Tell me, Micah, what is…"

A rider appeared cantering along the track at speed. His actions were quick and without hesitation. As soon as he saw the horse heading toward them, he pulled Imogen to his side and held her close on the verge.

A finely dressed lady in a beautifully made riding outfit, was sitting elegantly side-saddle, with crop in hand as she pulled the horse to a stop by them. Imogen did not think for one minute she had lost control of the animal.

Her manner was far too calm and the animal too obedient. It did not even whinny as it stilled.

"I do not know what possessed Wellington to rush so!" she exclaimed and looked down at Micah and Imogen. "I think there was a mongrel in the woods that spooked him. Honestly, I should have uncle send the gamekeeper to cull any strays!" She snapped and patted her immaculate hat that had not shifted at all.

Micah released his hold on Imogen who had gasped at the idea Pickles could be 'culled'. She had liked Micah's protective gesture; if only the 'lady' had not stopped, she would have enjoyed it a moment longer. He stepped away distancing himself from her.

"Perhaps he is too spirited for a lady to manage," Micah said, as he moved forward to stroke the Thoroughbred's neck. "I do not think that there are mongrels that run wild here. It could have just as easily been a trick of the light. I would not worry your uncle, whoever he may be." He turned briefly to Imogen. "I apologise, Miss Underwood, for being so bold…"

The lady smiled at him, but her eyes cast a less than friendly glance to Imogen who was for once at a loss for words.

"Mr. Arrow is it not?" she asked, ignoring Imogen completely.

"Yes, but you have the advantage upon me," Micah said politely.

Imogen saw the look on the woman's face as her eyes devoured Micah's. Oh, she would like to have the advantage of him, Imogen thought.

"Miss Beatrice Donaldson, sir. I believe you know my uncle, Sir Benedict Adams?" she said sweetly. "We are to dine together, are we not?"

"Yes, I understand that is so…"

"Excuse me, I must be on my way," Imogen said and walked on.

"Just a min…" Micah began, but the 'Lady' asked him about his parents' health.

Imogen let their words drift into the distance as she resumed her lonely walk into the village. Micah had wanted to be her friend, he would be, but Imogen realised that for him to be so could make enemies in the form of wealthier folk for her. She sighed; in her dream Imogen may win his heart. This lady might very well make Imogen's dream impossible to realise.

Chapter 10

Micah glanced at Imogen's slender back with regret as she strode purposefully away. He so wanted to set things right between them. Instead, he was faced with a vision, dripping wealth and finery. Why did she appear to him now of all times? Why at all? He should have stopped Imogen, he wanted to, or at least introduced her properly as a neighbour, but something had caused him to pull back from this and instead Micah let her slip silently away as if she had no standing at all.

"Who was your little friend?" the lady asked, and smiled innocently in Imogen's direction, but he was not certain if there was curiosity or menace within her words. "Such a pretty little thing, but she should not be wandering the lanes alone."

"A family friend and neighbour, the daughter of the village blacksmith. Mr. Wilfred Underwood is a local man who is well thought of hereabouts." He added the last comment almost defensively, yet why should he need to? Why explain anything to this stranger?

"Goodness, he must be someone special for you to hold a mere tradesman in such high esteem, and for you to be bold enough to walk out with his daughter alone, but then you are the Reverend Mr. Arrow's son, so she could hardly be in safer hands, figuratively speaking of course. They must surely trust you deeply." She then feigned a look of surprise as if a thought had occurred to her innocently. "Is there an understanding between you two perhaps? She wears such a pretty frock for the daughter of a simple blacksmith."

The final comment was one that made Micah want to deflect attention elsewhere. Imogen had a natural beauty about her and if she had put on her best dress to go to the village, perhaps she too had wanted to meet him and put their earlier misunderstandings behind them. He hoped so. She deserved to have more pretty dresses. It was something he would happily correct, in time… somehow.

"So where are you venturing to, Miss Donaldson? Is your chaperone lagging behind?" he asked, shifting the focus of their conversation, and denying her the answer she sought.

"Well, as I am going to be here for a few weeks, I was intending to learn something of the area. Uncle is too gouty to ride, and my dear aunt insists that I take carriage rides with her to call upon her friends… associates." She smiled and looked around her before adding, "However, the social circle in these parts is somewhat limited." She laughed. "So, I took advantage of the beautiful morning and decided to take a ride keeping my own company. I understand you are recently returned to war, sir. I hope that you find the quiet comforting after all your daring deeds abroad."

Micah nodded, she seemed remarkably well informed about him, which was disconcerting rather than flattering, as he had only recently heard of her existence. He wanted to change the focus again from his 'daring deeds'. Whatever flattery she was pouring on him was misplaced. But he was curious as to why she would have taken her ride past the church, and how she came to know so much about his circumstances.

"Then please come with me, Miss Donaldson, and I will introduce you to my mother, who is a gentle lady, but who will delight in your company for a few minutes whilst

I change and then I shall gladly ride with you back to Thurley Manor. That way, I can show you some of our beautiful countryside." His smile lacked sincerity as they retraced his steps to the vicarage. He would discover her motives for this 'coincidental meeting' and then set things right again with Imogen.

"How can I turn down such a generous offer?" She gently stroked the neck of her horse with her elegantly gloved hand, every gesture oozing sophistication and control as she flirtatiously caught his eyes. She walked the animal alongside Micah.

"Then do not," he said, swiftly changing his morning's plans. A flirt was a flirt, sophisticated or not, but why would she indulge in flirting with him? He was handsome, his looking glass confirmed that, but Miss Beatrice Donaldson's kind of lady was interested in money and position, and he was no more than a vicar's son whose family lived modestly. Far from being besotted by this beauty, he was curious as to why she would be staying in an area largely populated by sheep and had chosen to cross his path before her uncle's formal dinner, for he was certain she did little by chance.

He was beginning to suspect that word of his personal change of circumstances had travelled to Thurley Manor, first the invitation, now Miss Donaldson's interest. Lord Farrington would not betray his trust; he was certain of that. If his suspicions were correct it was going to make things awkward back at the vicarage. His father did not approve of secrets; they had a habit of emerging and causing grief in their wake.

However, Micah wanted to feel like the Micah of old again, a vicar's son in a small village, unobserved and happy. Was that possible after what he had seen and done for his King and country? He would enjoy a pleasant horse ride with a beautiful woman.

He found his father in the church and presented Miss Donaldson to him.

"My dear lady, you must come inside." Reverend Ezekiel Arrow's face lit up, but not as much as Mrs. Ruth Arrow's did as she welcomed her visitor into her home.

"What a charming home you have here, Mrs. Arrow." The words were deliberately honeyed.

Micah smiled as his mother preened and showed Miss Donaldson into their reception room, whilst he changed quickly into his riding coat and boots and saddled his own horse.

After a brief repast with his extremely excited mother, during which Miss Donaldson poured more praise upon Ruth's hospitality, they rode off together, an image he knew would please Ruth Arrow very well indeed.

Chapter 11

"Goodness, what a pretty sight you are this morning, dear." Mrs. Weeks' lively voice caught Imogen by surprise as she ambled by the stream. "I missed you at breakfast. I take it your mother did not." There was something about the way Mrs. Weeks asked her that made Imogen feel uncomfortable.

"I stayed over with Mama and Papa," she said defensively wondering if she had been seen talking to Micah by the inn. Surely Mrs. Weeks could not think she would so easily be led astray?

The woman hooked an arm through the crook of Imogen's elbow. It was a friendly gesture that brought a smile to Imogen's face as she dismissed all notion of such talk. Mrs. Weeks knew her better.

"I just worried that you were safe. Mr. Skaggs has had strange men walking around the woodland and the village recently. Shifty lot they looked to me."

They were making their way down from her laundry towards the forge. Imogen's family had grown close to her after Mr. Weeks was killed in the wars. His widow had become a frequent visitor to the cottage, even staying there for a few nights, when news finally reached her. Mrs. Weeks had developed a bond with Mary, before drifting back to the village. When she discovered Mr. Weeks had left her well provided for her life changed. The woman had always believed them to be quite poor, living sparingly. Her husband had saved and inherited but had lived frugally. From that day forward, Mrs. Weeks decided it was time to make a life for herself. She had offered to help

Imogen and taken her under her wing. Imogen had enough learning to teach letters and numbers to her laundry girls in return. Mrs. Weeks taught Imogen how to keep house and receive guests in her patron's home. She was quick to learn.

"Thank you, I was just going to see my father," Imogen answered. "I will be in the schoolroom later."

"Well, I am glad to see you in that pretty dress like a young lady." Mrs. Weeks smiled. "You really are quite striking."

"I hardly used to go around in rags, Mrs. Weeks!" Imogen exclaimed.

"You wear those riding boots under your skirt as if you were ready to mount up and head across country like a huntsman – not that ladylike, but ever practical. Much as you wish you could be a good son to your father, believe me, he loves you as you are. That wild hair is tied back so tightly normally that it is rarely seen in all its glory. Let it flow freely occasionally. I have some emerald ribbon somewhere in my sewing box that would look most striking."

Imogen bristled as she thought about the lady who had a horse and fine leather boots. What did Mrs. Weeks expect her to do, walk along Church Lane and cross the woodland path to her parents' cottage in her pumps or slippers?

"I need sturdy boots and it would not do to have my hair loose around a forge, would it?" Imogen replied, flattered by the compliments, but she preferred to be practical. "I am no child anymore so it would hardly be fitting if I turned up for lessons looking like a young girl myself. Besides, there are some people's attention I do not wish to encourage. Mr. Skaggs stopped and spoke to me recently. I did not like the way he eyed me up, Mrs. Weeks."

Her friend's expression changed instantly. "You keep away from that one. He is full of malice."

Her words backed up what Imogen thought of him. To some he was seen as a middle-aged man, of comfortable means, with a dubious fashion taste, but who could offer a maid a comfortable home. However, Imogen could not think of sitting at a dining table looking at him every day for the rest of her life or lying next to him as his wife – that made her feel nauseous. Imogen instantly replaced the heinous image with a more appealing one of lying next to Micah Arrow, as that thought pleased and excited her greatly.

Today she had hoped to impress Micah; show him that she could be civilised, and Imogen thought it had been working a treat until the gentlewoman arrived upon her fine horse, dripping words onto him whilst ignoring her. Imogen's confidence was not so easily dented, but the interruption had been very annoying.

She had stolen a glance back at the two of them - him the epitome of a tall and handsome, available man, with prospects, staring up at the vision of feminine gentility upon her fine steed. He appeared to be hanging on her every word. Was he so easily taken in by the woman's smooth turn of phrase? Men could be so fickle!

"I do not want Mr. Skaggs setting his eyes upon you. I have heard he is seeking a wife to add to the house he has bought in Gorebeck. You are meant for better than he, Imogen. Wealth he may have, but I do not approve of the way he accrues it. He bends, if not breaks, the law." She touched the side of her nose with her finger in a gesture of knowing. "Besides, he is a foul tub of a man and you, my dear, should be wooed by a handsome young gentleman."

Imogen laughed at Mrs. Weeks' candour. Imogen wanted Micah to see her as beautiful in the way Mrs. Weeks did. Imogen had always looked upon Micah Arrow favourably. However, their mothers' distaste for each other meant they could never be anything other than discreet friends, at the best, without causing a rift. She wondered how much of a rift he would be prepared to cause, for Imogen's mother would accept Micah. When he had left to serve, Imogen missed him, but he had returned to her and this time she would find a way to capture his heart.

"Don't allow tittle-tattle to sully that pretty face, Imogen. So, what do you think about our new neighbour?" Mrs. Weeks asked.

The question caught Imogen off guard. "I do not think I can comment fairly. I have only met him briefly as he is so newly returned and then by pure chance." Imogen stared ahead at the path hoping the colour rise in her cheeks did not give her true thoughts and feelings for Micah away.

Mrs. Weeks laughed and squeezed Imogen's arm gently. "Dear, Immi, I do not mean the attractive lieutenant - oh how marvellous he looked in his uniform! The white piping on his blue jacket set it off to perfection. What a figure he cut! Micah is not new here. Don't worry, my dear, I shall not share your interest in him with the village gossips. What with Mr. Skaggs' comings and goings of late they have enough to speculate upon. He has been showing men with measuring contraptions around the land north of the village, upstream. It cannot be a good sign. I am surprised that your mother has not been disturbed by them."

Imogen wished a wave would rise from the fast-flowing river and sweep her away with it. Of course, Mrs. Weeks had not meant that Micah was new to the village.

"Well, I would make for poor gossip on that account as I have hardly spoken to Mr. Arrow since his return, only meeting him by chance once…"

"I think you protest too much, Imogen. If you're meant for each other then God will find a way and you will meet Lieutenant Arrow by chance again and again – have your mother do a reading for you. No, I meant our new neighbour up at Thurley Manor, the honourable, or perhaps not so, Sir Benedict Adams. He is an enigma to me presently." Mrs. Weeks squeezed her arm. "I heard he is not the owner yet."

"Yes, of course you did, but I do not know anything about him." Imogen wanted to break away from her and go to the forge. Lose herself in the necklace she was finishing, it was special.

Imogen had been crafting a necklace with a set of jewellery making tools her father had bought her in York for her birthday the year before last. She treasured it. She had practised on simple wire and pieces of metal he gave her to make cloak pins and simple brooches. Recently he had declared her good enough to make proper jewellery and so had bought her some silver wire and small sheets of the metal, polished gemstones, Whitby jet, none-precious but all pretty or striking. The small pliers and fine tools were exquisite and the best present she had ever had.

"Imogen," Mrs. Weeks broke into her thoughts, "If it is true that Sir Benedict has offered to buy the land to the north of Dibbledale leading up to the moors then your cottage tenancy would transfer to him. He could evict your family at his will. If I hear more, I will let you know, but it may be prudent for Mary to look kindly on your father's plans to buy a cottage in the village. That way he could own the property outright and they would be safe from threat of eviction."

Imogen stared back in disbelief, realising what this would mean for her family.

Imogen was touched by her care and shocked by the news.

"But Mama relies on the woodland. It is her life's blood. Anyway, why would he want it? We have tried so many times to encourage Mama to move into the village, but she can be so stubborn." Imogen stopped in her tracks at this revelation. If true, it would break her mother's heart.

"Well, the river flows through that part of the land and I heard a whisper that he and Mr. Jethro Skaggs have plans for something concerning it." Mrs. Weeks stood facing her; there was no doubt that she was sincere and worried. "Men have been seen looking at the old oaks, but not in admiration of their longstanding beauty. I have heard they could be considering using the bark in a tannery."

"Never! Tanneries are foul places; they smell and what of the beautiful trees? They have been there for centuries. Mama will be distraught." Imogen was horrified; beautiful Dibbledale would be destroyed.

"Bark my dear... ash and all manner of noxious smells, of course they will use urine too, ugh!"

"But what of the fresh water needed for the laundry? The water will be filled with detritus." Imogen saw Mrs. Weeks turn her face to the sun. She had seen a tannery in operation as a girl when her father had been delivering some irons to it. It was a sight she would not forget, the smells lingered in and on her for what seemed an age.

Mrs. Weeks breathed in the fresh air deeply, before looking back at Imogen. "That is indeed my issue and everyone else's problem too if the rumour is true. We shall have to see what can be done about it. As the land is currently owned by Bishop Denton in Gorebeck, we could petition him, or try and collectively bid for it, then we may be able to stop the purchase, but that would require his goodwill and a miracle to raise the funds. We would also need a spokesperson who is well informed about Sir Benedict's plans. We can hardly approach the man armed only with a half-baked rumour."

"Have you asked Reverend Arrow to speak for us?" Imogen asked.

"Not yet, as I had hoped that we could perhaps encourage his son to take an interest in the matter. He may be able to persuade his father and other local businessmen to join; a united voice could form a collective." Mrs. Weeks smiled at her.

"You saw me talking to Micah, didn't you?" Imogen asked.

"Yes, and you did look well together. You have that spark between you. You rose to his bait and he to yours," she said and tilted her head on one side. "Oh, how I miss that. A good union should always have a spark to keep the flame going."

"You have been busy thinking about a lot of things, haven't you? But some sparks go out because of circumstances, they become smothered by opposition." Imogen's words were tinged with sadness as she thought of Mrs. Ruth Arrow. How could she win the woman around to seeing how lovely Mary really was? Imogen needed a plan, and friends like Mrs. Weeks.

"Then fight back!" Mrs. Weeks advised. "You are no simpering maiden. You have a backbone and brain that can think for itself. You use what God has gifted you with to catch and keep your man. Do not let any sour old woman stop that. She is his mother, so be careful to be more charming to him, and magnanimous, than Ruth Arrow is about Mary. Then you will claim the higher ground and he will love you for it."

"You are wise, Mrs. Weeks. I will heed your words, but I am enormously proud of Mama and will not stand by and have her maligned. If I cross Mr. Micah Arrow's path again, I will mention what has been said about Sir Benedict Adams and Mr. Skaggs' plan and see if he knows anything about it, and I could ask Papa."

Imogen saw the woman's eyes brighten at her latter suggestion. She intuitively knew that was what Mrs. Weeks was hoping for. "But he will not approve of me becoming involved in the politics and business of men, Mrs. Weeks," Imogen admitted, for all his willingness for Imogen to be involved in aspects of life and learning, he considered politics to be corrupt and therefore beneath her.

"Perhaps not, he would not approve of my asking him as he sees me passing the time of day. Unfortunately, he sees what he may think of a loose tongue, but he should have more faith in me. Wilfred is a good man and wise for one, but he makes the same mistake many do and undervalues women. I ask you, who would lose out the most? The village, yes, ultimately, but this plan would destroy Mary. It would expose her, and she would hate that. Have you ever asked her why? Is it purely down to her love of trees, plants and squirrels that keeps her hidden away? Mary is not a shy woman, so why does she fear living in a village?" Mrs. Weeks crossed her arms and tilted her head as she watched Imogen's response.

"She is not scared of anyone. Mama likes the peace and the beauty of nature." Imogen was always defensive of her mother, even when she knew there was more to the matter than that.

"And the cold, no doubt. You mean as she ages, as we all must, she enjoys the slog of fetching logs and water up to the cottage, or the hard winters to come..." She shook her head. "If you believe that then perhaps I have credited you with more brains than I should have."

"If you have something you wish to tell me, Mrs. Weeks, please do so. I have no wish to argue with you, which we will if my mother is criticised. Whatever her reasons they will be sound."

Imogen had asked her mother the same question many times and was always ignored, rebuffed, or given chores to do if she had so much time for chit chat. She did not like the reference to Mary aging. She was strong, always had been, and Imogen hated to think of her as fragile and old, or broken in spirit or body.

"I am being unfair, forgive me. I know how difficult your situation is and how much you adore her; but, Immi, ask her what happened to her grandmother back in her old country. I only know the truth of it because she let it slip once when we were drinking her dandelion wine. We had become close and yet no sooner was that bond formed than she withdrew into her shell again, and in the new morning I was back to being 'Mrs. Weeks', no longer fondly called Emily. Ask her when you next visit, but more importantly deal with our current problem and share this information with your father discreetly, please. This is all hearsay at the moment, plans were overheard by an interested party, but if it is true then we must act quickly in a united manner or say goodbye to the beauty of Dibbledale and you your parents' home in the woods."

"I will pass on your concerns. Mama never talks of her life in Ireland, she says it is a land of political turmoil where hatred has thrived. Yet she loves it so. She only sings the songs of a bygone time. They tell of battles won by a High King or of faeries and simple folk. Love stories that warm your heart, but her past is closed to us. It is her way," Imogen explained quietly.

"It is your heritage too, and you have a right to understand it. We will talk again later, now go see your father but do not be late to instruct my girls." Mrs. Weeks patted Imogen's back and turned away towards the laundry.

Imogen stared at her. Straight-backed and determined the lady walked briskly away.

Mrs. Weeks had given her already troubled mind much more to think on. Imogen would talk to both her parents when in the privacy of their cottage. She liked being able to go visit her mother and work alongside her father, when he was not too busy, using his small room at the back of the forge for her own work. She needed to leave her work ready to start later and ask Wilfred to buy in further supplies for brooches and necklaces for Gorebeck fair next month. Imogen was also making a lovely pendant, a special gift for her mama, as special as the woman was to her. With Mrs. Weeks' words of warning ringing in her ears she quickly made her way to the forge.

Chapter 12

Micah was enjoying the gallop through the dale before him, as it melted into the woodlands and then moor above. The lady had a fine seat and controlled the horse easily. Although fashionably pale, Miss Donaldson had energy and a taste for the outdoors.

He slowed as they reached the moor road and looked down upon the town of Beckton. Mill Lane stretched out towards Thurley Manor. Would the lady return his earlier action and invite him in, he wondered? If so, should he accept before the forthcoming dinner? Perhaps not.

"You ride well," he said, as she came alongside him. The horse was, like its rider, quite beautiful.

"Thank you. My father bred racing horses, so it is hardly surprising." Her smile was genuine. "I was put in the saddle of a miniature pony as soon as I could walk," she said and laughed as if recalling a sweet memory. Then with her composure regained she added, "He could be a fraction dramatic on occasion when it came to my safety though."

"Then you are in the right county, miss, Harrogate, Northallerton, Thirsk, York - there are so many racecourses in this beautiful part of Yorkshire. Is that why you are visiting? Is your father buying new blood stock?" he asked innocently, as they moved along.

"No, I am afraid I no longer have a father. He served in the wars and died from wounds he received at a place called Salamanca, where there was a nasty battle." She turned her head away.

He realised that for all this woman's bravado and pretence, where her father was concerned at least, true emotion peeked through the veneer of indifference. She still grieved.

"I am sorry... I too was there." He stared ahead hoping she would not press for a detailed account of what he had seen. He tried to forget so many memories, there was no glory in war, but much gore. If only mankind would learn lessons from the past and stop them.

He was in the heavy cavalry, Captain Matthias Donaldson. Did you know him? I heard he died valiantly, but so many soldiers are reported to have done so, it makes me wonder if every officer died such a death. If so, I am surprised that the French did not fold years before. Men died nobly and bravely – but they died all the same."

"Perhaps it is best to believe what you are told. He is beyond reach of pain and battle, in a more peaceful place than Salamanca was. I am afraid I did not know him. I was in the Light Dragoons. It was a hard battle, a significant victory, but not for the many brave soldiers who fell. Is Sir Benedict Adams your guardian now, Miss Donaldson?" he asked, curiosity aroused. If so, she, like her horse, had been given her head and a great deal of freedom for an innocent maid who should surely be out in the marriage market.

"Uncle Benedict married my father's sister. So, temporarily he is acting as my nearest male relative should. He insists I stay here until Julian, my brother, returns. Then we shall travel to Belton Hall and Stud, down in Wiltshire, at that point, in law at least, my wellbeing will fall to my brother.

However, I hope that he will arrive quite soon. Like you, many officers are now making their way home, selling commissions, and hoping for more peaceful times. I do not wish to offend my uncle for he is a man of some temporary influence over my life." Her tone sharpened.

"And your mother, is she visiting with you?" he persisted, as she was so willing to openly discuss her family circumstances.

"She stayed in Oporto where she had been awaiting Father's return and now remains there with friends until Julian can fetch her home."

"So, you were left on the estate on your own… in mourning?" he commented, and saw her smile broaden at the surprise in his face.

"I changed from blacks to my sombre colours and am now venturing into pleasanter new hues blissfully waiting to be seen in such a pretty colour as your young friend! I have been running the estate with the help of a particularly good landsman, trainer, and the many stable hands. My grandmother was there, so it was fine. However, sadly, she died, leaving me quite alone. That is when Uncle Benedict stepped up." She shrugged. "I know the business better than anyone as I was always following my father around. Horses were our life's blood." Pride glowed from her as smoothly as the words she uttered.

The passion that drove her words was strong, like her formidable character. This beauty had run a stud farm, surely this would make for interesting conversation in the withdrawing rooms when ladies gathered after functions, he mused.

"You are…"

"Am I?" she said quickly cutting him off and kicked her horse onwards making for a copse at the brow of a hill skirting the moorland without letting him finish his sentence.

He followed her. Once in the shelter of the copse she dismounted, looping the reins over a low branch, and stood in the shadow of an oak looking down the slope at Thurley Manor, its grand Jacobean chimneys clearly seen across the splendid lake that was at its front.

"What is your uncle like, Miss Donaldson?" he asked, as he stood beside her.

"Other than gouty?" she laughed. "Oh, he is rich, ambitious as most men are, likes his own way and tolerates few who obstruct his wishes." She shrugged as if there was little else to say about the man.

"Does he have ambitions for you too?" Her delicate scent wafted across his face; combined with the exquisitely fitted riding outfit, they permeated an air that conveyed stylish wealth. In her riding hat she was nearly as tall as him; he admired the sensuous line of her lips, that mouth, if not so eloquent in her choice of words, was as inviting as a quality harpy's. Her tongue gently traced the contour of her lower lip.

She glanced up at him, chestnut eyes brimming with life and mischief. "Oh, yes, he has a stallion in his eye line who he would pair me with." Although she smiled, her eyes did not.

He laughed. "You have a very stark way with words, Miss Donaldson. A way that I have not heard expressed in the assembly rooms."

"Really? Do you gentlemen not speak of ladies so, in the quiet recesses of grand halls?'

'But I see that I do not shock you, soldier, and neither do you appear greatly offended by my indelicate choice of words. I have failed to scare you off."

What a strange thing for her to say, Micah considered. "I have heard far worse, but not delivered in such an elegant way, or off a lady's tongue." He tried not to offend her even though her comments were beyond forthright.

"Do not doubt that I am a well-bred lady, sir, even if I speak with a directness that you are unfamiliar with."

"What is it you want of me? You are being too frank to be simply toying with me for your amusement." Micah felt his stomach clench. Far from being seduced by this woman she was someone he would rather keep at a distance.

She leaned against the tree trunk behind her. "I would like to befriend you, Mr. Micah Arrow."

"Why?" What on earth could this woman need from him? She had wealth, confidence, freedom, and a fine horse, so why focus on him? She could catch the attention of many an eligible gentleman who at least on face value would have greater prospects than a vicar's son.

"Because, if 'we' are to be matched, I would know the man first, and cut down the painfully long courting ritual." She flicked her crop by her side and tilted her head up challenging him, but to what?

How brazen she was! The lady had not realised that she had crossed a line and he was genuinely offended. Micah would enjoy courting and unravelling the character of a lady worth taking the time to know properly. His desire was that both would enjoy each other – a lady like Miss Imogen Underwood.

Miss Donaldson may resent it being a man's world, but he wanted to cherish his life partner, not be dragged around by her on a rein, like one of her prize horses. Micah was unsure if it was her attitude; one that knew too much of the world for her own good and standing, or her involvement with the 'plan' whatever it was that Sir Benedict Adams thought he had in store for Micah. Whichever, he wanted none of it. He could not be bought.

"Ah! At last. I have managed to truly shock you!" she added. "Believe me, Mr. Arrow, I do not wish to insult you, but whatever it is that my uncle has found out about you, he aims to use to his advantage. If that involves me, which from the way he is praising you in front of me, is most certainly his intention, then I would also know, or I shall not play along with either of you." She folded her arms with her riding crop hanging loosely from her right wrist.

"Miss Donaldson, I do not know the man. We have never been introduced and have no knowledge of why he should take any interest in my affairs, for my parents are humble people. You have seen my home and met them. I do not think that Sir Benedict sounds like a highly religious sort to be so influenced by my father's preaching. However, flattered I may be by your attention and the upcoming invite to dinner, it can be no more than a friendly gesture upon his part. We do not mix in the same circles." He stared back at her.

"Tell me, do you prefer the fresh-faced blacksmith's daughter to the lady from Wiltshire?" she asked.

"Good day, lady. You go too far!" He walked back to his horse.

"Arrow!" The word was snapped out. "You are hiding something, but I tell you this for your own good.

Uncle has received a letter from his legal representatives last week. I listened to some of the conversation he had with the man who delivered it. He mentioned your name and the words 'considerable inheritance'. If that is true... If he really could be asking you to take interest in me and my dowry, I would have you know that I am not entering any marriage to suit my uncle's whim, or anyone else's. I will run my estate as I always have done. My brother has no interest in it, so as long as it funds his lifestyle, he will happily leave me to it." She walked over to him. "I will only take a husband if he pleases me."

"I will only take a wife, Miss Donaldson, of my own choosing, in my own time. When I do, I will live on my own land, where I will share the joy of matrimony with her. You are welcome to your horses, your brother, your land and your life. I have no intention of being any part of it. However, I would thank you for sharing this information with me. I am happy to be your friend, but no more." He mounted his horse. "Good day, I hope you find your true match, in time." Micah touched the edge of his riding hat as a farewell, then rode directly back to Dibbledale without a backward glance.

Chapter 13

"Imogen, you have such a gift for doing this kind of fine work. That heart shaped, stone pendant catches the light as if it was really beating with life's blood. The colour changes as you move it. Quite beautiful!" Wilfred looked at her with pride; he admired delicate work that his large hands were not capable of creating. Set him to making an ornate pair of iron gates for an estate and his craftmanship was second to none.

"Thank you, Papa, I thought I would give it to Mama when I next visit." She watched his expression lighten and saw that the idea pleased him greatly.

"Aye, she'll be well pleased. I must confess that I've not given her many trinkets over the years." He glanced at her fondly. "You have a kindly soul, Immi."

"You give her so much more!" Imogen watched as he sat down on his favourite tree stump. He looked tired; his usual spark dulled somehow, his words softened with sentiment. Imogen missed seeing him each morning and walking into Dibbledale with him. The lines under his eyes had darkened and there were bags there where there had not been only weeks before. "Are you alright, Papa?" she asked. The words resonated in her mind as she could not remember ever uttering them before.

"Of course I am," he said, and was about to stand up and continue his work. "Nothing a jug of porter won't fix once I'm done here." He laughed, but even that seemed short of his normal spirit.

"Sit a while. Talk to me. I won't hold you up for

long as I have to instruct the girls shortly." Imogen touched his arm and he hesitated.

He handed the pendant back to her and then sat with his hands placed on each knee, ready to hear what she had to say. "I am flattered that you would want to chat with your father, with such a busy life as you have now, but tell me what is it you want to know? Ask it, and let a man get on with his work, or maybe have a drink." One quizzical eyebrow rose.

Imogen decided to get straight to the point.

"Two things: firstly, have you heard any rumours that our woodland may be under threat of purchase by the new owner of Thurley Manor, and secondly…"

Imogen shifted uneasily on her own high stool.

"Go on, woman, you'll burst with it if you don't ask it."

"What happened to Mama's grandmother back in Ireland?" She had to stifle a smile as he looked shocked at her unexpected question. Both of his eyebrows shot up.

"Well, the first is gossip that is gathering the possibility of having some truth within it, but I have no idea who began it. The second question was a bolt from the blue – I did not see that one coming from you! Makes me wonder why it has now." He stared at her.

"Is it true about the woodland being bought? Is there anything we can do about it? Will it threaten our home?" It was Imogen who was shocked now. It would destroy their beautiful world, their home – Mary.

"One question at a time! First, we need to know if it is true, which may involve a trip to Gorebeck, like for the fair."

He winked at her, obviously it was a plan Wilfred was already plotting. "We need to find out all the facts and then see what can be done. Usually there is something that folk can do if they work together and put their minds to it."

"And my second question...?" Imogen saw the troubled look return to his eyes. Mrs. Weeks had told her something of a family secret that she had been shielded from, but why? In her heart she knew there was something kept from her.

"You should ask your mother." He stood up and faced the forge.

"Papa! Don't do that. It is precisely why I don't ask Mama. She will ignore me and walk away. But if it explains why she stays away from folk in the village then understanding it would be a way forward to helping her and us. We both want to live as a family again in the village in a home of our own, don't we? If we lose the cottage in the woods, then we shall have to move into the village. Mama would have no choice. So, what is it she fears? You know she will not let me do the fetching for her – she holds out hope that I may make a 'decent marriage' so long as my hands are not rough." Imogen raised her eyebrows this time. If a man was only concerned with whether she worked or not, then a marriage would never happen. After seeing the fine lady on her horse, what hope was there for her? No, her dear mama was wrong. Micah was not eyeing her hands before the woman disturbed their moment.

"Don't you think I know this?" He spun around and faced Imogen. She could see the creased lines on his forehead that laid his concern bare.

"So..." Imogen raised her eyebrows to stress her point.

"To tell you would break her trust in me and that I will never do. Go and ask her yourself. But do so with an open mind because your mother suffered much in her young life, so allow her some idiosyncrasies, especially at her time of life."

"But Papa!" 'Idiosyncrasies was one of her mama's favourite words, but secrets were what he really meant. Imogen had not realised that they had any between them. Now she doubted – what had they kept hidden from her? She was hardly going to challenge her father when she had managed to fluster him so.

"No, Imogen, you will not have your way on this. You take her your gift and if she will tell you then so be it. If not, then accept that not everything in our lives needs to be shared – I am sure you have your secrets too." His head tilted to one side.

"No, Papa, I don't. I told you the truth about the woods and meeting Micah Arrow." Imogen braced herself because she did not know what he was referring to. Surely he had not guessed her desire for Micah. She wanted to push him for more information but knew that it would only create a bad feeling between them. Wilfred was fiercely loyal to Mary.

"Then no doubt you will have in the future. Now go and leave me in peace. The first question relates to a situation I am giving a deal of thought to. The second one is between you and your mother." His mouth closed. The conversation had ended.

"Very well, Papa," she said, and gave his cheek a quick kiss before leaving him to continue hammering at his work. It took a lot to make her father agitated or for him to refuse her, so she had to respect that he was a man of his word. Annoying, though, as it had proven to be on this occasion.

Imogen was distracted during her lesson but could not wait to be free again. The younger girls were keen to learn, and Mrs. Weeks had plans for starting a village school. The notion of teaching in a classroom and having to spend every day inside with them made her fearful. She had been brought up to wonder in nature. Her mother told her all sorts of things, from knowing what to use if your skin broke out in a rash, or your belly became bilious, to the legends of old and tales of Roman gods, Sagas from a bygone age, to know how to weigh and measure things. She taught her quick ways of figuring out number puzzles. Most of this had been done outside. Only spending time indoors for her slate and practising her letters. Was she her mother's daughter - did she too desire to be with nature? If so, how would she ever settle to keeping house for her man?

"Mama! Mama!" Imogen hailed her outside as she had not found her in the cottage. Pickles lolloped around the corner and knocked into her legs as he skidded to a halt for his greeting. Imogen laughed straight away; her troubled mind unknotted from all its mulling over of questions.

"Here, pet," Mary said, as she came around the corner of the cottage carrying a pail of water from the well.

Imogen went straight over and took it off her. "You should not be labouring so.

Mary followed her into the cottage and when Imogen turned around the woman was standing staring at Imogen with her hands on her hips. "Was there something you wanted to say to me, Imogen?"

"Yes, I love you!" She handed the heart pendant to Mary.

For the first time she could remember in Imogen's life, her mother was totally surprised. Moreover, a tear escaped from the corner of her eye down her cheek as she inspected the heart-shaped stone and spun it in the daylight from the open doorway. It glistened.

"Where did you get this?" Mary watched it, mesmerised.

"I made it for you, at the forge. Papa bought me the jewellery tools; you remember?" Imogen swallowed. Time seemed to stand still for a moment as Pickles bustled into the cottage after them.

Mary nodded.

"Well, I've been using them regularly and as soon as Papa felt I was good enough he gave me some things to turn into necklaces, cloak pins and brooches."

The woman nodded and swallowed back waves of emotion. "Aye, you have inherited a rare gift..."

"From whom... my grandmother, perhaps?" Imogen asked innocently, but as she watched her mother's head turn to face her, she knew that she had somehow struck at her heart in a way she had not intended. "Mama, don't shut off from me, tell me, what happened to her, please?"

"You have the gift... how else can you have known there is something to tell..."

"I could lie to you, but I will admit the truth. Mrs. Weeks was telling me some unsettling news about the woodland. It may be that someone is planning to buy it from the Dentons and, well, as we chatted about you not wanting to move into Dibbledale, she said I should ask you about Gran. Whatever it is that you keep from me, I should know as I am no longer a child, and it is my heritage too."

Mary sat down still looking at the heart shaped stone in her hand.

"Imogen, I was raised by my grandmother. She lived in a small cottage with a peat fire. It was not as comfy as this one, but I loved it. She was full of tales, and she knew how to read the seasons, use the plants, see beyond the obvious and I so wanted to be like her. The local folk used her potions, asked about what they should do – she was wise and kind. She even knew her letters and taught me as I have taught you. Then a man of religion came, he started to tell folk not to listen to her, not to drink her poison, and when someone she tried to help died as their wound was already festering when they were brought to her, he stirred them up against her. They blamed her for the man's death." Mary closed her eyes, stopping tears from flowing.

"Was she arrested for his death? Did they accuse her of murder, Mama?" Imogen was horrified.

"No, but they whispered she toyed with the devil's doings." Mary shook her head.

"Did they burn her … as a witch?" Imogen asked wide-eyed, gripping her shawl tightly around her body, as a chill swept through her.

"No, lass, but three local men came for her when she was foraging. It was said that they took her up to the bog and, well, that they sent her down to the underworld to appease her gods of old. I had nightmares about it for years. I was taken in by nuns and my mind was supposedly cleansed. But she never was a witch. She never traded potions, poisons, or spells; she was just a wise woman who knew how to survive off the land. She believed in a god, whether it was the God or a greater spirit, or a mother of all the earth, but her instincts were acute."

"Mammy sensed trouble… you know how it is, knew how to help folk when she could, and hated cruelty. However, she never thought they would turn on her, but she did not realise the fear that a bitter man could stir up in them and, so in their ignorance, they believed his lies."

"That's horrid, Mama," Imogen hugged her and for once the woman let her, allowing her moment of raw emotion to be seen by her daughter. "Did they arrest the men?"

"There was no witness to what they did, it was all hearsay. It was claimed Mammy ran away and deserted her home and family. My brothers were older and had their own families. I never saw them again. Those men paid the price though, and no one knew what happened to them either. One by one fate had its way." Mary did not expand upon the comment, but a strange, distanced air pervaded the silence that drew out between them before she continued. "I learnt the plants and remembered all she taught me. I tried to pass this onto you, but that's why I always told you not to tell others. Our knowledge brings danger from those who envy us."

"And what of the tea leaves?" Imogen could see how that knowledge could have been used against her great grandmother.

Mary laughed. "I learned them from a woman in a country fair before I met your father. I wanted so desperately to be that 'wise woman', to be able to tell when trouble was coming, but now I realise that I could be accused like her. Don't you see, Imogen, we are surrounded here by moors and bogs! History repeats itself – you mark my word I could suffer the same fate!" She blinked nervously and Imogen's heart felt tight. Not her lovely Mama!

"Oh, Mama, never say that! Papa would not let anyone hurt you. But you hide away from people. Don't you see that could make you look more like the witch of old? Think of Papa too. He needs to be in the village. He's tired and you are too. The winters are hard." Imogen did not mean to make her mother sad after bringing her the moment of joy with her gift, but the words had to be said. "The fate of one does not need to be the fate of all. Papa and I would never let that happen to you, but you must face this fear down. If not for yourself, then for your husband, you owe him that."

"I know, but I really love the woodlands. The animals... I don't trust people. I never will." She put the necklace on. "Imogen, you may not wish to hear this, but you are so like her. Granny could turn her hand to anything like this and, well look…"

Mary went to a cupboard, she opened a small wooden box and pulled out an old metal chain from which was hung a small heart made of amber stone; a stone that once again, when held to the daylight, had a sparkle to it as she twirled it around. "Your granny made me this. It is all I have of her, and I give it to you now, Imogen, because the gift of foresight I so eagerly wanted to inherit from her you have running through your veins, and do not deny it."

Imogen stared in wonder at the pendant, but never uttered one word of denial.

Chapter 14

Wilfred hammered as hard down on the anvil as he could until happy with the effect his labour had upon the red-hot metal. Strange that it seemed to take longer than normal. Then plunging it into his tub of slack water, he took a moment's rest as it spluttered and hissed, eventually giving up its heat. His job was surrounded by fire, and effort, yet he felt a shiver run down his spine. He shrugged his muscle-bound shoulders dismissively. Wilfred had been feeling off-colour for a couple of days but did not want to worry Mary or Imogen.

Glancing over to the small waiting room at the entrance to the forge he saw the rotund, garishly dressed figure of Mr. Skaggs standing flicking a crop impatiently about his leg. He harrumphed loudly to get Wilfred's attention and in a gesture of complaint at being kept waiting.

"Good day, sir. Can I be of service to you?" he asked, wondering how quickly he could get rid of the man. Wilfred felt tired, he wanted his dinner, to sit by his fire and chatter to Mary, then take his rest.

"Yes, my good man, you certainly can."

Wilfred did not like Skaggs who had a reputation that Wilfred knew well enough from the tavern in Gorebeck. Wilfred breathed in deeply, trying to clear his tired mind. He felt strange, and this man's presence did not help any.

"I would talk with you, man to man." Skaggs stood, legs centred, holding both ends of the crop with each hand.

He was standing his ground, making a position that was ready to bargain, but why? Whatever this man wanted Wilfred would have none of it. If it involved man traps, then he would give him short shrift. He would not have another man's blood on his hands.

"You have a fine forge here." Skaggs did not even look around.

Skaggs seemed to wait for the compliment to be acknowledged. Wilfred did not disappoint him. Wilfred wanted to perch on his favourite tree stump, but Skaggs stood proud, so Wilfred centred his feet also. Why was it so cold?

"My thanks. Can I do something for you – does your horse need shoeing?" Wilfred asked hoping it was not an urgent job. He wanted to go back to his Mary, she'd give him something to take that would stoke the fire in his blood again.

"Yes, you have a good-looking forge here, like your daughter," Skaggs said.

"Pardon?" Wilfred was confused. What was this buffoon doing standing in front of him praising his forge and likening his daughter to it? It was a clumsy attempt at flattery. Had the man been drinking?

"Your daughter, Underwood. She is a beauty." Skaggs' smile grew.

Wilfred stood straighter. His daughter was perfection itself in her father's eyes. This man had no right to make comments about her. Wilfred was glad he had replaced his long tongs, or he might just commit an act that would see him thrown in gaol for life. He was not a violent man, but every man had his limits and where his Mary and Imogen were concerned, he would let no man deride them.

"You deserve better than this though, Underwood," Skaggs said as he curled a lip and glanced around

Wilfred's neat and organised forge. The product of years of hard work and devotion.

"I do alright, sir. My family are well-provided for and loved." Wilfred tried to sound upbeat and not offended, but he had to focus on standing straight and keeping eye contact with this worm of a man. He felt as though he could sway – or, heaven forbid, fall. God knew he was tired, but this was ridiculous.

"No, they aren't, man, and you know it. Your woman dwells in a forest hovel and your beautiful daughter in the house of a widow who takes in laundry." Skaggs shook his head with contempt. "I admire the way you have tried. You work hard and you have given life to a rare beauty. But is it fair to her that you keep her locked away with a dried-up widow-woman? When she could be a lady in her own house and raise fine sons?" Skaggs raised his grizzled eyebrows.

"My wife keeps a tidy, homely cottage in the woodland that we both love. My daughter resides in the house of a decent, recently widowed, lady who runs more than one successful enterprise. But what interest is all of this to you... sir?" Wilfred asked, realising where the conversation was going. With incredulity he gave effort to being civil, as he also struggled to stay upright.

"I make you an offer, man. I need a wife, a young one who will provide me with heirs for my growing number of successful businesses. Your Imogen would be ideal. She is somewhat headstrong, that can be managed as I do not want a simpering maid with no backbone for life, and she is strong of body and knows her letters. I am telling you to bless our union and I will offer you a position of overseer/manager to a new enterprise, a tannery I am undertaking here in Dibbledale..." He widened his eyes as if making the greatest offer to Wilfred he would ever receive.

"Imogen is young and…" Wilfred's words caught in his throat. The thought of this poor excuse of a man laying with his daughter made his stomach turn. For a moment Wilfred actually thought he may be sick. He breathed deeply whilst taking in the meaning of Skaggs' next words.

"Precisely, she is young and strong, and I like that about her. I do not wish to break her but show her how she could also be formidable in this backwater with me leading the way. Imogen will see how I can provide a good home for her, make you overseer of the tannery, see that your woman is protected from idle tongues…" He flicked his crop casually at his side as he spoke. The menace he meant was palpable.

Wilfred grabbed the iron framework of the bellows to steady himself. The man's words were a threat not an offer. "I provide adequately for my family, Mr. Skaggs, and when Imogen is ready, she will marry a man of her choosing as her good mother did." Skaggs intended to use Imogen as a brood mare, buy his approval with promises of Wilfred working for him – more like be indentured to him and his wicked ways, and threaten Mary at the same time. He could stir trouble up for Mary, Wilfred knew this, for whispers and hints build on fear… they might have to move. Skaggs had influence; Wilfred swallowed hard. His worst nightmare could be realised.

"This," Skaggs circled his arm around the room dramatically. "This is not providing, Underwood. This is merely existing."

"You will lose your strength as you age, your woman will lose her lair, you your business, and the laundry wench hers, which would leave Imogen vulnerable and homeless. Then I may not offer a wedding for her, but she could still humour me, for a while."

Wilfred stood forward; rage welled within him. But Skaggs prodded him with his crop in his already painful chest. "Think on it. I will return here in one week; you will have had time to see the reason by then. You should be honoured. My own father was a tanner, so I can live with a father-in-law who used to be a smithy, who could manage one of my businesses. Keep it in the family so to speak." He strolled away.

Wilfred stepped after him and reached out. He wanted to ring the blighter's neck but as he stretched out an arm the pain within him grew.

Wilfred sank to his knees; his head felt the smack of the earth as he crumpled.

Breathe, breathe… he was cold, he was sweating, shaking and his heart felt as though it would break…

"Mr. Underwood… Wilfred… talk to me…" the woman's voice was familiar, but it was not his Mary. A tear slipped from his eye, "Oh God save them!" he muttered.

"Calm yourself, Wilfred," the voice said. He felt something placed over him, warmth… his coat perhaps.

"Please… you must help Immi, he can't… he mustn't… I failed them…" Words drifted off.

"Who is he?" Mrs. Weeks asked.

"Skaggs, he can't…" Oblivion ensued.

Chapter 15

"Miss Underwood." Micah stepped in front of her as she slipped out of the church, hoping not to be noticed. He had pre-empted her path and waited.

Imogen's heart quickened immediately on hearing Micah's voice.

She liked singing and seeing people, usually with her father, but today he had not joined the service. Always seated at the back, or at the end of the pew nearest the side chapel, they were regular attendees.

"Mr. Arrow." She avoided gazing directly into his eyes lest she become lost in them. Imogen was still annoyed with him for not introducing her to the lady and allowing Imogen to slink off as if she was of no consequence. They had once been childhood friends who would laugh and smile together. As they turned from children to adults, opportunities to meet faded away, the world raged, and war broke the lives and destiny of many.

"I did not have the chance to introduce you to our new neighbour the other day - our temporary one, that is. Miss Beatrice Donaldson was out exploring Dibbledale when she stopped to engage in conversation." His words were softly spoken, but they had the desired effect as her head shot up, defiant eyes meeting his curious ones.

"I did not think you had noticed that I had gone, Mr. Arrow," she said, and stifled a smile as his expression changed to deliberately humbled puppy-dog eyes. The congregation had dispersed through the main doors to shake hands with Reverend Arrow before Imogen had slipped out of the church through the side chapel.

"I sincerely apologise, Imogen, for I was remiss, but I too was taken by surprise at the lady's directness. Believe me I wish she had not interrupted us." A disturbed note entered his voice.

Imogen stood closer to him, perhaps too close, but he did not back away. "Micah, you were clearly quite taken with her." Her words were out before she had the chance to phrase them carefully or temper the raw jealousy that had threatened to overwhelm her. She had no claim upon Micah, and they had parted as childhood friends, with no promises or agreement on their futures. Now it seemed that they were ready to renew their acquaintance. Imogen breathed in his musk, as he leaned towards her. Would he kiss her?

Imogen would not resist if he did, but then he whispered, "How quickly you judge me to be a gullible fool!" Micah led her away from the side of the church to seclusion behind the vicarage where they could stand near the path that cut through woodland to her cottage. He continued, "I was unsure why the lady was riding alone and here. That made me curious. I was shielding you from unwanted attention if that makes sense. I will not have your reputation besmirched by being seen walking out with me alone." His words seemed heartfelt. "It appeared we met by chance as you returned from the vicarage, so all was well."

"We were not exactly 'walking out', Micah, although we were out walking..." Her words trailed off.

"Exactly, the difference is subtle." He looked around them. "Prying eyes are everywhere." He shrugged. "I was protecting you, Imogen. You can choose to believe me or not."

"I would hate for your name to be 'besmirched' with mine, Micah Arrow." She folded her arms. "It would never do for you to be seen dallying with the likes of me behind the vicarage and on a Sunday too! Whatever would the village gossips make of that?" She deliberately put her hand to her mouth as if shocked by the sudden recognition of their predicament.

He smiled in that warm, melt-her-heart way. Whether her wisdom was lost, or her senses were confused she could not mistrust this man. In the blink of an eye, he kissed her lips tenderly. She returned the gesture, overwhelmed with the need to embrace him. His arms encircled her, time lost meaning, the moment lingered, bodies ignited with a mutual desire to do so much more. When they parted the cold air that filled the void between them seemed to accost her confused senses.

"No one will see us here," he said in a husky voice.

"Micah Arrow! What else do you think we shall do here?" Imogen's eyes sparked with mischief as she asked, almost daring him to commit to a greater folly of propriety.

"Other than Father, possibly, when he returns and he knows both of us well enough not to judge and jump to the wrong conclusion about our intentions," Micah reassured her. He cleared his throat.

Imogen wondered if Micah really believed that. "Then we had better reassess our intentions for that kiss promised so much more, Lieutenant Arrow, but we can go no further as I am not so easily won over, and we have our families to consider. I hope that your mother does not come across us or you will be in for a right earwigging! After all, my mother lives in the woodland and does not enjoy tea at the vicarage as so many ladies within the village community do,"

Imogen watched the flash of admission cross his eyes, even if he did not wish to admit that his mother damned the Underwoods to Hell and back, she knew the truth of it. Imogen only had to look at Ruth Arrow for her skin to prickle with unease.

He pursed his lips as if holding back his initial response. "She is a good woman, Imogen." His words were defensive.

"Aye, so is my mama, but I do not think that your mother would ever say or see it." Imogen was not meaning to speak unkindly, but she was still raw from learning the fate of her own grandmother and Ruth Arrow was placed in a position to cause them serious harm. She may not intend to, but her ignorance could blind her to the dangers she was creating.

"Imogen, let us stop this. We clash whenever we meet, and I would change that. I believe we should and could be good friends, close friends...more than just friends. Wouldn't you prefer or like that?" His expression reminded her of Pickles when he had done something wrong and wanted to be forgiven.

Imogen had to resist the impulse to raise her hand and stroke that beautifully defined jaw line. His features darkened. His spirit, like his hair, was pure gold, and she always felt his warmth when they were near. She certainly sensed some powerful force that drew her to him.

Her shoulders relaxed. "Yes, you are right. We act like two spoilt children. I would have us be true friends. One minute we kiss, the next we fight. You came back here for a reason, and I would know if I was part of that reason. We need to be honest with each other for there are things, Micah, that I would like to discuss with you that affect our village and everyone within it…

But I am concerned about the way your mother reacts to and speaks about my own. If she knew that you were so familiar with me, what would she think? You must speak to her, make her see the danger..."

He was taken aback by the last comment, but she would have it said and perhaps between them they could find a solution to it.

"Imogen, I thought of you often but there are things I would share with you also. Important news that you need to understand and, well, now seems as good a time as any..."

"Micah, Micah! Where are you?" Reverend Arrow's voice was heard loud and clear as he approached them. The usually calm man seemed to be in a fluster, the urgency increasing audibly with every rushed step.

Micah placed a hand on Imogen's shoulder. "You must stay out of sight. Go along the path and back to your cottage. I shall call for you later. Take care... and for your own sake stay out of sight."

"Surely, we have not been seen! He cannot hate my family that much that the very sight of us together gives him such cause for concern!" She saw the perplexed look that Micah gave her as she shook her head. It was simply not in the Reverend Arrow's nature to hate, and she had done him a huge injustice.

"Wait here a moment then if you must, but then go. I will find out what has happened, and I will come to you before the day is out and we will talk further. There are things that we must address, as you have so frankly pointed out. We shall talk as soon as I have seen to Father's troubles; whatever they are I am sure they will not be great..."

Imogen nodded. Her instinct told her that whatever the problem was it would not be so easily dismissed. She stilled as she prepared to listen to what was said.

"Oh, there you are, Micah. Have you seen Miss Imogen Underwood? I know the dear child was in church for I saw her in the shadows of the column. Mary Underwood has come for her in such a frantic state, I must find her…" He stopped to catch his breath.

Micah had stepped around the corner of the vicarage to greet his father and knew that Imogen was beyond sight, but she had been listening and appeared by his side, much to the apparent surprise of his father and the frustration of Micah, for they knew he should not have risked either of their reputations by loitering in the vicinity of the church alone.

"What is it, sir?" Imogen asked, glancing around for her mother. Mary had sworn that she would never set foot on Ruth Arrow's hallowed ground. It was not the church or the cross that kept her outside but the hatred she felt for the woman inside – or was it just the imagined retribution she feared could be called upon her? Something dramatic must have brought about this turn in events.

"Mrs. Underwood waits on the path by the lychgate. Imogen, your father has collapsed; you must go with her, in haste. Mr. Underwood is in the village, and I fear that your mother too could collapse with worry for him." The reverend's words were, as always, kind. "Be swift girl!"

Micah watched Imogen run nimbly down the church path towards her mother. This was concerning news for Imogen and her family, and Micah felt guilty, possibly for his immediate plans could be affected if Wilfred was struck down by some ague.

He licked his lips savouring the feel of her kiss. He would have Imogen as his wife one day, but there were so many problems to sort that stood in their way. He had no doubt that she wanted to be with him, he felt her desire as it met his with equal measure.

Most of the villagers had dispersed. Only a few looked back and realised something was amiss with the Underwoods. However, Reverend Arrow waved their interest away and so they went about their business, speculation dripping from their lips.

"How bad is it?" Micah addressed his father. His question was not purely mercenary as he respected Wilfred like most of the villagers did.

"I do not know, Micah, but let us hope that it is not as bad as Mary fears." Ezekiel grabbed hold of Micah's sleeve and stopped him from following Imogen. "Tell me, with honesty, what were you two doing around there on your own?"

"We were conversing, Father." Micah's attention was on the path ahead; he must follow and find out what was occurring.

Ezekiel shook his head. "Have you no sense, son? She could make any claim against you, and you would have to stand for her or destroy a young lady's reputation, and she struggles to carve a respectable place for herself under the guidance of Mrs. Weeks as it is. Her mother lacks any social standing. She may have a good heart but precious little else to ingratiate her to the local wives of Dibbledale. Think of your good name and your future. Your world is just opening. Do not be so keen to be trapped, my son," he said and patted Micah's shoulder, who knew that his words were well meant.

"She may be a sweet child, but there are many more fish in the sea, and you have just begun to swim within it." Ezekiel looked pleased with his words.

"Not now, Father... please! Besides, have some faith in me too, and respect Imogen for the woman she is and not for the image created by others. Poison may have been dripped into your ear over the years about her equally good mother but be a bigger man than to heed any of it," Micah replied and did not wait for a reply as he ran to catch up with Imogen. If events had not happened so quickly Micah would have thought the sea metaphor quite humorous, but this was no time for quips.

Chapter 16

"Mama, where is Papa? What happened? Will he be alright?" Imogen skidded through the lychgate and into her mother's arms. Mary hugged her quickly and tightly.

"We must make haste to the village. Wilfie collapsed inside the forge and was taken to Mrs. Weeks' cottage," Mary explained, as they dashed down Church Lane toward Dibbledale.

"I will come with you," Micah said as he caught them up.

Mary stared at him and stopped stock still for a moment as her eyes cast a glance to the church behind them.

"The shadow man, Imogen, and the sign of the cross..."

Imogen's body stiffened. Not now, Mama, she thought. A bemused look crossed Micah's face.

"Mama!" she said and swept her off along the road, glancing at Micah's puzzled expression. "Thank you, Micah, I will need your help. There will be things to do at the forge once we have made sure Papa is safe and well." She swallowed as she could not allow herself to consider for one moment that he could be anything else.

"If you know, tell me what to do, I will provide the muscle needed to do it. I have not been sat behind a desk these last few years, Imogen. But if he needs the doctor, I will fetch you a good one," he added, and saw Mary's eyes dart a warning at him.

"Thank you," Imogen said, ignoring her mother's prickling pride. Looking at the shaky state her mother was in, she could hardly be thinking clearly in the moment. Her father was too precious for his care to be given to chance.

Micah nodded and was there at their side as all three rushed towards the village. Mary was only just holding back her tears, which made Imogen braver, even though her heart felt as though it would break at any moment.

Mrs. Weeks' cottage was no more than twenty paces away from the forge. She had been passing by when she noticed Wilfred lying motionless on the floor by the doorway. The silence within the workshop had been eerily strange and had drawn her attention.

"Thank God he had not fallen into the flames," she said and saw Imogen flinch. "Sorry, that thought should not have been voiced."

Mary ran straight into the woman's parlour where Wilfred lay limp on a chaise longue, his large frame listless. She knelt by her husband, feeling for his pulse, placing her other hand on his forehead. Tired eyes opened.

"Wilfie, what have you been doing? Speak to me Wilfie..." Mary asked gently. Her voice trembled, so unlike her normally formidable self. "Thank goodness you are not cold and clammy. Whatever ails you, it is not your heart giving out. But you gave mine quite a start."

"Too much," Mrs. Weeks whispered to Imogen, who knew it to be more than true. "He has been doing far too much," she added.

"I shall get the doctor. If he is not in town, I will ride to Beckton and fetch Doctor Speers back with me," Micah offered.

"It is not his heart, his colour is good," Mary said. "He just needs a few days' rest." She patted his hand as she laid it down carefully next to his thigh. "We need to get him home, where I can tend to him. I'll make some of my restorative broth and you see, he'll be back on his feet in no time. We'll need to borrow a wagon." Mary forced a smile at her husband, but he did not smile back. He squeezed her hand weakly.

"No, Mrs. Underwood, this time you must stand aside. I have Doctor Speers here and he has a gig waiting outside. Fortunately, he had been visiting the vicarage after being in church in Beckton with Mrs. Speers. They brought a letter for you, Micah, apparently from a mutual friend." Ezekiel glanced at his son, who looked a little surprised and sheepish at this news. His father continued, "We will take Wilfred to the vicarage and have him tended there. You need not worry, Mary, for chicken broth will be prepared and he will want for nothing."

Reverend Arrow had spoken out from behind Micah. He pulled his son back and Doctor Samuel Speers stepped inside the room, honey-coloured eyes taking all around him in.

"You cannot do this, Father," Micah said to him quietly in the corridor.

"Yes, I can and will. The village needs that man, and he requires rest. It will be no inconvenience and he will regain strength. His wife is right about that, but he will do so under God's protection in a warm house. Speers is a good man who will care well for him. I think you two should know each other, for you have our community's welfare on both your hearts. You see to the girl and the forge and let Mrs. Weeks pacify Mrs. Underwood. She can come to her husband when he is resting.

Do not allow her to interfere, her nurturing will be needed once he returns to their home."

"But Mother will…" Micah began but was quickly silenced.

"Your mother will do exactly as I ask, Micah, her Christian duty!"

Micah and Imogen exchanged knowing glances.

Inside the room Mary protested but stopped when Wilfred raised a weak hand. "Mary, let it be, please? Just give me a few hours to sleep. All will be well, but you must trust… You must stay safely with Mrs. Weeks and Imogen. Keep her safe… Do not go to the cottage on your own… do as I say…" His voice faded away, but the grimace on Wilfred's face made his order sound like a plea.

Mary backed away, eyes wide like a cornered animal, thrown off balance and cast aside by her pack, and she edged into the kitchen and looked as though she would flee. Wilfred's words held a warning of some kind, but what it was she did not know.

Doctor Speers took all in, but his focus was on Wilfred who he tended immediately. "I will see you well, Mr. Underwood," he reassured everyone in the room.

Mary retreated, looking for the back door, but Mrs. Weeks blocked her way. "Mary, stop. Do not run. He needs you still, just not in this minute. You may be right, it will not be his heart giving out, but that could happen if he does not rest now. Leave the Arrows to give him a good warm bed and calm that pride of yours. Then you will have a man to tend to in the future." She pulled out a chair from the kitchen table. "When they have gone, we shall make tea."

Mrs. Weeks raised her eyebrow at Mary who, although trembling, clasped her hands in front of her small frame. They heard the men carry her man out to the doctor's vehicle. Mary swallowed back her pride and nodded, peering along the hallway she caught Wilfred's eye as he glanced back. Despite her feelings, Mary knew she had to let him go. Listlessly, she sat back into the chair.

Imogen stood in the narrow hallway, Micah at her shoulder, as Wilfred was assisted into the coach. She was torn between wanting to go with him and supporting her mother. Then there was the forge to tend to…

"Imogen, you need to lock up the forge, securely," Mary reminded her.

"I'll go with her," Micah offered and stepped forward.

"Good, stay with her please. I do not think that Imogen should be on her own just now." Mrs. Weeks glanced at Mary as she spoke.

"Mama, will you be alright?" Imogen looked at her mother's crestfallen face.

"Do it, Immi. Do what you need to and take your shadow man with you. Let him return you to your pa. I will meet you at the cottage later." Mary sniffed. The woman looked to her cottage as her own sanctuary so why she should not go there Mary could not fathom and had seemingly decided that Wilfred was being over-concerned or muddled in his thinking.

"Mama, you must go with Papa," Imogen said. "He said not to return to the cottage."

"You think I will be allowed inside that woman's house?" Mary glared back at her. The words were spoken so harshly that it caused Imogen to take a step back. She bumped into Micah who had appeared behind her.

"Do you think she would have her sanctuary defiled by the likes of me?" Mary looked down at her hands; she was holding them to stop their shaking.

Micah stepped around Imogen. "No, because you would not defile it. Yes, you will be admitted to our home, a house of God, because 'that woman' also has a good and kind heart and I would end this travesty of distrust between you! You two cannot see plainly that good exists within each other. Right now, I will go to the forge with Imogen, make all safe and then we should all return straight to the vicarage and see how your husband fares. I will not hear otherwise!" He turned to Imogen. "Come, we must be about your father's business."

"We will see you soon, Mama," Imogen said and left following her shadow man, before Mary could respond further.

Mary looked up at Mrs. Weeks. "You found him, just lying on the ground?"

"Yes, I was returning home when I noticed Mr. Skaggs riding away. I thought he had been to see your husband but could not swear to it. Anyway, I decided to detour and ask if Mr. Underwood knew what the man was about, but there was no sound of singing, humming, clanging or banging as there normally is. Something felt strange and so I entered. He was on the ground where he fell."

"Do you think Skaggs did something to him?" Mary asked, her fists balled.

"No, I do not. Your Wilfred could easily floor a man like Skaggs if he had a mind to. No, I fear this was something else. Still if Skaggs had been there, I wondered what he wanted." Mrs. Weeks paused as her mind turned options over.

Mary watched her in silence for a moment. "You told Imogen about her grandmother!" she said accusingly. "How could you? I will never trust another soul again."

"No, I did not. I told her to ask you about what happened to that poor woman. Did you tell her?" Mrs. Weeks folded her arms as she watched her friend closely.

Mary nodded.

"Good, then she might now trust her own instincts more, especially where Micah is concerned. And, Mary, since when have you ever trusted a soul other than Wilfred?"

"I trust Imogen!" Mary declared.

"Perhaps now you do as you have shared the secret of your own mother's fate with her."

Mary shook her head. "It is dangerous, Mrs. Weeks. Make that tea, let me see if I still can use my skills for the good of my family even if they reject my care." Mary sniffed again.

"Mary it is time you acknowledged that your man suffered this last winter, trekking back and forth in all weathers to your beloved cottage because of your stubbornness and fear. He must live in the village. You need to break free of your own invisible chains and let him have an easier life. He is strong but is still only human. Whatever would you do without him?"

Mary could not answer that question, for of all her fears that was her greatest. Wilfred was her man, lover, friend... her life. Tears poured; she rested her head on her arms as she leaned over the kitchen table. She too was so tired: tired of all the physical work, but more tired of the constant fear that she would end her days by being thrown into a dark bog in the heart of a cold moor. Yet she had been unable to deny her true nature and the person she had been brought up to be. Could anyone? she wondered.

So, what did Skaggs want with her man? Why did he warn her to stay with Mrs. Weeks and Imogen? Mary had a bad feeling, one that was confused as she did not think she could ever feel worse than the day something untoward happened to her Wilfie. Mary wanted to obey her man, but despite that she would return to her cottage, it was her home, one she knew destiny was set to take her away from. That would happen soon enough but for now it was hers.

Chapter 17

"Well, that should keep all safe here for now, but he has jobs left unfinished. We must smother the fire and if needs be remove any burning embers into the slack tub."

Micah picked up Wilfred's thick glove and tongs and was going to set about the task.

"Micah, here…" Imogen slipped Wilfred's heavy cow hide apron over his head, fastening it behind his waist. "Take care, Micah, because sparks can fly and splashback is not uncommon, even on a neglected and dying forge fire."

He smiled at her as together they set to their tasks. Imogen moved the bellows and replaced hammers, wedges, chisels and nails to their rightful place. Wilfred usually kept an orderly forge to prevent injury or for it to burn down. The waiting area had a small stove and seating. This was kept clear so that customers could watch safely if they wanted to wait for a small job to be done. The forge's fire, chimney, anvil and bellows were grouped closely together. Limited light filtered in through the small windows.

"I am surprised that your father could actually see to work in this light, yet his work is always to a high standard." Micah placed the last ember in the tub and placed the tongs carefully down before smothering the smouldering ashes that were left.

"That's so he can judge the colour of the flames. Papa says they speak to a trained eye and tell the smith if what they are doing is right or not."

Micah removed the apron and hung it back on its hook by the forge doorway. Imogen was wiping her hands on a dampened cloth having tidied and secured as many tools as she could. Staring at Micah her eyes moistened. "No work - no pay! Papa is a good man, but I hope Mama knows where he keeps his money, unlike Mrs. Weeks. Mind, she was shocked to discover how much her husband had stashed away."

"Your father will live, Imogen," Micah said. His expression showed surprise that she would talk about her father's money.

"This is a mess - there will be a doctor's bill to pay, not to mention him staying at the vicarage. What are we to do, Micah? Mama will not accept charity, but Papa always sorted the bills and the business. I can sell my brooches next week at the fair, but that will hardly be enough to keep things going." Imogen felt her heart was being gripped by an invisible hand. How would they cope without him? Papa was always so strong, and a forge needed muscle to run it as well as a strong mind. "I do not want him to return to this too soon and end his days prematurely. He needs help. If only I had been a son, instead of another daughter."

Micah stepped into the shadows of the back room of the forge, where the supplies were kept and gently pulled Imogen to him, as if shielding her from her own fear.

She should have resisted, but as he held her close, warm and secure in his embrace, some of the overwhelming physical torment lifted from her, replaced with a more comforting sweep of emotion. She was not alone.

Imogen had no idea how long she stayed like that but when he stroked her hair she looked up into the depth of his eyes and realised what her mother had said was true.

They stood in the shadows, entwined, and four words formed in her mind: I will have you. They were meant to be together; a simple kiss had reassured her of that, but right now Imogen must stand on her own strength as Mary would need her to be at her side.

Micah must have read her thoughts because he bent his head down low, and his lips found hers. Savouring the moment deepening their first kiss, their skins touched, sensations sparked as each held the other close. Succumbing willingly to his embrace, she slipped a hand behind his neck as he lifted her to him. Heat burned inside her as hot as any fire, united in that moment, a bond was being forged.

Instinctively, breathlessly, they separated. Neither thought it the right time to explore this new openness further, not here, not now! Eyes burned into each other – a silent promise made.

"We both go too far, Micah," she said unconvincingly, yet knowing her father was relying on them, guilt gnawed at her moment of joy. Mary needed her too. Imogen did not mean a word of it for she would have liked to have gone so much further, but she would not let either of her parents down or shame them by her behaviour.

"No, we do not. Imogen, I am not taking advantage of you. We are drawn to each other but, unlike the moth that is incinerated on the flame, we are meant to bring warmth, safety, and happiness to each other. We shall continue this conversation once we have dealt with the immediate crisis and the troubles beyond that."

Imogen nodded. "I cannot deny it. Now is not the time and we have much standing in our way." She began to tidy up her father's small bag he carried back and forth from the cottage. He must have knocked it over off the table as he fell. "You have helped me to leave this place in order, Micah. I know you are right. I must go to Mama and see Papa as soon as we are done," she said, taking hold of his hand tightly.

"Yes, quickly," he said. "I will not have my mother unwittingly offend yours. I mean that, she is a good person, but fears what she does not understand, as does yours."

Imogen nodded her agreement.

"I will pay Doctor Speers anything that is owed," Micah said.

"Mama would never allow it, or Papa. They are saving for a cottage of their own in Dibbledale. He will use that money. Papa will have it secure somewhere. He hardly drinks and has never been a betting man, so he will have some savings." They worked silently to finish securing the forge and make all safe. Imogen tried to sound confident, for she had never realised before that, if anything serious happened to her parents, she would have no idea what to do. Hopefully, her elder sister or brother-in-law knew. Imogen shook her head, clearing such dismal thoughts. No, they would be a family again and for years to come.

"No – no need. For I have a suggestion to make. Allow me to pay for the doctor. Trust me on this. When he returns, he can tell me what to do here and I will be his strength until he recovers, or an apprentice arrives, to clear the jobs that he has outstanding. It will give me time to know him, and you can do your jewellery which you told me about. It may be a very useful skill that you could use when I have established things here."

"We couldn't possibly… We are not poor, but we have limited funds and Papa depends upon working to pay for our livelihood. What apprentice?" she asked, her pride dented, for had she not already confessed to Micah that she should have been the son they craved?

"Yes, you can because it may well save your Papa's heart from breaking completely. Besides, we have plans to make, we three. The things you would speak to me about are to do with Sir Benedict Adams, are they not? I would like to use your father's knowledge and he could do with using my influence... and we both need you." Micah smiled. "I am so grateful that you were born his beautiful daughter and not a son."

"Thank you for that, but a son could do more. And yes, they are concerning Sir Benedict Adams." She laughed at him. "How do you know? Do you possess second sight?" she asked as he laughed.

"No, that I would not claim. The lady on the fine horse had a reason for cornering me. I dine there soon. So let us see to the drama of this day and then we shall talk further. I would go to this dinner knowing as much as I can about the village and what has been heard." Micah kissed her forehead tenderly before turning away.

"Micah, you may need to speak to Mrs. Weeks and Bishop Denton in Gorebeck who owns the wildwoods."

"Of course." He picked up his coat that he had shed as soon as they entered the forge and smiled at Imogen as she straightened his collar.

"Imogen, we shall be more than just friends, believe me, for I have never felt more certain of anything in my life. I only hope that you feel the same way about me." He stepped back; Imogen removed the protective apron she always wore around the forge.

"I think you know the answer to that, Micah, but we have many obstacles in our way."

"Then we shall have to overcome them." Together they stepped out of the shadows and into the daylight, Micah deep in thought about the obstacles in their way.

Chapter 18

"Doctor Speers, thank you for attending Mr. Underwood and transporting him. Please allow me to recompense you for the intrusion into your day," Micah offered as he escorted the man from the vicarage. His wife, Mrs. Lydia Speers, was still at the vicarage doorway. Micah thought she was trying to extricate herself from his mother's presence as she poured yet more apologies for this highly unusual occurrence.

"There is no need, Micah. I was delivering a letter on behalf of Lord Farrington for your attention. I know Wilfred, or at least by reputation and his good work, so I am delighted that I was at hand. He does need to heed this warning though, perhaps take on an apprentice – like all of us he is aging."

"Yes, I shall pass on your wise words. Thank you for delivering the letter personally. He must trust you greatly," Micah said and watched the expression on the face of this tall, personable man, with his smart clothes and upright posture. He was a fine gentleman, perhaps too fine for this small village.

"I think Dibbledale is a haven amongst an area of natural beauty. He looked toward the village and added, "We shall miss it." His soft words seemed like a thought spoken out loud. "And yes, I am proud to say that Farrington shares at least some of his trust with me, as he must you also. Did you serve together in the wars?"

With his tall hat, Doctor Speers was a good foot above Micah in height and looked down into his eyes.

"Yes, in a way. We met at Talavera, and he saw something in me, I suppose. We have been close acquaintances ever since." Micah did not wish to expand upon this simple explanation if Farrington had not already told Doctor Speers. "Are you leaving us?" Micah asked.

"Life moves on, Arrow, and we all must. Not yet a while, but we have established a fine hospital in Gorebeck and improved the asylum immeasurably. I will seek to leave both in good hands with a strict system to be adhered to. But I have an estate that I must return to for a time. Please do not mention this as it is still a few months away and I do not wish to cause undue concern. I have a new man arriving in two weeks who will be trained and ready to take over before I leave."

"I had hoped that we may become acquainted as I have plans concerning the village that I would like your thoughts on," Micah began to explain, but hesitated, as he did not wish to talk openly of them before he had the funds from Farrington. Micah's father-in-law's estate should have been left in order, it was just time that was needed now and that was moving painfully slowly.

"Then I am sure we shall find the time when it is opportune. Ah, my dear wife, are you ready to leave now?" he asked as Mrs. Speers joined them. Her cheeks flushed slightly at his question, for she looked mightily relieved to be ready.

"Mr. Arrow, I hope that Mr. Underwood recovers quickly." The lady looked at him politely smiling before Doctor Speers offered her his hand so she could climb up into the gig.

"Miss Lydia! Miss Fletcher, isn't it?" Micah's face

beamed at her. "I'm sorry," he said as Doctor Speers looked directly at him, questioning his familiar outburst.

"Yes… Micah?" she responded in equally familiar tone.

Doctor Speers looked from one to the other. "You two are acquainted?" he asked.

"Yes…" Lydia began

"In a way…" Micah explained. "Both our fathers studied for the priesthood and were friends."

"It is alright, Micah, Samuel knows my father and all about him losing his position for standing up for the working man." Lydia sat back, sounding proud at this declaration.

Micah stared at Samuel. "Then, Doctor Speers, you are certainly a man who I would like to talk to about my vision for Dibbledale and the returnees." He glanced back along the path as Ruth Arrow was walking toward them, no doubt to see if there was a hold up or if she was missing out on some piece of tittle-tattle.

"We really must be going, Samuel," Lydia said. "Perhaps you could visit soon," she hastily addressed Micah.

Doctor Speers took the reins and Lydia waved to Ruth. "I will leave word with Farrington for when I am available to meet with you. He will pass it discreetly as is his way. Good day, Arrow," he said before moving off.

Micah was surprised. Lydia Fletcher had lived in a cottage on the Bagby Estate with her fallen from grace father when last he left Dibbledale. Now she was married and travelling around like a true lady. When her father was thrown out of the church and lost his living, her mother's family the Denton's had disowned her. How fortunes changed.

"Micah! You must come with me and talk to your father. He brought that man in and I had guests. Whatever would they be thinking?" Micah placed a conciliatory arm around Ruth's shoulder and walked her back to the vicarage.

"I believe Doctor Speers actually brought Mr. Underwood, Mother. How is the poor man?" Micah asked as they approached the door.

"He is in my house!" she stormed inside.

Micah glanced back. He must speak with Speers before he left the area, especially as his wife was directly connected with the Dentons – or reconnected he hoped.

Chapter 19

Imogen had managed to convince Mary that it was her wifely duty to return with her to the vicarage, despite Ruth's presence.

She insisted on freshening up first. Instead of her normal heavy skirt, thick cotton blouse and shawl, she washed quickly, brushed her hair up into a neat bun and wore her best navy dress with cream lace around the neckline. She swapped her hobnailed boots for a pair of hardly worn polished leather shoes and stood, reluctant but proud, on the threshold of her cottage. "Wilfred is strong, I know it, he will survive," she declared.

"You look lovely, Mama," Imogen said, and noticed the glint of the heart shaped pendant that Mary was wearing with pride. If it had not been for the dominant worry lines around her eyes, and the tired rings underneath, Mary would look years younger than she did. Her fear, Imogen realised, was aging her prematurely,

"Aye, well, we can't have people saying Mrs. Mary Underwood does not know how to be respectful of folk, can we? Now come on, let us go and see how my Wilfie is doing." Imogen smiled.

They walked in silent companionship to the vicarage where Micah opened the door and led the two anxious women inside his home, with its woven, colourful rug creating a striking contrast to the clip mats Mary made for the cottage. They had wiped their feet on the coarse mat outside before entering. Walking on Mrs. Weeks' carpet had seemed odd to Imogen after the flagstone floor of the cottage. In passing, Imogen glanced in admiration at the pretty red weave of the carpet's pattern.

A large vase held umbrellas by the door, featuring a

bird with long legs and a fine beak; the hallstand was laden with hats and coats all neatly arranged. How many coats does one person need? Imogen's thoughts were interrupted by a sharp and startled voice.

"Oh!" Ruth Arrow rushed into the hallway to see who was at her door. Clearly flustered, her lace cap flopped wildly over her neat greying bun. "Has Lady Speers returned?"

Stopping in her tracks when she saw Mary, the woman gasped.

Her sinewy hand shot to the gold cross that adorned the front of her emerald-green dress. Micah stared at her pointedly. However, he registered the title 'Lady Speers' which he had no knowledge of previously. Had Miss Lydia really married herself a Lord? What on earth was the man doing tending the village sick? Micah had more questions to ask his father when he had the chance. So much had changed whilst he was away.

Ruth's hand slid down to meet her other one in a tight grip. Her spine straightened as she forced civility into the words directed at her unwanted guests.

"Your husband sleeps in my guest room." Mrs. Arrow's voice was not offensive, but neither did it express any compassion. There was no attempt to address Mary by her proper title of Mrs. Underwood, or to welcome her inside the vicarage cordially.

Imogen felt the chill in the hallway was far colder than the air outside. How rude!

"Ladies, I will take you up to our guest room. We shall not rouse Mr. Underwood, Mother, but I am certain that our neighbours will sleep all the better for seeing him safe in his slumber." Micah still held his mother's gaze.

Her head tilted backward a little as if she was bracing herself to cope with the situation that was being forced upon her, lest she be rebuked openly by Micah. "Very well, I will see to your tea," she said, and was going to turn away from them when Micah answered her.

"That would be a lovely idea, Mother. We will join you in the parlour when it is ready. Come, ladies." He led the way up the stairs.

Ruth Arrow stared at him in clear disbelief. That was not what she had meant, and they knew it, but Micah was going to have his guests treated kindly, Imogen thought, and it made her feel proud of him for it showed he was a man of true values and of his word.

"Thank you, Mrs. Arrow, for your generosity. My family will be forever in your debt." Mary's words, so clear and seemingly sincere, caused three heads to turn and look at her in surprise. "Should we?" Mary asked, making her way up the stairs behind Micah, not even glancing back at Ruth Arrow as she passed by, polite but distant, her usual way.

Imogen sensed her mother's moment of inner triumph as she had been more civil than the lady of the house. Mary was facing one of her biggest fears - Ruth Arrow - on a day when her beloved Wilfred, had collapsed.

"I shall call when it is ready," Ruth Arrow stated, vexation clear as she disappeared to the kitchens to instruct her maid accordingly.

They entered the bedroom quietly. Mary made straight for the man, laid in the bed with a pretty floral quilt covering him. He slumbered peacefully. His colour was returning to his normally rosy cheeks and his breath was even.

"I will leave you two ladies here and fetch you once tea is ready. We will share a light meal together as friends, all of us," Micah said.

"There is no need to do that, Micah, although the gesture is kind enough in intent." Mary spoke, as she slowly rubbed her husband's brow. "I do not wish for you to cause your mother further discomfort on our account."

"Yes, Mrs. Underwood, there is need, and I hope that you will see why when you join us." He left with only the briefest nod at Imogen.

"Your shadow man has strong form, Immi," her mother commented but her focus was on the man laid before her. "He has heartfelt opinions. I hope that yours and his align."

Imogen picked up a small bottle from the bedside table and studied it. Her mother never bothered with the doctors or apothecary and so Imogen had little knowledge of what the common cures of the day were.

"The liquor of the poppy, Imogen, otherwise called laudanum," Mary said without even examining it. "In small, short doses, it serves its purpose. It can send a person into a dream world that they begin to grieve leaving it if its use is continued."

"Mama, is it safe, though?" Imogen asked to reassure herself as she admired the light within the room. The high rectangular window, pale yellow curtains and pretty little birds drawn onto the wallpaper. No wattle and daub here. No old oil lamps or smell of tallow. This was like Mrs. Weeks' home, what a real house looked and felt like and one like it, or smaller, could be a home to them all. She looked down at her father. He would live, she knew it, believed it, he just needed rest. The burden had been too heavy for even his strong shoulders to bear.

"It is safe, Immi, as I said, so long as it is used only for a short spell. It must not be continued, or he will have dreams and visitations, and Wilfie cannot do with such. He is far too practical a man to put up with visions."

She smiled at him, and Imogen felt warmed by the love that shone from her eyes.

Mary was sitting on the bed next to him, staring longingly at Wilfred's face. On the wall above the bed was the cross of Jesus. Mary stared blankly at it for a moment as she continued to gently stroke his arm.

"Are you praying, Mama?" Imogen asked softly, and Mary nodded gently.

"Have done all my life, child. It is said He made all the creatures and the wildwoods, so why not pray to one that can create so much beauty. Tis' his other creation, mankind, that does not do it justice." She looked back at her husband.

"Mama, you should not hide away so. People should be able to see the good in you for themselves." Imogen stroked Mary's back, knowing how it ached.

"People see what they want to see when they want to see it, Immi. However, when he wakes, we will tell him to make plans for the house in the village, but I'll not give up my cottage. We can afford to keep our tenancy. I can go there to tend my plants and forage and I will walk back to the town and forge daily instead of the other way around. But we will have to set to earning our way. I can sell herbs and you your fine jewellery. We shall thrive, we always do."

"Those are the first wise words you have said all year, woman," Wilfred muttered without opening his eyes, his voice slurred and sleepy.

Mary chuckled with delight. "Sleep you dote and come back to me as soon as you are free of the drug. You didn't have to scare me half to death to addle my wits and get what you were after." She kissed his cheek.

"Aye, lass, it was not planned. I would not do that to my girls. Listen to me, Imogen, before my senses go again.

Mary, it is not safe for you at the cottage on your own. You must take care. Try to stay at Mrs. Weeks' cottage, Pickles can sleep in her yard."

"Papa, I will return to the cottage with Mama and keep her company, never fear." Imogen was surprised by Wilfred's eyes staring at her struggling to keep her attention and his focus. "Stay with Mrs. Weeks. And listen, you keep hold of Micah Arrow, he's a good man." His eyes had closed again as he slumped back. "You need him now more than ever." Imogen's face turned cerise as her father had not seen Micah appear in the doorway. "Don't let that fiery pride of yours walk away from him. Imogen, you need a man's protection."

"Father, please rest…" Imogen wiped his brow with a damp cloth and saw his worry lines ease slightly.

Mary looked at Imogen, both knew that this strange urgency for their safety meant something had happened, but Wilfred was in no fit state to talk further.

"I will say my piece. You do not brush him away. You are good enough for him… I'm not a pauper, but you must stop that mouth of yours running off with itself when you get the bit between your teeth. There are worse men out there and you are now an attractive woman. Now, I'm tired," Wilfred forced his words out and yawned. "Let a man sleep."

Mary smiled nervously. "Mr. Arrow is tea ready?" she asked quietly.

Imogen stared at her father, transfixed, not knowing whether to speak, stand or run. She did not care to face Micah straight away.

"Yes, Mrs. Underwood," he said, clearly amused.

He seemed not the slightest offended. Imogen looked from one man to the other – her destiny seemed cast. Her past, her future? But how? Was it true that greater forces chose a person's fate or was it like doors that opened? You had to be brave or wise enough to walk through them? She glanced at Micah; walk by at your peril, she thought.

"He does not know what he is saying, the juice of the poppy frets him so," Imogen began explaining.

"Come then, Imogen, it is time we stepped out of the shadows." Mary walked past both young people and made her way downstairs.

"Your father talks perfect sense, but we have time enough to cast our future, our way." Micah spoke quietly to Imogen who followed her mother, as she regained some composure but listened intently to his words.

Chapter 20

"Excuse me, ladies, I shall be but a moment." Micah winked at Imogen and moved ahead so that he could meet Ruth outside the kitchen where the maid was busy preparing their food.

Ruth bristled and hissed at him. "You have invited them to stay here and eat in my parlour, Micah! Is it not enough that you brought that man into my house and placed him in my guest room? Doctor Speers – you do know he is a Lord, don't you? Only by default of course, because his elder brother died, but nevertheless the doctor inherited the title and lands, tending a blacksmith in my humble home and all. Whatever will they think of us? Could you not have left the man with the laundress? At least she would be able to see to cleaning the mess after he had slept in her sheets!" Ruth spat out words although they were only audible between the two of them. Her 'guests' were to be seated at her table. Her best circular, walnut, inlaid table.

Micah ignored her protestations and instead walked to open the door to the parlour to show the ladies inside.

"Micah… can you help, dear?" Ruth called Micah out on the pretence that he was needed to help the young maid carry the large tray. Ruth did not like being ignored.

"That man was filthy!" she whispered with venom.

"Mother, the man works in his forge, what do you expect him to be like?" Micah lowered his voice in response and to avoid insult.

"Oh well why don't we ask any farmer who needs a rest to drag dirt through my house, or a miner who needs a break from his God-given toil! Perhaps they could use my guest bed at their convenience?" Her eyes glared at her son whose equanimity was unchanged.

Micah did not like this side of his mother's nature and if her voice became any more audible and travelled to the Underwoods' ears he would tell her so in front of them. However, he wanted to have a peaceful half hour with these women seated together in the same room. That way, there would be less of a barrier when he and Imogen walked out officially together. Their relationship was something that he had every intention of pursuing, for her presence filled him with a sense of joy he had never experienced before. Micah sensed the effect his presence had on her when he was physically next to Imogen.

"Mother, for God's sake! And no, I am not using His name in vain. I mean it literally. Wilfred Underwood is a friend of Father's, and you should be glad that he has survived, his heart did not give out, and God has blessed him with a safe place to recover. Besides, he did not look that dirty to me," Micah said.

"No, he is not now because between Doctor Speers, a true gentleman, and Betsy they managed to clean him up some. His clothes are another matter; his woman can take them with her and bring fresh ones to him." She breathed out, her nostrils almost flaring in indignation. "For now, he sleeps in one of your father's older nightshirts. Literally taking the shirt off his back!"

"That 'woman' you refer to is his wife! Before God, they were wed, and you will show some respect and human kindness. Stop your nonsense for Father would be extremely disappointed in you. You must bury that pride;

it will not bring you any joy in life if you do not. Now where is this tray?" Micah strode past her and picked up the laden tray. "Follow me and put your prejudice on hold!"

"Micah, soon we shall dine with Sir Benedict Adams. What would he think if he knew we had the blacksmith sleeping in our home and his wife a…"

"He would think that you and Father practice what you preach!" Micah snapped his words out at her over the tray and saw her shrink back. He did not feel proud of rounding on her but, somehow, these women would share sustenance together, and accept each other in a way that would smooth the path for him and Imogen to build upon the newfound friendship. If all worked out well between them, then Ruth would be seeing a lot more of Wilfred and Mary. Miss Donaldson had inferred Sir Benedict had knowledge of Micah's secret wealth, in which case he would be sitting down with his parents in a few days and explaining all to them. In hindsight his planning of events had lacked wisdom. He should not have tried to recreate and wallow in his nostalgic image of his past before he told them of his future.

How Imogen would view him when she knew about his marriage and all that had befallen him since, he knew not. That concerned him. Imogen was beautiful in a wild and untamed way, she was hardly going to suddenly blend into society, like Carolina had. Her exotic bloodline had been one that came from position and wealth. Her natural grace along with determined and striking features had singled her out as his wife amongst the other officers at their regiment's gatherings. Micah had been proud to be seen with her, and in a way awestruck. However, now he had returned Micah had no intention of following the fashionable to the latest ball or soiree. He had done his share of feeling like a poor relative amongst the army's officers, rubbing shoulders with the sons of true gentry.

Money opened some doors, but old money had invisible barriers, ones he did not even want to cross. Micah needed time to himself, in his beloved Dibbledale, to sort out what was important in life and what was not.

"Ah, Micah, I am just in time, am I?" Reverend Ezekiel Arrow's face was a welcome surprise as he opened the vicarage door wide.

Micah smiled at him over the tray. "You are, indeed, Father," he said. "We are taking tea in the parlour. Mother is just coming…" he said. Ezekiel cast a glance behind him and seemed to sense the strained air between them. Micah would make all well but for now she was just too angry.

Intuitively, his father nodded and went to speak to his wife.

Minutes later they appeared together in the parlour.

"Mrs. Underwood," the reverend greeted. "I am so pleased to hear Mr. Underwood is looking better already. He gave us all a nasty shock. Our blacksmith is at the heart of our village life, his fire burns for us all.

I fear he may need an apprentice, though. We tend to think that the strong never weaken, but our bodies will often belie that notion. Ah, fresh parkin! Divine, Mrs. Arrow, you must compliment Betsy for me." He smiled warmly at his wife.

"An apprentice - that might be a good idea," Mary said. "There must be many a lad who would be glad of a job. Times are hard and it is a lot safer than becoming a drummer boy or taking the King's shilling. Of course, we shall now be moving nearer the forge," Mary added before anyone suggested it to her again. "There is a vacant cottage on the end of Church Lane. Perhaps you could make enquiries for us, please." Mary looked at Reverend Arrow, ignoring Ruth's sharp intake of breath.

"What, Mrs. Underwood, you would be prepared to leave your de… cottage?" Ruth exclaimed.

"Yes, Mrs. Arrow, for Wilfred I would do anything. I would even live in the village and use the cottage for its herb garden and for drying and pickling produce," Mary said. "It is a good place for quiet reflection."

"And prayer," Ezekiel said.

"Aye, that too," Mary said and smiled warmly back at him. "Nature is a blessing."

"Dan… Micah, er Mr. Arrow, we could ask young Dan if he would like to be apprenticed," Imogen broke into the silent impasse that had formed between the two women. It was obvious to her that Ruth had been going to say 'leave your den' and it took a lot of self-control for both Mary and Imogen not to stand up and walk out, but for Wilfred and Micah's sake they stayed.

"Now that is an excellent idea." Micah nodded at her. "I'll speak to your father when he is rested and then ride over to Gorebeck and see if Dan would be willing."

Ruth's head shot up. "What is he?"

"A stable lad, Mother, but a good one. His father is a tenant on the Kinsley Estate." Micah shrugged. "Lord Farrington knew the family."

She stared blankly at him as the ensuing silence began to stretch. "You spoke with Lord Farrington?" she asked.

Micah fell silent.

Ruth glanced around awkwardly then suddenly commented, after Ezekiel nudged her under the table, "What a lovely pendant." In the absence of any other topic, she could relate to she managed to find one close to

Mary's own heart, literally.

"Thank you. Imogen made it for me," Mary said proudly.

"Really?" Micah had been looking for craftsmen in the area but had not realised he had already found such a gifted craftswoman. He could see it was made of silver and of an unusual but not precious stone. However, if she had gold and real gemstones to work with it would have made a splendid piece. Imogen had mentioned she made jewellery, but this was beautiful work. He would be able to develop her skills in the future. Perhaps she could teach young fingers to do such work and use her eye for design. "Imogen, you are very blessed."

Imogen blushed her gratitude at the compliment.

Micah turned to his father. "Have you heard any news of an intention that Sir Benedict Adams is reported to have for the village, buying up land – to be specific the woodland, from Bishop Denton? His associate Mr. Skaggs has been seen riding around the area with surveyors."

His father raised a hand politely. "Micah, this is hardly the time for discussing that kind of business talk. I am sure the ladies have enough on their minds without adding in speculation."

Mary spoke up. "Perhaps it is exactly the time for discussing it, Reverend for we, like the villagers, would be greatly upset. The water runs pure through the land we call our home. Nothing should be allowed to taint that," Mary said. "Many a living would be affected as well as the good health of your parishioners."

"On that I would concur," Ruth added. "We do not want the countryside to be fouled like some of the cities. We should be stricter about what influences it or makes claim to it. I read a newssheet that had been brought in from York by the bishop which he left here. People are actually revolting about it!"

Mary ignored any slight if one had been meant by references to 'foul influences' and continued.

"Your flock would be turned from happy self-sufficient farmers and cottage workers to being no more than the parts of a mill machine or put out of a job by the destruction of their homeland. Do you want that for Dibbledale?" Mary spoke her heartfelt words.

"You have a clear mind and a direct tongue in that head of yours, Mrs. Underwood. But although I have heard the villagers' concerns there has not been any proof of them. Perhaps our dinner invitation will shine a light upon the truth," he said, and looked over his teacup to Micah.

"Yes, it may well, whilst you take port together with the men folk and I chat of more ethereal matters with the lady of the house and the elegant Miss Donaldson. They are so eager to meet Micah." Ruth was smiling sweetly as she glanced over at Imogen and Mary. "Our own hero," she added whilst Micah shifted his weight uneasily.

Imogen resisted commenting that Micah and Miss Donaldson were already 'acquainted'; that could risk it backfiring upon her own destiny, knowing that to link those two together could dismiss any hope she had of becoming permanently acquainted with Micah. She must place her faith in destiny, but there was no harm in nudging it along and preventing their paths from being obstructed.

"Thank you for your kindness," Mary said and stood up nodding at Ezekiel and Micah and then giving an almost imperceptible gesture of a nod to Ruth.

Imogen stood next to her mother, so proud of how she held herself when in unfamiliar surroundings. "We really appreciate your kindness," she said looking directly at Ruth Arrow. "Father will be returned to us as soon as he is strong enough and will not bother you and your household again. The tea was exquisite!"

Ruth nodded, without responding.

"Yes, an unadulterated loose leaf from Asia, I believe. You are truly fortunate to have a supply of such quality and I thank you for allowing us to enjoy some. We mainly drink our own brew from the forest's bounty once dried. I shall be pleased to send over some of my rosehip tea. It is excellent as a pick-me-up or to clear the skin. Come now, Imogen dear." Mary walked out of the vicarage her head held high.

"Mama! Did you really just hint that their tea was smuggled?" Imogen said as they strode away. "And I do not think that rose-hip tea will improve her natural pallor."

"Getting outside in the air and feeling the sun on her face would do that woman's face and body good. She hides away like a mouse. Aye, lass, I did hint for she may not know where it came from, but I can tell that it was too high a grade for the local store in Gorebeck. But she may have no idea, and it could have been gifted to the reverend in his innocence," she winked, "Most likely by Bishop Denton when he visited here." Mary laughed.

"You should not bite the hand that fed you," Imogen warned her.

"No, but I will be happy to return to my 'den' again." Then she glanced back at the vicarage. "This is a warning to us, Imogen. That man who has such a big heart is not as strong as we thought. So, we must do what we must. Find out from Mrs. Weeks about a home in the village. We will see if the good priest will open the door to the one at the end of Church Lane. Ask her on my behalf to see if she can get a fair price. She has a business head on her that frightens menfolk, she knows the properties well as she is good at snapping them up. I do not want to pay rent to her or anyone. We will own our home outright. Do not give offence to her for we need her help," Mary admitted and then hugged Imogen.

"Yes, we do, and we need Micah too…" Imogen let her mother pull away. "Pa said not to go to the cottage."

"Aye, well, I have things to see to. Wilfie was under the influence of that drug. It breeds fear. No, lass, you need Micah and he you. You know it and what is more it is clear to read, that he concurs, but he must cast off this Donaldson woman, for I saw a look of interest in his eye when she was mentioned. He has a secret troubling him there. He finds her attractive, but not in the way he is attracted to you, but do not ignore her influence as the balance of any scales can easily tip the wrong way."

"She came by here to seek him out. Mama, Miss Donaldson is beautiful. I do not know what he sees in me after being in the company of such a well-bred lady." Imogen's downcast eyes found a subdued Pickles lurking around the lychgate patiently waiting for their return.

"You make her sound like a horse – they are all well-bred or inbred – but you ride horses, you don't marry them, and you and he will be wed."

Mary laughed openly at Imogen's shocked face. "Come now, I have lived a life and know more about what goes on behind closed doors than most. Do not forget that some folk trust Mary and happily share a confidence with me. I'll make our home right and you go see Emily Weeks and let her know what has happened and find out all you can of what we need to know. Perhaps ask if I might stay tomorrow night – just the one, mind." Mary and Pickles fell into step as they began to turn for home.

"Mama, heed Papa's warning!"

"I won't be scared off; he was just worrying... it was the drug talking!" her mother stated emphatically.

"Mama…" Imogen struggled to find the right words to ask the question which had troubled her greatly since she spoke to Micah.

"Spit it out, lass." Mary ordered.

"It is about Papa," she began.

"He is closeted in a clean home with good food. We will have him back and I will not renege on my promise to move to the village, God help me." She glanced up.

"No, Mama, it is not that. Are you certain that we can buy the cottage? I always thought we would have to be tenants as most are," Imogen said, watching a smile grow on her mother's face.

"You think I say things without substance? My dear Immi, you should have more faith in me. Your father works hard, he has a good eye for what he does and for turning a fair profit. He owns that forge; he does not pay rent on it."

"Oh, good." Imogen had not thought about that. "But if he sells the forge to buy the house then he will not have a business…"

"Imogen, I did not mean that. He can afford to buy it. He has been saving for his precious house for years. You think I do not know what my man makes?" She shook her head. "You must think I spend my life with my head in the bushes. That man is dedicated, he does not drink, nor gamble away his hard-earned coin. Instead, he places it safe and watches his nest build. I know this, for he shares his joy – his pride, with me."

Imogen hugged her mother. "I feared that you did not know about his business and therefore were very vulnerable whilst he was ill."

Mary's face fell and Imogen placed her arm around the woman's shoulder.

"Oh, Immi, I know what is where and what I should do if his health failed, but I tell you now, if that man falls, I am lost." Mary clamped her jaw shut, lips thinned, and her eyes moistened.

Imogen embraced the petite frame tightly, but she soon stepped away and addressed her mother firmly, whilst Pickles ran around them both waiting to be acknowledged too. "Do what you need to, Mama, and I shall see Mrs. Weeks. Together, we will be ready for Papa's return and have some good news waiting for him. No looking at tea leaves today – look up at the sunshine instead!" Imogen paused. "Mama, the thing that frightens us the most is fear itself. Face it, no more hiding, we… I need you."

Imogen walked off down the lane leaving Mary watching her. She nodded, but under her breath replied, "Look to your shadow man, girl, find your own future, Immi, and leave Wilfie to me. Come on Pickles," Mary walked on with her dog at her side.

Chapter 21

Gorebeck was quiet as Micah rode over the bridge by the Norman church. He left his horse with an excited Dan who was thrilled at the possibility of becoming a blacksmith's apprentice instead of labouring endlessly as a stable hand at the Hare and Rabbit and walked back towards the church. The day was bright, but he had not paid it a great deal of attention as Micah had much on his mind.

"Morning! Arrow, isn't it?"

Micah turned to see where the stranger's gruff voice came from. An uncouth looking figure was leaning against the back door of the inn, pipe in one hand and tankard of porter in the other. His ill-fitting greatcoat covered a somewhat garish waistcoat. The breeches did nothing to enhance his rotund figure.

"Yes, sir. You have me at a disadvantage," Micah said as he removed his riding hat, carrying it in his hand as he stepped forward.

"Mr. Jethro Skaggs, Mr. Arrow. We shall have our proper introductions soon at Sir Benedict Adams' dinner party. But as our paths have crossed perhaps you would join me in a tankard… or two now, eh?"

"Another time perhaps." Micah smiled and replaced his hat ready to walk around the building to the main street.

"You have pressing business?" the man persisted. "I have an errand to complete for my father. Thank you, perhaps another time. Good day," he said and walked on before the arrogant man could push his nose any further into Micah's business. It seemed Skaggs had him marked out, but why?

Micah thought for a moment about going straight to his rendezvous, as he would be certainly watched, but decided that he was not going to raise suspicion should his errand take him into Gorebeck's church. He crossed the road and entered through the church's iron gate entering Saint Hilda's by the main doors. Slipping inside he made his way to the front pew where Lord Farrington sat staring at the line of Celtic saints on the grand wooden reredos behind the altar.

Micah nodded his respect to the cross and sat next to his friend.

"Thank you for meeting me again, Lord Farrington. There is a man who apparently watches me, named Skaggs. He knew who I was on arrival, yet we have never met," Micah reported to his ex-senior officer as he would have expected to if on reconnaissance.

"He is a letch. I will have him brought down as soon as I can. It appears I must wait before I slip away then."

"He will be at Sir Benedict's. This he also knew about."

Lord Farrington nodded thoughtfully at this piece of information.

"Thank you for meeting me, sir," Micah repeated.

"Arrow, for goodness sake. You are a man of means now, you do not need to keep thanking me like you owe me. Put those fine shoulders of yours back and walk tall, as if you still had your uniform on." Lord Farrington smiled at him.

"I will try to. It is just all so new to me. The funds are through?" Micah could hardly contain his excitement.

"Yes, you are now a man of considerable means. I may have to come with my cap in hand to you one day," he said and laughed. "We will venture to my local, legal representative because a large sum has been deposited via my account at Coutts in London to your account, £5000 is held locally, which will be exchanged today, but there is also a deposit in gold which I will give you the safety box key to – that is in London also." Lord Farrington watched Micah closely.

He swallowed, having dreamed of this moment. His wife's father, Philippe, had kept his word, and upon his death had left a sizable inheritance to Micah, so he would keep his own promise to himself that Dibbledale and at least some of the war's returnees would also benefit from it.

"Well, speak, man…" Lord Farrington said. "Do not hit the ground like the blacksmith! Come to the offices of Bellingham and Crouch in Northallerton the day after tomorrow. I will send word that you will be available to sign where needed at 10 o'clock. I shall be there to make sure all is completed in the correct manner and then my concerns with this matter will be relinquished."

"You heard about Wilfred Underwood too, so soon," Micah was amazed.

"Yes, I heard. It is my life's blood to hear things, Micah. I may have retired but my network of ears and mouths still keep me informed. It is my duty to protect the people I live amongst. Insurgence still lurks in the troubled shadows of this land."

"I want to stop the scheme of Skaggs and Sir Benedict Adams that would destroy the woodland, pollute a beautiful fishing river that is the village's lifeblood and some properties in Dibbledale, if indeed the rumours I hear are true." Micah did not wait for a better moment to state his intentions.

"The retired Bishop Denton is as bent in stature as

his staff. He wants to sell off land and is open to offers as he has no heirs other than his disowned daughter's daughter, who has married a lord, but the old fool still will not acknowledge her."

"You mean, Miss Lydia Fletcher as was, now Doctor Speers lady wife?" Micah was surprised for he had always thought Miss Lydia to be a fine woman. Her father may well have spoken out for the working man and been labelled a rabble rouser by the church he represented and society, but it was a shame that the sins of the father had meant his daughter was cast off too."

"The very one. A lady who is a close friend of my dear Lady Farrington," he said, and again Micah felt that emotions ran strong.

"Does Reverend Mr. Fletcher still live?" Micah asked and realised his mistake straight away. I mean Mr. Fletcher."

"Yes, and he happily co-habits with his common law wife, but that is a different story. I am content that he is not seditious. Speers finds him an honourable and likable chap, so I shall not judge. But I will always be there should Lady Speers need help."

"Can I prevail upon your support, once again, to introduce me to Bishop Denton, sir?" Micah realised that Lord Farrington had closed the conversation regarding Miss Lydia.

"Consider it done but, Arrow, I would warn you that Skaggs is not a man who takes being crossed well. We will be at the dinner with them. Act as if we have met on the field of battle, as a matter of fact but with distance – ranks apart. It would not serve us well to have them know of our business."

Farrington stared at him.

"Yes, sir, but as he is here and presumably keeping an eye on my travels, I shall lead the man's attention away as I retrieve my horse. I suspect they may know something of my personal business!"

"Do as I say. You go and I will slip away, as I so frequently do."

Micah left. Lord Farrington with hands resting atop his cane stared at the altar before them, deep within his own thoughts.

Chapter 22

"Mrs. Underwood, is it not?" The gruff voice bellowed louder than necessary, as he walked his horse towards the cottage clearing.

Pickles ran out of the cottage, stood with his four paws set in the earth in front of Mary and growled. The man took firm hold of his crop, so Mary quickly sent Pickles inside the cottage where he skulked across the threshold. "Stay, boy," she said softly. Reluctantly he stayed.

"Mr. Skaggs, I presume. What brings you to my door?" she addressed the man as he walked his horse near to their well.

Mary was tired from the recent events and had no intention of inviting this man into her home, especially after Wilfred's garbled warnings. His visit was somehow connected, but how?

"Ah, has your husband spoken to you already? I thought you did not venture to the village. Oh, and this door, like these woods are not really yours, are they? Your presence here is... transient. But if you guide your husband wisely, woman, your future will be safe enough."

Mary knew she was being goaded but calmed herself with a fresh intake of woodland air. She would not rise to his torments. Her family's future had nothing to do Skaggs, she did not need to read the leaves to know that. "Mr. Underwood is currently indisposed. What is it you are wanting, Mr. Skaggs? Most folk have seen you hereabouts and know you by sight."

She did not add that his rotund figure was testament to a greedy personality and his dress sense, a total lack of taste. Mary may live simply, but she had a good eye for colour, balance and harmony and Skaggs affronted all three.

"Is your daughter here today? I did not cross her path in Dibbledale." He asked his question whilst glancing at the cottage window. With no visible movement inside, he tethered the horse to an iron hook in the well wall and took a step forward; Pickles made a low growl and moved to her side. Mary did not chastise him; instead, she patted the dog's head. It stayed near; hackles raised.

Skaggs stopped and looked around as if unperturbed, but his eyes showed that he would like to take his crop to Pickles. "These trees are well mature. Excellent. They will be fine for purpose."

"These woods have stood for centuries. It is what gives them their beauty and the wealth of diverse plants. When nature is left on its own, it thrives," Mary explained but doubted that the man had an appreciative bone in his body.

Skaggs faced her. "I see you know much about your plants, Mrs. Underwood – you are Mr. and Mrs. Underwood are you not?" he asked.

"Not that I can see how it is of interest to you, but yes we were wed before God and have lived happily together for many years." She paused because the vision of Wilfred lying helpless in Mrs. Weeks' cottage flashed before her eyes and her fear returned. Mary fought hard not to show her feelings to this man who made her skin creep.

He smiled; those cold eyes bored into hers. "Good, it could have been one hurdle I would have had to overcome if Mr. Underwood sees the wisdom of our discussion."

"The wisdom? Your discussion?" Mary queried. He may be sly, wicked and greedy but wise was not a word that Mary felt sat right with Mr. Skaggs.

"Yes, I had hoped to find Miss Underwood here. Please pass on my regards. As I told Mr. Underwood, I shall soon return for his answer."

Mary realised Skaggs had no knowledge of Wilfred's collapse. She decided not to enlighten him.

"Mr. Skaggs," Mary saw a grin appear on his pock-marked face. If he thought she was going to pry into his conversation with Wilfred, she would disappoint him, "When did you speak to Mr. Underwood?"

"Why, morning before last. I gave him a clear explanation of my intentions. Do remind him that you have less than one week now to agree, or say goodbye to your... home," he said, and mounted his horse. "Good day, Mrs. Underwood." He pointed his crop at Pickles. "Keep that hound under control or lose it."

He rode away. Mary sank to her knees and wrapped her arms around Pickles as he licked her cheek and leaned into her. Why, she wondered, had they been sent these torments? All she wanted was to live in peace, with her man and dog, in her home. Was that too much to ask?

Skaggs was after Imogen, and he must have said as much to Wilfred. Was that what broke her man's heart? Is that why he collapsed?

Chapter 23

"Mama!" Imogen stopped as she chalked on the blackboard. The girls were copying the words on to the slates before them.

Six curious faces spun around to look at Mary's anxious figure as she peered into the room used as a school at the side of Mrs. Weeks' house. This small space was sufficient for now, to bring some learning to these young laundry workers, but Mrs. Weeks wanted to use the village hall for a grander scheme, including as many village children as could attend an open school.

"Girls, continue to copy the letters until you are happy that you have done your best. Then leave the slates on the table by the door as you leave. Oh, and please don't be late for work tomorrow, Sarah. Mrs. Weeks is a generous employer, but she will not turn a blind eye more than three times, so be sensible and not a lazy girl." Imogen stared at the blushing girl pointedly.

"Yes, Miss Underwood," a downcast Sarah replied.

"Good!" Imogen said and made a beeline for Mary, putting a caring arm around her mother's shoulder to guide her into the nearby, pristine sitting room.

Mary fidgeted with her hands; her workday, warm skirt and shawl seemed shabby and out of place in Mrs. Weeks' renovated home.

"It's Pickles, Immi, he was there earlier, but now he's nowhere to be found." Mary was fraught as the dog was always there for his dinner, yet today there was no sign of him.

"You've called him throughout the woods?" Imogen asked, knowing that Mary would have. Her stomach knotted.

Mary just nodded.

"Right. Give me a moment to leave a note for Mrs. Weeks and I will come with you. We'll check the forge…"

"I did," Mary admitted and shrugged her shoulders to show her lack of result.

"Very well, sit down I'll only be a minute."

Imogen left her mother standing looking at the fine tapestry covered winged chairs by the empty fire grate, knowing she would not let herself sit on them.

Within minutes Imogen and Mary were heading down to the path by the river. From there they could cut back into the woodland. If he did not come to their calls, then they would head across into Sir Benedict's land and carefully check the traps. Both women knew that if there was silence from Pickles… well, they felt sick at what they might find.

Other than calling the hound's name the women were silent.

"Mama, we have to go up and check the traps." Imogen saw Mary's eyes were moist. Pickles was her companion, like her last child, he was scatty and loyal, but never went far from her; they had an almost intuitive link.

Mary nodded, but as they took steps away from the river, Imogen touched Mary's shoulder and stillness descended. Breaking through their silence, above the sound of rushing water was a faint whimper. Imogen ran in the direction it had come from.

On the bank of the river lay a mass of wet hair. Arriving first, Imogen placed her hand on the dog's side. Pickles' sad eyes sparked to life. Mary, breathless, fell to her knees at his side as he struggled to find his paws and stand. He whimpered faintly, pathetically happy to be rescued.

"He's been beaten, Immi," Mary said through her anger and disbelief. She placed her hands on his side and saw his tail wag. "He may be broken but can be fixed."

Standing, she laid her shawl flat on the ground.

In silence and without a word of instruction, both women carefully lifted Pickles onto the garment and then each took an end and lifted him. All the time his tail wagged slowly, as Mary hummed a soothing Irish lullaby.

Once he was safely placed by the fire on one of Mary's clipped rugs, they gently dried his fur and Mary fed him by hand.

"This is Skaggs' doing," Imogen said, as she stood defiantly. "I'll…"

"You will do nothing."

"Nothing!"

"You cannot prove it. It could have been one of them surveyors. Even if you feel you know this, you can do nothing but will that whoever it was comes to justice." Mary's voice was cold and angry. "We were led to him, Imogen. It is not his time yet to die. I suspect he got away and swam to safety. He is bruised and shocked, but his bones are not broken."

"Papa might be right, Mama, we should not stay here on our own."

"He so often is. We stay here with Pickles tonight. Tomorrow we will do as Wilfie asked and all three of us will descend on the hospitality of Mrs. Weeks."

Imogen nodded.

"Do not run and tell your father. Time enough to share this with him when he is back and on the mend. Come, Immi, I'm tired and Pickles needs his rest. Latch the door and sleep with me this night. Tomorrow we all go to Dibbledale." Mary fondled Pickles' ear who had already slipped into a peaceful slumber.

Imogen followed her into her parents' cosy bedchamber and saw the resignation on Mary's face to her plight. She would have to live in the village for a while. Mrs. Weeks was kind and Imogen knew she would not object.

"Hang my good dress on the peg, Immi, I don't want those gossips thinking I don't know how to dress properly," Mary said and sniffed as she pulled on her nightgown and slipped under the blankets.

Imogen did and smiled as, even tired as she was, Mary's reluctance to be in the village still led her thoughts. However, for the good of her family, Pickles included, she would face her fears. Such was the strength of love she had for them.

"What are you doing, Mr. Underwood? You are under doctor's orders to rest and yet I find you trying to swing your legs out of bed." Micah entered the room, and with one careful gesture swung the man's legs back into the bed and under the coverlets before Wilfred landed in a heap on the floor. Wearing only a nightshirt, as none of his clothes were back from the washroom yet, Micah could not imagine where he thought he was off to; he could give his mother the fright of her life.

"You don't understand, lad, I am needed at home. I must protect Imogen…" Reluctantly and with a sigh as the wind escaped his lungs as he fell back on the pillows, Wilfred laid back down. "Please fetch my breeches, I must go now."

"They will manage fine for a few more days without you, and we have secured the forge and made all safe. No one will interfere with it and all flames and embers are out. I will look in on the ladies today and make sure that they want for nothing." Micah smiled but the concern upon Wilfred's face did not lift. "What is it, Mr. Underwood, that concerns you so?"

Wilfred shook his head. It was as if he did not know where to begin.

"Tell me then, why you were so desperate for Imogen to snare me?" Wilfred's eyes found Micah's, he feared something, which was strange for such a solid man who had been the strength of the village until this recent fall.

"Oh, lad, what will you think of me? I am no gold-digger. I did not mean Imogen should 'snare' you to improve her lot in life, for she is doing nicely, but... I know you are from a good family, as is she, but..."

Micah tried not to bridle. He liked Wilfred, but if word had spread of his good fortune to even the blacksmith's ears, then Dibbledale would be rife with gold-diggers and opportunists. How reliable were the offices that Lord Farrington was using? Then Wilfred went on.

"She is young, and he cannot have her, I will never allow it. If I die here, who will protect them if not you, Micah... Your father cannot for he has no right to stand against such a man, and he is God-fearing." Wilfred grimaced.

"Well, you are not going to die here, or anywhere else soon, but you need to rest a few days. Who is 'he'?" Micah folded his arms and stared down at Wilfred, trying to make sense of what the man's ramblings meant. It was possible he had been dreaming.

"You are the vicar's son, a good match for any village girl. She likes you, always has. Imogen cannot hide her heart from me. She may appear wild, but Micah, she has a good spirit. Skaggs would kill that spirit, or she would die in the fight, unless he had something over her to use against her, and that would be the wellbeing of me and Mary. Immi would do anything for us, I know."

"Skaggs!" Micah could not believe his ears. "He has designs upon Imogen?" he asked.

"Aye, and if I do not agree to the match, he will spread rumour about Mary and make our lives hell. We will have to move away and begin again, but we are not as young as we were when we came back here. Besides, I knew the place. I am sorry, lad, to tell the lass to grab you. Can you not see why I am so desperate?" Wilfred looked up at Micah who, stunned for a second, burst into laughter.

"You know how to flatter a soul, Wilfred. Would I be such a bad choice to make you 'desperate' for her to choose me?" he asked. Micah hurried on not wanting to upset an already worried man. "I think Imogen is too good for Skaggs. He will not lay a hand upon her." The notion of it made Micah want to call the man out.

"No, lad, you'd be fine, but I know that we hold her back. She is our daughter, but is gifted and, well, could do better. But your Ma and Pa are hardly going to consider her suitable even if you did."

When Wilfred said the last few words, Micah thought he saw a glint of hope in the man's eyes as he looked up.

"What is Skaggs to do with this?" Micah asked.

"He wants to make Imogen his wife, and his carrot that he dangles is that I oversee his new venture. If not, he will destroy us… and Mary in particular." Wilfred rubbed his tired eyes with the flat of his calloused hand.

"Leave this matter with me, Wilfred. I will promise you that Imogen will be safe. Skaggs will not have her, your cottage, or your forge. I need and want Imogen and you involved in my plans for Dibbledale. I had meant to talk to you later but now would appear opportune. Wilfred, I would like you to take on an apprentice. Dan, the stable hand at the Hare and Rabbit, is keen to be that person. I also have a man, Jamie, who lost his foot at Talavera arriving in the next few days. He is gifted with turning wood and metal, in his early twenties and deserves to have a life and a future. He could work at the forge and help out in return for some workspace, and you could take Dan on to do some of the menial work. Please think on it. Leave Skaggs to me." He opened the door.

"Micah, how can you do so much, you have so recently returned?" Wilfred asked.

Micah looked at the cross on the wall and smiled. "Wilfred, have faith and believe. Because I make no false promises here... I will make Imogen safe; you have my word. I will confide my plans and trust you to keep them between us, until such time as I am ready."

"Very well," Wilfred said.

Micah revealed his intentions for the ex-servicemen and his hopes for the future of the village. Wilfred greeted them with enthusiasm and willingly agreed to support them in whatever way he could.

Micah ran downstairs, grabbed his riding coat and headed out. It was even more imperative now that Lord Farrington disclose all of Skaggs' underhand dealings.

Chapter 24

Sir Benedict greeted his niece as he entered Thurley Hall. "There you are, my dear!" he exclaimed, but the cold glare he received in response could have sent ice daggers into his heart, if he had one that could be so easily targeted.

"Where else would I be? Seeing as my horse is being guarded by one of your henchmen and other strange men lurk outside the main door. Are we under siege, Uncle?" Her delicate skirts swished around her slender, straight form. Tall and elegant, the only curves were provided by her firm bosom that rose and fell with her deep breaths. The skirts of the muslin fabric hung straight down, not an ounce of fat bulged. If he were not already married, and she not his niece, Sir Benedict could have been tempted to take her as his mistress. He'd have fed her up a bit to put some meat on her bones. Normally, Beatrice was a vision of composure, but today she was angry, and it showed. Beatrice's cheeks flushed betraying her frustration as he eyed her, lost to his thoughts. Her chin tipped upward.

Sir Benedict laughed and walked into his study ignoring her affront. Her highhandedness might work on the young bucks she was used to associating with, but not on a mature man of his experience. In his day he had bedded finer than her, but never had he fallen for their waspish ways.

"Do you think you can keep me here as your prisoner?" she demanded to know.

"Yes, I do. For you have behaved badly. My

'henchmen' are there for our protection. So, until you learn how to behave like a young lady should, and to respect me and my guardianship of you, you will not leave this manor without my permission and never on your own." He leaned on the heavy walnut desk that had belonged to the previous unfortunate owner, Lord Bagby.

The room was dark with lines of heavy leather-bound books stacked on layers of shelves. There for show, never read. What light entered did so from a tall window at the end of the room. It smelt of smoke, brandy and a past where it may have once thrived.

"My brother will return and…" her words spat out, defensively.

He stepped around her and slammed the door shut.

"Listen to me, Beatrice, your brother will return with your mother to find you attached to a young, naïve, rich lieutenant. The man has had a vast fortune transferred to him. I learned of this by pure chance through a clerk in my pay in Northallerton's legal offices, and Micah Arrow is here… alone and vulnerable. You will ingratiate yourself to him. If the funds have not raised his ambitions in life, then you will whisper sweet endearments into his ear and turn his head."

"Why would I lower myself so as to toy with a naïve fool?" she asked. "I have no interest in the man."

"Because his resources will place Dibbledale and our tannery on the map of new money. We will provide the best saddles and harnesses throughout the whole of Yorkshire. Anything that needs a supply of fine skin we will provide. Who knows, he might even help prop up your family's stables. But first we must catch this fish on your sweet and sharp hook; reel him in, Beatrice, before others spend the fool's fortune for him. Young men and sudden fortunes need guidance." He smiled and poured himself a glass of cognac.

"What makes you think I will go along with this plan, sir?" she asked.

"You will marry in time perhaps. However, I am proposing you hook his attention. Marriage may be out of the question for now. My dear spoilt niece, you have already flaunted yourself in front of him. I need time with him, I just hope you have not scared the dote off. He is a vicar's son and not one of your society toffs. Although I have known men of the cloth that slip between the sheets of wanton harlots when they think no one notices. Arrow does not know how the flirting game is played out... and you certainly do not know how to restrain your forthright nature, for your previous meeting was seen by one of my 'henchmen'! If you have scared him away, I will see to it that you reside in Beckton Abbey to keep you safe until your family reclaim you." He folded his arms in front of his rotund chest and stared at her.

"You would not dare!" Miss Donaldson exclaimed.

"Oh, I dare, for you are not so clever as you think," he nodded at the door, "Now, you go and sit with your aunt and make sure that all is planned for our forthcoming dinner." He sat down in the Chippendale chair behind the desk, having poured another glass. He sipped it as if this time he savoured the fine French taste. He must remember to praise Skaggs for this supply. It was superior to his expectations.

"Arrow has served and fought in many battles. He was at Salamanca. You may well find that he has a mind of his own, for he has been out in the world, or how else has he made it to such affluent heights?" she asked. "Where did this fortune come from?" she enquired; curiosity piqued.

"Destiny is unpredictable. The man was married overseas to a foreigner. She is rich, so now is he… and he is here… she is not. Make play for him, my girl, he could set you up in your own apartments," Sir Benedict said, as he sat deep in thought.

"If he is married then how can I become engaged to the man. Uncle, surely you are not suggesting any other… arrangement?" she asked incredulously.

He waved her concerns aside. "The woman is foreign. We are still seeking some answers. However, the transfer of money is real. So, use your guile and catch our fish. We need him on side and you, my dear, will act all innocent. He will be so taken and flattered by your attention that he will set all else aside, whilst he takes a step up in society within our care. I intend to take him to Harrogate to begin with. You will accompany your aunt to the spa. That will be the first step. I will wine him, dine him, and introduce him to my club. Yes, that would be good, but I will keep him away from the gaming tables. I do not want any cardsharp to pocket our good fortune and bleed him dry before we do. You can dance with him at the assembly rooms. But keep the other maids away from him. He must have eyes for you only."

"Uncle…"

A knock on the door interrupted their discussion. "Enter," Sir Benedict shouted.

"Mr. Skaggs to see you, sir," the butler announced.

"Good, send him in." Sir Benedict waited for the door to close again. "Now, go, Beatrice. I have business and make sure that you stay within this Hall until this dinner is done. Then I shall tell you where you may go and with whom. I will not have you cavorting around the county like a harpy. You will have the young man all to yourself soon enough." He looked very pleased with his plans.

"I value my reputation, Uncle, even if you do not." She reached for the door handle. "I will not play these sorts of games. It is beneath me, and I am surprised that you would suggest such a shame upon my family."

"Really, so what will your brother say to you about your reputation when I mention to him your friendship with your stableman?" Sir Benedict could not help the smug expression spread across his face.

Her hand tightened on the brass doorknob as she glanced back and calmly responded, trying to control and steady her voice. "I do not have a friendship with Jacob Stanley, he is in our employ."

"Surely your tryst is not so forgettable, Beatrice? The man helped you run the stud. Doing such an excellent job he was. I understand that since your father died, he has taken your understanding of horse-breeding to a whole new level. Offering you a helping hand and lifting your spirits as well as your skirts!" His voice hardened as he spoke.

Miss Donaldson froze. "It is a lie… Who told you this falsehood? Stanley merely advises me about stock and the welfare of the beasts."

Her calm, cool eyes watered slightly, and Sir Benedict knew instantly that the suspicions of his agent were true. The stupid woman had whored herself to a glorified stableman. The ways of women confounded him.

"Guilt drips from your every pore, but my lips are sealed unless you refuse to play Arrow for all he is worth. Be a good niece, Beatrice, and you shall be rewarded, but play me for a fool instead and I will have you locked away in an Abbey cell, a fallen daughter, whose shame will taint her family name so deeply she will never return to her much-loved beautiful horses, home and lover."

The door opened wide, and Beatrice jumped back to prevent it hitting her face.

"Pardon me, Miss Donaldson." Mr. Skaggs burst in.

Beatrice walked briskly out.

"My apologies, Sir Benedict, I didn't know you had company." Skaggs' eyes followed the departing figure as she ran upstairs. "Has something upset the young miss?" Skaggs asked innocently.

"Yes, me," Sir Benedict said and laughed. "No matter, she needed a few shocks. I look forward to having her on her best performance to entice Arrow. What more have you learned?"

"Well, he would not drink with me in the inn at Gorebeck, but I suspect he was meeting someone. However, he went to the church on an errand for his father, but I did not see any other priest there. Then he returned to Dibbledale straight away."

"How go your own plans." Sir Benedict pointed to the decanter and Skaggs quickly poured himself a drink into the crystal glass at its side.

"Excellent," he said on sipping it. "More French cognac will arrive from my 'friends' a week Friday."

"Good, keep me informed."

"The surveyor said the river would do nicely and plans are being drawn up, labourers will be sourced from the northwest – Irish maybe – they come over all the time, but our men will keep them in check. I have set up an appointment for us to see Bishop Denton at the end of next week. By then we should have Arrow's funds on side. He does not seem much of a nut to crack."

"Good, man," Sir Benedict said.

"Who else will be at this dinner, sir?" Skaggs asked.

"The Arrows, Farrington, Speers, Beatrice, my good wife and us."

"Why ask Farrington? He snoops everywhere. I don't trust him."

"Then you are a wise man. We want this to appear above board. He will snoop as you say, so we shall present all openly. He has no interest in Dibbledale, his river flows from a different source at Kepstone Hall so his fishing will be good and his property even more sought after. He may even decide to head back south taking his young wife with him."

"So, you are keeping your enemy near," Skaggs said, liking the idea.

"Aye, something like that. I do not want him as a foe, although we will never be true friends – an associate will do. He has a pretty wife you know. Lucky bugger!"

Both men laughed, and at the other side of the door, having descended the stairs to listen as soon as the study door was closed over, Beatrice fumed. He knew about Jacob! She could scream. As if she wanted to spend the rest of her life with either Jacob as a lover or Arrow. She needed neither. The latter had eyes only for his little friend in the woods, but they did not know that. She would have to let Jacob go, that hurt because he was good at his job, knew to keep his mouth shut, and had been entertaining, but she just did not feel the physical need for a lover. However, she had been careless in her play, and that she could not afford to be once her mother returned, which could be anytime soon. Jacob would definitely have to go.

Beatrice returned to her aunt, picked up her embroidery and thought deeply. She would appear as perfection itself, a dutiful niece, at this dinner but would make sure that her uncle's plans failed miserably.

She smiled sweetly at Aunt Ashley. What a waste of

a life she thought tied to the likes of Sir Benedict, whilst he could rove freely. With no children the woman had nothing but needle and thread to occupy her and a host of servants to do everything. That would not be a life for her. No man would stand in her way. The thought of childbearing repulsed her. But for now, in an air of serenity she charmed her aunt, a lovely lady, kind and, if Beatrice was honest, quite simple.

When inspiration hit, she put her embroidery away. "Aunt, I have been quite remiss. I wondered if I could be excused, I meant to write to Mother, but quite forgot."

"You must, my dear. Mothers worry so," she said before her attention returned to her needlepoint.

Beatrice heard the regret in her aunt's voice. Three stillborn children had made her resigned to being barren, perhaps it was a relief to her not to have to go through the heartache again. Perhaps they no longer... no matter. Beatrice slipped out of the orangery into the garden. Crossing swiftly to the stables, anxious not to be caught as Mr. Skaggs left, she hurried.

"Matthew!" she snapped the name of the young stable lad.

"Yes, miss," he replied after a moment, as he appeared from one of the stalls.

Beatrice saw him tucking his shirt quickly into his breeches. Guessing correctly, she rushed forward and caught sight of the dairy maid running out of the other end of the stables. Excellent! she thought. Now, she would own his silence.

"Miss... I can explain..." he began; his colour had drained.

"Please do not bother. I am not blind. It is plain that you are having relations with one of the house staff. Both of you could be dismissed without references or pay!" she snapped her words out.

His eyes were filled with the fear of a trapped rabbit, face frozen as his livelihood hung in the balance.

"Please..."

She lifted her gloved hand to silence him. She had little time to use as it was.

"I need you to exercise my horse for me," she glanced back to make sure there was no one within earshot.

"Anything," he said.

"You will take a message to the vicarage in Dibbledale, for Mr. Micah Arrow, the reverend's son. "Make sure you speak to him alone, no one else. If he is not there, find him. If anyone asks you about where you are going you are exercising my horse."

Matthew nodded.

"Ask him to attend the chapel here tomorrow at noon."

"That's it?" he queried.

"Repeat my message."

Matthew did.

"If you tell a soul, you, and Muriel - yes, I know her name - will be out on the streets. Now, go!"

She retraced her steps, slipping back into the orangery unnoticed as Mr. Skaggs took his leave and left by the main door.

Chapter 25

Micah was livid; no one was going to force Imogen into marriage. Skaggs was moving faster with his plans than they had expected. Having a wealthy backer, in the form of Sir Benedict Adams must have gone to his fat and delusional head.

He entered Dibbledale ready to cross the stone bridge when he saw a rider approaching on a fine horse. He recognised the animal instantly and wondered what a country lad was doing atop it.

"Stop!" he ordered, and the baffled youth pulled the animal up short by his side. He could certainly ride well; his expression could easily be taken as one of guilt. Yet if he had stolen the beast, he would have to be a village idiot to ride through the town so openly and not expect to be questioned.

"How did you come by that mare?" Micah asked. His brusque manner was influenced more by his inner anger at Skaggs than this latest mystery.

"I am Matthew, sir, on an errand for Miss Donaldson and exercising her horse." He steadied it as the Thoroughbred was skittish.

"Why isn't she riding her own horse? Does the lady ail?" Micah thought the old Bagby Estate was big enough for any stable hand to exercise their horses on.

"No, sir, she doesn't. Please, I need to go to the vicarage." Micah could see Matthew was unmistakeably flustered about something.

"Why?" Micah asked, and now Matthew looked like he was ready to make a bolt for it. "I am Lieutenant Arrow, son of Reverend Arrow, so you can tell me what is so urgent." Micah softened his tone, "I may be able to help." To Micah's surprise the boy looked instantly relieved.

"I have a message for you, sir. Miss Donaldson asks if you could come to the chapel at noon tomorrow." He turned the horse around ready to leave.

"Why?" Micah spoke his thought out loud.

"It's not my place to ask, sir," Matthew stated.

"Tell her, yes," Micah responded, wondering why he had been summoned by a messenger, knowing he would only find out if he attended her meeting.

He watched the lad ride off then continued up from the dale to the moor road and then down to the larger village of Beckton. He urgently needed to speak with Miss Lydia.

Since their brief meeting when Wilfred collapsed, Micah had learnt from his father that Doctor Samuel Speers had carved out quite a name for himself in the two years he had been in the area. The previous doctor, a man named Brown had been unmasked by Speers as a charlatan, and now languished in York gaol.

Beckton would soon have another doctor as Speers' responsibilities, Ezekiel had confided to Micah, lay elsewhere with his family's estates.

He approached the spacious Rowan Cottage and Micah felt reassured that Miss Lydia would still talk to him. Rowan Cottage was a humble home for a lord, but with a beautiful well-tended garden, with budding wisteria flourishing abundantly around the entrance.

Micah tethered his horse by the gate and walked between two carefully laid out beds; one side had an abundance of roses and wallflowers whilst the other was more practical with burgeoning herbs and vegetables.

Before he could knock, the door opened and the lady he had affectionately known as 'Miss Lydia' stood before him in a finely made dress, the colour of sunshine with tiny white flowers embroidered around the bodice. She looked younger than her years. Marriage suited her, he thought, as he removed his hat and was warmly greeted.

"Lieutenant Arrow!" she said and stepped back. "Please, come in." Then, as if struck by a thought, her expression changed quickly. "Is it my husband you seek? Is all well with Mr. Underwood."

"He fares well. No, Miss Lydia... Mrs. Speers... Lady..."

"Micah, please call me Lydia, for you knew me when I was just a..." her words faded as her confidence ebbed.

"Just a lady who I greatly admired, and perhaps was a little smitten with, but how things have changed. You are married to a lord and yet still living in a country cottage. Grand as it is."

"Well, everything in life is temporary or transitory." She ushered him inside. The hallway was narrow, but as they followed it to the left, they were soon in a sunlit room, with casual chairs arranged around a fireplace. Everything from the delicately embroidered sampler on the walls to the highly polished inlaid cherry wood table by the window felt loved and homely.

"This cottage actually still belongs to Lord Farrington; we use it when Samuel is seeing patients here. It has fond memories for us," she smiled at him but then tilted her head on one side and asked, "But what is it that bothers you, Micah? You have come to see me, but why?"

"Lord Farrington is arranging for me to meet your grandfather, Bishop Denton. I wondered if you and he had any contact, since your circumstances have changed so much. Sometimes wisdom comes with age." Micah watched her eyes sadden.

"Not in his case, despite him being a clergyman of learning. My grandfather rejected my mother when Father spoke his mind to protect the common man. He was a priest then, and as you know Bishop Denton wanted him to toe the line and follow in his own footsteps. My mother, the bishop's own daughter, never recovered from her family's rejection of her. She was cut off. So, the answer is no, Micah, I have never had any contact with him." She smiled at her old friend. "I forget my manners; would you like a drink or some sustenance? My maid can easily fetch something."

"No, thank you. I wondered if you knew anything about him. He owns the woodland and the river source. There is word that this may be up for sale and if so, I hoped to show interest." Micah felt that he was grasping at straws.

Lydia shrugged. "I know he is old, but he is not desperate for money, so why should he sell it? He has no one to leave it to. One uncle was killed during the wars, another died in infancy; as he has no male heirs, I cannot see why he would suddenly sell."

Micah stood up. "I really am sorry to have intruded and perhaps stirred up memories you would prefer to forget."

"Sit, please, you have not stirred up anything. I have no feelings other than regret, for my mother and I came to terms with that a long time ago."

Doctor Speers appeared in the doorway. "May I join you?" he asked and stepped inside the room.

Micah was still on his feet. He realised that Speers had overheard their conversation. "I apologise for calling unannounced and disturbing you, sir."

"Sit down, man, and tell me what you know about the plans of a Mr. Skaggs?"

At his mention Micah's face reflected his inner rage.

"I know that he must be stopped. He and Sir Benedict Adams will buy the land and build a tannery if he holds the deeds. I also know he bullies those who depend upon it and would try to force innocence to his will." Micah sat down.

"Then you need help," Doctor Speers declared, "And possibly money, for how else could you show interest and be taken seriously by Bishop Denton. Save your breath if you merely wish to utter words of persuasion to the man, for he is deaf to any heartfelt pleas or compassion. Believe me, I know," he admitted and then glanced at Lydia.

Micah realised he must have tried to build bridges with the bishop and been rejected.

However, Micah saw no indication that Doctor Speers had any knowledge about his arrangements with Lord Farrington. The two men were good friends, so Micah's respect for Lord Farrington grew even stronger if he had not confided in another of his 'friends'.

"I merely hoped that you may now be on good terms with Denton and could help support the cause."

"Sorry, Arrow, but that door is closed to us for good," Doctor Speers declared.

In order that his visit was not entirely in vain Micah changed the focus of his conversation. "I could do with information about the man Skaggs. I would protect those who I value, and I have plans that will protect Dibbledale whilst keeping the village's beauty. This man is proving to be an ever-growing threat."

"Tell me about them," Speers said and pulled over a chair. "These plans you have, Micah."

Some minutes later Micah had finished explaining his ideas for an artisan village of ex-soldier craftsmen providing a living by their own skills, supporting each other's efforts. Doctor Speers sat back thoughtfully, pondering what he had been told.

"You have thought this through. I applaud your vision. Tell me, Micah, did you come here hoping my wife would be able to convince her grandfather to act as a sponsor? I warn you he may be a retired bishop, but he has never been a generous spirit. Or do you harbour hope that I will be your benefactor?"

"I am not here seeking to beg money or favour, sir! I merely want to understand if there is a way to approach the old man so I can stop a grave wrong being committed to the home I both value and love."

"Is Farrington investing in this?" Doctor Speers asked, and Micah began to feel uncomfortable.

"No, sir, he helped me with some personal matters. We served together. It is just that Skaggs' plans may be moving forward more quickly than we realised."

"Micah, you are a man with a dream. Dreams require funds to bring to fruition. If Farrington is behind you with this, I too will consider investing, but leave Skaggs to Farrington. His area of expertise is with dealing with the likes of him. Interfere and you could get hurt."

"I appreciate your well-meant words, and with the help of Lord Farrington I will deal with Mr. Skaggs. My plan is more than a dream and has been costed out. I am a practical man, sir. Believe me, I am not naïve and blinkered, I served behind the enemy lines. We will bring Skaggs down. Now, if you will excuse me, Lord and Lady Speers, I must be on my way."

Micah stood up and was shown to the door by Lydia.

"Pride comes before a fall, Micah," she whispered. "Samuel only meant to help."

"Please accept my apologies if I sounded ungrateful. I have much to sort out in a very short time." He left, wondering what his next steps should be.

Chapter 26

Imogen praised the girls for being so diligent in learning their letters as they went on their way home. She soon had the room ready for the next day and was enjoying a moment of quiet. The girls worked hard in the laundry, but Mrs. Weeks saw to supplying a bowl of hot oats before they began their lessons. Imogen found her care touching. Stepping out of the small school room she saw a man leaning against the forge doorway. He looked ill at ease and restless.

Imogen made her way over to him. She could see how exhausted he was.

"Can I help you, sir?" she asked. Imogen tried not to show her surprise when she realised the young man was missing his lower right leg. The peg leg looked worn and tired like its owner.

He pushed himself upright and leaned on a crutch, his eyes sheepishly found hers. "I was looking for the blacksmith, but the forge is all locked up. I hoped he would be able to fix this." The young man showed her the end of his crutch which had split; the wood would soon be useless unless it was protected.

"I am his daughter. The forge will be closed for a few days," she explained, and saw how downcast he was at this news.

"Sorry, to have bothered you." He hobbled around to begin his walk away.

"I am Miss Underwood. You are?" she asked, as he balanced precariously for a moment before correcting himself.

"Mr. Jamie Campbell," he said in a gentle tone. "I hoped I was expected."

"Are you staying with someone in Dibbledale?" Imogen persisted.

"I received a letter and instruction from my old lieutenant. He paid my fare here and said I was to present myself. Mr. Underwood would tell me where I can find him. I have the lieutenant's letter in my pocket, miss, if you would care to look."

"Would that be Lieutenant Arrow?" she asked.

"Yes! Do you know him?" A spark of light glinted in his eyes for the first time.

"Yes, I do. I can and will help you. Stay here a moment and I will fetch the forge key. We will do a temporary repair on that," she said and pointed to the damaged wood, and then I will see if Micah, Lieutenant Arrow, is at the vicarage. His father is Reverend Mr. Arrow."

Jamie's face lit up. "Bless you, Miss Underwood. I had no idea what to do next. Mind, I am not surprised that he is the son of a priest as he certainly has good Christian charity in his heart."

Imogen smiled as she could not agree more with him. "Wait here for me, I shall not be long. Are you hungry?" she asked and saw by his expression that pride was stopping him saying just how much he was.

She nodded and ran over to Mrs. Weeks' cottage where she could fetch the forge key and pick up some scones and milk for him to eat and drink.

Imogen heard a horse approaching as she left the house.

"Miss Underwood, I have been hoping to catch up with you. You are like an elusive butterfly; you flit from place to place. I think it is time you settled and nested."

Imogen's spirits instantly sank, unlike the flit of a butterfly. "Mr. Skaggs, why ever would that be? Why would you give the matter any thought at all?" Imogen asked, hoping he would soon pass her by, wishing she had followed her father's instructions. This was likely the man who had beaten Pickles; it took strength not to accuse him.

He dismounted, obviously trying to do so in a smooth movement, but the effort of swinging his leg over the saddle caused him to land heavily and sigh loudly with the effort.

"Have you spoken to your ma or pa?" He stepped nearer to her seeing that she was carrying a basket. He lifted the cover cloth with his crop.

Imogen pulled away. He must not have heard about her father's circumstances, she presumed. Good, for some strange reason she would feel more vulnerable if he did. "Perhaps I could join you, help you devour that?" He laughed. "I like a woman with a good appetite."

"I think not, sir, as it is a gift," Imogen said and tried to step around him.

Skaggs' hand shot up, placing his palm on the side of the house, blocking her path. "Miss Underwood, it would be in your best interest and in particular your ma's if you were more commodious toward me." His grizzled face was too close to hers; she could smell stale ale on his sour breath.

Imogen tried to mask her anger. She could see Jamie watching them from across the road. The visitor must have realised Skaggs was being intimidating, but Imogen did not want him to place himself in danger. Jamie's face betrayed his growing concern.

"Mr. Skaggs, if you wish to speak to my father then you need to talk to…"

His breath was vile as he leaned into her. Any nearer and she would strike him, but Imogen knew that anything she did rashly could cause the family actual harm, he had powerful allies and her papa was unwell.

"I have spoken to your pa already and made him a proposition." One of his stubby fingers traced the line of her jaw. She pulled back, appalled.

"Well, he is a busy man, and I am sure he will get back to you in time. Now you must excuse me as I…"

He placed the tip of his crop under her chin.

Wide-eyed she glared at him, her hand gripping the basket ready to swing it and run if needs be, but first she would kick the man hard where he was most vulnerable and see him double up.

"My proposition is simple. You willingly consent to being my wife and all will be well, or you refuse me, Imogen, and see your family be destroyed."

Imogen's mouth opened to dismiss this ludicrous idea, but he continued.

"If you speak rashly to me now and reveal your true wild nature in all its coarseness, this will go badly for you. Those eyes betray what that small mind of yours is thinking. You will agree to my demands, or your father will lose his business and your ma… well that old witch, Mother Shipton is long gone, but people still fear what they do not understand, don't they, Imogen? Superstitions feed fearful minds."

She backed away so she could step around him, realising that to retaliate now would be foolhardy at best or even dangerous for her family.

"Ah, I see that you care deeply for them both. Good, because if I take you as my wife, they will be linked to me by marriage, and some re-educating will need to happen.

So, you will make your ma acceptable enough to be seen publicly, not that I would display her at a dinner party, I am sure we will have some entertaining evenings until you produce my heirs. Yes, I want a strong woman, not a simpering pale shadow that is only good for tapestry and fits of vapours. I will handle your pa. And you, my dear, will be the most obedient wife a man could wish for, for their sake. I like that fire, but slow the burn to a simmer, for the sake of family - the one you have now and the one we will have together in the years to come." He glanced around as Jamie was slowly crossing the road toward them. "What the hell do we have here? Cripples walking the village streets! I'll chase the blighter away. Beggars, I cannot abide."

"No!" her word was snapped out. Skaggs immediately turned his head and stared at her, lifting an eyebrow.

"Please, don't, he is just passing through on his way to the vicarage. He has obviously been at war."

"Then he was not very good at it," he smirked. "However, my dear, as you ask me so nicely, I will let him pass through. But remember, charity begins at home. Your home will be with me, or your family will be homeless." He laughed and placed his leg in the stirrup of his horse and with a gargantuan effort heaved his bulk up into the saddle. It was no more elegant a move than his dismount. Skaggs galloped off casting Jamie off balance as he passed by. The two young people's dislike of this man somehow created a silent bond between them.

"I take it that he is not a friend?" Jamie remarked.

"Do not be intimidated by him, but best avoid direct conflict if you can." Imogen offered her advice whilst watching Skaggs disappear into the distance. She knew in her heart that Skaggs' words would come to nothing, but they still sickened her. No one made threats against her kin and got away with it.

"Miss Underwood, you are truly kind and mean well, but I lost a limb to worse men than he and am still standing. I am not so easily intimidated, but I am hungry and tired."

Imogen now saw the mature man, not a figure deserving pity, who had experienced the cruelty of life. She felt respect for him, but her heart had not ceased to pound at the threats to her family Skaggs had made. Did he really think she would ever marry him? Beget children and propagate his line? Like hell she would!

"Come inside, sit and eat, then we will find Lieutenant Arrow, Micah. He will know what to do to help us both. For I fear we may both need him."

Imogen wanted to consult her shadow-man. She set her basket down by the chair her father kept in his small reception area. Wrapping her apron about her dress she set to using a small strip of scrap metal to hammer into a protective cap to hold Jamie's crutch together.

"I would never have thought you could wield a hammer so deftly, Miss Underwood. You amaze me," Jamie said, as he tucked into his scones and sipped milk from the leather flask.

Imogen pictured Skaggs' leering face with each controlled strike. She was careful not to split the wood further but was burning with a desire to vent at the loathsome man. It would do no good. She had to think quickly; somehow she would defeat Skaggs. "Perhaps we should not judge by appearances." She tried to lighten her mood. "Where do you hail from?" she changed the topic, wanting to bring some fresh thoughts into her troubled mind.

"I was born over Skipton way, but before you ask, my father could not look me in the eye when I returned a cripple." He stared bitterly at the flask before downing the last thirsty gulp. "It took me quite a while before being able to glance at my own reflection."

"That is awful!" she said. "You have given so much for your country. What of your mother?" she asked and stopped hammering to use her father's long-handled pincers to fasten the metal to the wood. Once in place, a nail secured the cap she had made, which was also hammered gently until its head was flush. Satisfied her work would hold at least in the short term, she removed her apron and returned the crutch to its grateful owner.

"Thank you kindly, miss." He nodded as he took hold of it, relief instantly apparent. "Mother felt differently. She saved my letters and one that had arrived from my ex-lieutenant. That was what changed my fortunes; a timely invite to come here, it included a banker's note for the journey costs. Mother gave me lodging and clothes until I could catch the coach to Gorebeck. I hitched a lift on a wagon from there over to Dibbledale. She made me promise I would write as one day my father may change his mind. I told her I will write her once settled, but my view of him has changed for ever."

"Have you known the lieutenant long, Mr. Campbell?" she asked.

"We went over on the same transport from Southampton to Oporto. Of course, he was a young green officer and I a green young lad keen to earn his King's Shilling. What a fool I was." He glanced at his leg stub.

"Lieutenant Arrow fared much better in the years that have passed by; our paths took vastly different routes.

He is a hero, made to do daring and bold acts. I was destined to be cannon fodder." He shrugged.

"I can understand your resentment of his good fortune," Imogen said, trying not to sound critical as she feared it was at Micah and not the war. "But you are a hero too."

"Oh, I am only resentful at my own incompetent officers, not at Lieutenant Arrow. He recognised me from our first journey when he saw me being carried off the battlefield and placed me in a small convent for my recuperation. I was going to be sent home as no longer fit for active service. My leg had not had a chance to heal properly. I would have perished with the badness if it had not been well-tended. Those two months gave me time to make a decent recovery and attune to a new life. The peace and wisdom of the nuns, who treated me kindly but firmly, taught me to value what was left of me – my life - rather than die with my severed foot."

Imogen was filled with admiration for this young man, and pride in Micah for his generous spirit. She knew that Skaggs would never be her husband but could not see how to escape his threats at present. Compared to these two soldiers, Skaggs lacked courage and compassion.

"I cannot imagine what you went through. Or what you have experienced since you returned. However, I could never imagine my father turning away from me because I was injured. Surely, he should have been filled with joy that you lived?" Imogen asked, but the man just shrugged, realising that she had momentarily forgotten what Skaggs had said. Then his words returned to her, and she realised that he had spoken to her father, and her mother! Had he caused her father to have some kind of attack? She must go to the vicarage and talk to him. Then speak to Micah.

"Well, Mr. Campbell, if you are feasted," she smiled at him lifting the conversation and deciding to hurry things along, "we shall locate Micah."

Jamie stood up, tried out his crutch and nodded. "Fine work, miss, I can pay a few pennies," he offered as she locked up the forge.

"No need. It was only a piece of scrap metal and, besides, my father will do a better job, next time."

"I will make a better crutch myself, once I have settled somewhere. The oak here is good, as are the other trees. This is an ancient woodland." He looked around as he moved along.

Imogen was pleased that he managed to keep up a decent pace although the ruts of Church Lane were tricky for him to manoeuvre. "You know how to turn wood? I think you would get on well with my mother too," she said. "Here we are!" They approached the church lychgate.

Jamie stood straighter after pausing for a moment and straightening his jacket. "Miss, do you think they might turn me away if Lieutenant Arrow is not in?" His words and his step were uncertain.

Imogen paused and straightened his collar for him. "There, you are fit to meet the King," she said and smiled at him. "Where is that confidence you had a few moments ago?"

He laughed. "You get used to rejection so quickly, without even realising that it has happened."

"Did I reject you?" she asked, hands on her hips.

"No, you are like your friend, Lieutenant Arrow. You have good hearts; I hope they are in some way connected."

Imogen's face instantly flushed. She turned away and opened the small gate. "Come, you need to rest for I fear the exertion of your travel has affected your mind and loosened your tongue. You are very bold, sir." She walked ahead.

"I spoke out of turn, but honestly, miss."

Imogen glanced back at him. "I know you did."

Ruth Arrow was watching out of the window whilst waiting for Ezekiel to return when she saw Imogen and Jamie approaching together. "Whatever now! Micah! This really is too much."

"Mother, what is it?" he asked, as he entered their reception room.

"We are being turned into a nursing home by the Underwoods," she snapped her words out. "This is your father's doing. He does not know where to draw a line."

Micah looked over her shoulder to see Jamie and Imogen approaching.

"I will speak to you later, Mother, for your comments are really too much." He darted out of the room, leaving the vicarage door open wide as he rushed outside to greet his young friend, and Imogen.

"Jamie, you made it. How marvellous! Come inside, we shall have food brought and…"

"Miss Underwood has already fed me once," Jamie replied, as Micah stood before him and patted both arms in an awkward pincer movement.

Imogen sensed Micah wanted to hug Jamie, but that would hardly be appropriate.

"Miss Underwood." Micah acknowledged Imogen, equally awkwardly.

"Micah, I need to speak with my father, may I go up, please?" she asked, knowing Ruth was watching from the window.

"Yes, yes… thank you." Micah was tongue-twisted, which surprised her, but then Jamie represented the meeting of his two quite different worlds. One as an officer and gentleman, the other a man at home; the two images of him must be totally different to his young friend.

"I will leave you two gentlemen to catch up. Lovely to meet you, Mr. Campbell," she said before making haste up the stairs to see her father.

Micah ushered Jamie into the vicarage whilst Imogen slipped in to see her father, who looked well and rested.

"Papa," she said.

"Is everything alright, Immi?" His face instantly filled with concern as he threw back the coverlet. "I'll come. You need me there!"

"No, Papa, all is well!" She covered him back up and tried to reassure him that both she and her mother were well. She would speak to him of Skaggs once he was up and around. On seeing him Imogen decided he was worried enough without her adding to his burden. She needed time to think – time which she lacked.

Chapter 27

Micah approached the chapel warily. There was no horse outside and little sign of movement around it. He had taken the woodland path to avoid entering down the Hall's drive. No problem, for as a boy he had explored these woods regularly. Oddly, the gates now had a man garrisoned there. Micah was assessing the situation; it seemed that Sir Benedict either had enemies or was afraid that he may soon have.

Before leaving the cover of the trees he watched for signs of movement by the old chapel. He was expected at noon, or so the mysterious message had said, so he had decided to arrive an hour early, keeping watch to ensure there were no unwanted surprises.

The only person to enter was Miss Donaldson, moments before midday. She had not ridden from the Hall but walked apace along the pathway to the chapel. All the while she glanced about her as if making sure she was not followed. Once she was inside, he waited patiently. Haste was the downfall of many a man, Micah had learnt to bide his time. When no one followed, he tethered his horse under cover of the trees and entered.

The lady was already seated, head covered piously in front of the altar. He walked up the short aisle and stopped by her side. Micah crossed himself, giving quick thanks to his maker for sparing him in the wars. He had been in this chapel a few times with his father when he was a boy.

"Please sit, Lieutenant Arrow, for my time here is limited. However, you are welcome to stay and reflect once I have left. But if you are seen, please do not mention that I was here." Miss Donaldson looked up at him, her manner intense.

The lady was ill at ease here. "Tell me what it is that bothers you and why I was summoned?" Micah saw a glint of humour cut through the watchful glare that had greeted him.

"It is you! You are the reason I am here."

"I am flattered," Micah said. What game did the lady play? He felt like a country mouse being toyed with by a city tom cat.

"Don't be!" She shook her head. "Let us cut through to the bone. My uncle and the obnoxious Skaggs want whatever it is you have - your wealth – all of it. They wish to use me to lure you into their web so that they can bleed you dry. If I do not play their wicked game, they will disgrace me whatever way they can. Arrow, I speak frankly, I do not care to be with a man – any man. I wish to have a choice in this matter. I have no more desire to have children than I do the pox. Once my brother returns with Mother, I will go to my home and help to run it. However, apparently, I must flirt with you at the dinner they are hosting, so I would ask you to go along with their plan, but do not fall into it." She pursed her lips and awaited his response.

"Why would you warn me, Miss Donaldson? Why not play your part and please your uncle?" he asked, intrigued by this amazingly outspoken and direct woman. It seemed unnatural to him that a woman should feel so, but if the idea of having children was so abhorrent to her, then he hoped that she did not have any. A child deserved to be loved and nurtured – not compared to the pox! If she had met him before his service overseas, he may have been an easy catch, but then if he had not married, he would not now be worth the catching. It seemed that part of his past they were unaware of.

"Because I hate him! Oh, do not look so shocked. My uncle is a fat lazy oaf who has his minions do all his dirty work. Skaggs thinks that Uncle treats him as a friend. As soon as they have bought the land, built whatever it is they wish to and have the thing making money, Uncle will move on and have collectors pick up his share at regular intervals. Then when the day comes that Skaggs decides to short Uncle of his share, for he is greedy and stupid and so will almost certainly, he will find out that he has no friend in him. My uncle has men who are efficient at getting Sir Benedict Adams exactly what he desires."

Micah rubbed his face as he pondered the very descriptive explanation. "How do you know all this?"

"Because I listen at doors. I followed my father around the stud. I know how men talk when they think that innocent ears are closed. So, please save me any chastisement."

"Perhaps you have been unfortunate in the male company you have had to endure, Miss Donaldson. I do not consider all ladies to be made up of the same character, so please allow some room in your judgement for honourable men who respect women."

She stood up, brushing his words aside. "I must return as I am under house guard, and they will be sure to look for me shortly. Will you help to bring those men down?"

"Very well, we will play a game together to our mutual end."

"Good. By the way, my uncle seems to be provided with tax free, excellent French cognac, which will be restocked next Friday I understand. Skaggs sees to its distribution."

"We have a mutual aim, but for different reasons. Thank you for giving me the warning, Miss Donaldson, but please understand I am no man's fool." He watched as she stepped past him. He could have added 'or woman's'.

"Good," she said.

"One thing, Miss Donaldson," he said, and she paused.

"Make it a quick thing, Lieutenant Arrow." She glanced back.

"Tell me, is it all men you hate, or just these two?" he asked. His words hung unanswered in the air.

"Good day, Lieutenant Arrow, please be discreet when you leave and go back through the woodland."

He watched the elegant figure slip outside the side door of the chapel. Was there a man that Miss Donaldson could respect? He doubted it. Micah acknowledged the cross and returned to his horse. Miss Donaldson was a bitter woman, beautiful, wilful and one dangerous to be crossed. He did not flatter himself to think that she was doing this to save him from naive fiscal ruin. He was merely one of her loathed men that she willed to control to achieve her own ends. Micah urged the horse onward and when he came to the long stretch of the moor road, he gave it its head. Whichever man or men had wronged the lady in the past had tainted her for life. He would play her game to buy time, but the thought of being in her presence alone for any length of time did not appeal to him. Imogen was warm, refreshingly outspoken but not in a cruel way, whereas Miss Donaldson would make ice look warm in her presence.

Lord Farrington would, no doubt, be interested to know about the contraband cognac, but it was becoming imperative that he talked to his mother and father about his wife. Where to begin...?

Chapter 28

Imogen had been so lost in thought as she left the forge having checked all was still well, that she had not seen Micah approaching at a fast pace.

"Imog… Miss Underwood," he shouted over to her.

She nearly dropped the forge key. However, his presence made her troubled thoughts lift with a spark of hope. "I need to talk to you, Micah," she said as he came up to her. "I had hoped to have a discussion with my father when I brought Mr. Campbell to the vicarage, but he was so peaceful that I did not wish to risk upsetting him further. So, I did not explain my problem."

"He looked well this morning. I think he is already planning to return to his old life. I have mentioned Jamie and introduced them. Dan is ready to join as soon as he is needed. I know they will all work well together; an apprentice and a skilled carpenter means Wilfred will have plenty of help. Jamie is staying with Abraham Harkness over at the general store for now as he has a small room at the back that will do him fine until he is more settled. Abraham loves hearing about the battles fought so Jamie will not be lost for conversation."

He stood next to Imogen, who resisted the urge to wrap an arm around him and bring their bodies close. Micah's eyes and his half smile showed they shared the same thought. Imogen longed to feel his warmth and the security that loving arms can provide. More… she wanted to feel so much more with this man, whatever there was to experience.

"So, what was it that caused your father to be so upset to the point of collapse?" Micah asked.

Micah's question replaced her feelings of desire with a shiver as she remembered Skaggs standing next to her. "Micah, let us go to see Mama. I will explain as we walk. She returned to the cottage earlier and I fear that Mr. Skaggs may have upset her as he did Papa."

"Skaggs has been here intimidating your parents?" Micah's smile dropped instantly. She nodded and started walking. "Very well, but Imogen there is much I need to talk to you about too," Micah said falling into step with her.

"Mr. Skaggs spoke to me," Imogen began, ignoring Micah's comment being totally lost in her own troubled thoughts. "He came up to me in the street, his manner arrogant and insulting."

"Has he threatened you?" Micah stopped mid step, but Imogen gestured they should keep walking.

"In a way, but more worryingly he has threatened my mama and papa if I do not do as he wishes." They crossed the small stone bridge and entered the sheltered peace of Church Lane.

"What did he want you to do?" Micah asked.

"He wants me to marry him, bear his children and then my parents will be safe. Otherwise, he will destroy my father's business and my mother will be ridiculed. She cannot be. I will protect them to my last breath!" Imogen words stopped when Micah took hold of her hand and gently pulled her to him.

Facing her he looked down into her striking blue eyes. "That he will never do, for I will not allow it," Micah declared.

"How would you intend to stop him?" Imogen asked. She had no intention of giving in to the man's demands, but was curious what Micah thought the solution was. Part of her wondered if he would propose to her there and then. Hoping, perhaps…

"Do not give in to him, but neither reject him at the moment." Micah offered his advice.

Imogen stepped away and continued her journey again as she nodded, as if taking in his instructions but her mind felt befuddled. Was it disappointment she was feeling? Could she really expect this handsome, eligible lieutenant to offer himself up so easily? Imogen told herself to focus more on her problems and finding a solution, and less on daydreaming about her returned hero. Hadn't he declared he had feelings for her, and made his intentions clear – surely he meant to marry her.

"Let him think you are considering it. A bully is easier to catch off guard when they think they have won their prey's obedience. Meanwhile, I will be working to undermine the man's plans. Trust me, Imogen. You will be free of him soon enough to do as you will. No one should force your hand."

Imogen looked up at the golden flecks in his hair as the sunshine caught them. His face was alight with enthusiasm. Yet, he had not made an offer to step in and ask for her hand. Imogen smiled back at him; she did not want to appear so transparent. "What will you do? Micah, you are no longer at war. You cannot pick fights with powerful men over here. Skaggs maybe uncouth but he has a powerful friend in Sir Benedict Adams and your father serves this community. He too could be vulnerable if you openly stand in their way."

"Imogen, I too have powerful friends. I fought alongside them. Don't look like that, I do not mean Jamie, although he is as brave as they come, I refer to a man of power who is a friend of Wellington himself. Take my word on it. I will win this war."

Imogen could feel his truth burn into her heart. He would protect her; her family would be safe. But not a mention of their future did he utter, yet in the forge hadn't he made a commitment? Or were they sweet murmurings uttered into distressed ears as her father had crumpled? Imogen could not see hers and Micah's future clearly: emotions overwhelmed her whenever he was near.

"You said you wanted to tell me something, Micah. What is it?" Imogen tried to sound curious rather than desperate to hear what he had to say as they left Church Lane and followed the path to her family cottage.

He stood square in front, blocking her way forward. "Imogen, much has happened to me in the last nine years. I am not the boy I was. I am a man full grown in every way."

"I can see that," she said impishly.

"Serious, woman, please?" he rebuked.

"Sorry, Micah."

"I need you to listen to me and take in my words. When I was in Spain my life changed irrevocably. I did something through desperation... not mine, but..." He sighed ran his fingers through his shoulder length waves and took in a sharp breath. "I would not have you think badly of me, Imogen, but you have not experienced the world and its ways," he fumbled over his words.

Imogen tried to keep her face impassive, but who was he to tell her what she had experienced when he had not been there to see it? She may not have gone to war, but she had lived through the troubled and uncertain times at home. Men were away, shortages abounded, and civil unrest was never far from people's mind. Look what happened in France! Well, perhaps he had some right to his point, but she tried not to show her disapproval of what he said.

"When I was in Spain, I met someone who was in desperate straits and as a favour I…"

"Woof! Woof! Woof!" A rough bundle of grizzled fur stumbled past Micah jostling him into the ferns and stopped in front of Imogen barking incessantly at her.

"Calm, boy, calm!" Imogen sat the troubled hound down and crouched by its side. "What is it, Pickles?" she asked.

Micah brushed mud off his trousers. "Perhaps you will spare a few moments to listen to the hound!" he snapped.

Pickles ran awkwardly along the path a few feet in the direction of the cottage, stumbled and then stopped. When Imogen did not follow straight away, he began barking once more.

"Can't you see, Micah, he is telling me Mama is in trouble?" Imogen said as she rushed past him following Pickles. "He was attacked – I believe Skaggs may have had something to do with it, if not struck out himself."

"I will avenge him, you will not live in fear of this man," Micah declared, as he conceded defeat about sharing his own troubled thoughts with Imogen. Another time then, he thought and followed. Who knew what the dog was saying to his mistress now? Apparently, Imogen did!

They passed by the cottage, but Pickles did not stop. Instead, he led them up through the woodland until they stepped out onto the edge of the moor road.

"Where is he going?" Micah asked as both slightly breathless people followed the dog to the old milestone, where he stopped.

Imogen began to run as she saw Pickles nudge something and realised it was a huddled figure. "Mama!"

she shouted as she approached.

Pickles began to jump around excitedly as Mary stood up, shaking, as she looked into Imogen's eyes. Her daughter grabbed hold of her.

"Mama, what happened?" She rested her forehead on her mother's as they nestled together. "You've been crying."

"Oh, Immi, it can't end here, not in a bog, not like Ma?" she muttered. "I had to come and face my fear. The moor here is beautiful but the bogs frighten me so."

"What can't?" Micah asked, obviously totally lost as to what Mary was muttering about.

"No, Mama, it will not! For one thing these bogs blanket the land, they are not very deep. The cold would get you before the land could swallow you up. But stop this now, for my shadow man is here and is finding us a way out," Imogen said, and was relieved when Mary held her head straight and looked at him.

"See, I told you, didn't I? He is the way forward." Mary said, "Forgive me for my spell of weakness. It will not happen again." She began to walk along the woodland track, not stopping or looking back with Pickles walking at her side looking up regularly at his disturbed mistress.

"What is this about the bog?" Micah asked.

"No matter," Imogen said.

"Is she alright?" Micah asked, clearly thinking that Mary was far from it.

"Yes, she had a moment where the past came back to haunt her. Tell me, soldier, in all you have seen does that never happen to you?" Imogen did not mean to sound waspish, but she needed to protect Mary against anyone who doubted her or the state of her mind.

"Good point. But she has not been at war..." he began only to be cut off again.

"She is from Ireland. Have you no knowledge of life over there?" Imogen was wanting to follow her Mama. "What was it you wanted to tell me about... Spain?" she asked, changing the subject.

"No matter. Go and see to your mother and dog. We will speak again when your world is more peaceful." He strode off along the road, heading for the lane that led back down into Dibbledale.

Imogen let him go. Men could be so single-minded; they knew their own mind but undervalued women and what they had to deal with in life. Disappointed that Micah had not proven himself to be any different, annoyed that their conversation had been interrupted and frustrated as she wanted to know what he had done in Spain that was so difficult to state, she ran to catch up with her mama.

Chapter 29

"Mother you look divine. Stop fussing, please?" Micah watched Ruth straighten her skirt for the umpteenth time as they waited for the door to Thurley Manor to open. Looking down upon the top of her bonnet he wondered if he had grown so much since he was away. Or was his mother's bearing becoming more fragile. Somehow, she seemed reduced in stature, yet when he glanced at Ezekiel, with his head held high, shoulders broad and back straight, he seemed just as he had been all of Micah's life.

Ruth's head shot up; her disapproval of his slightly patronizing comments obvious. "It is important that we make the best first impression. Your father's work requires the patronage of people like Sir Benedict Adams and you, my dear son, could do well to practice your conversational skills with a real lady like Miss Donaldson, instead of being flippant with local girls. You are far too outspoken these days. A common girl could drag you down to their level instead of raising you up!" She sniffed as her nose raised a little higher.

Micah did not respond but he knew which specific 'local girl' she referred to. Now was not the time to challenge her. Soon he would have a conversation in which she may well feel a bitter sting and that he regretted.

"We do not want to appear common. Straighten that back of yours. See how your father keeps his bearing. Be proud, Micah, you are our own hero, stand like one." She straightened her own and stared at the door awaiting to be admitted.

Ezekiel glanced across his wife and met his son's

gaze, reading annoyance clearly. He gave Micah a warning shake of his head, to instruct him to let all pass for now.

"Mother, we will talk about this later; calm your worries and just be yourself. If that is good enough for Father and God, then it will have to be good enough for Sir Benedict Adams." Micah was trying to apply the same words of wisdom to his own manner.

"Well said, son." Ezekiel patted his back as the door to a grander world opened to them.

The hallway was brightly lit by many candled chandeliers, their flickering light so captivating. There was no whiff of tallow; instead, their senses were filled with the pervading smell of lavender and pot-pourri. A tall housekeeper with keys at her waist greeted them and a maid relieved them of their outer clothes. Micah cut a fine figure in his dinner jacket and breeches.

There was music playing in the drawing room to their right as the Arrows were shown in and announced. Ruth had positively preened as they were greeted by Lady Ashley Adams. A large fire burned in the ornate marble hearth, atop which stood two fine oriental figurines.

"Lady Adams," Ruth gushed. "How beautiful your home is," she added.

"Come, dear, warm yourself and meet Lady Speers and Miss Donaldson. Reverend Mr. Arrow, Lieutenant Arrow, how fine you both look." The lady fussed until they were all introduced to Lord Farrington, Lord and Lady Speers, Sir Benedict and a man already supplied with a glass of port, Mr. Jethro Skaggs.

After some long minutes of 'chatter' Micah found himself slightly away from the others. He took the opportunity to look around him. Skaggs was in conversation with Miss Lydia - she would always have that title in his head - who looked very demure in an embroidered overdress showing a rich coloured skirt underneath. He tried not to glower, the man's girth was wrapped in a hideous overworked scarlet and gold waistcoat under his dinner jacket. Pearls before swine, Micah thought.

"I hope you are enjoying home life, Arrow, and are in fine fettle," Lord Farrington cut across his thoughts. "We were both at Talavera I believe - bloody battle. How fares civilian life?" Lord Farrington had discreetly made his way to converse with him.

"I am indeed, sir. Are you and your good lady wife in good health?" Micah glanced around.

"Alas, Lady Farrington could not attend." He bristled and added quietly, "This Hall holds unhappy memories for her." He quickly changed the conversation. "Have you met everyone here before?" he asked more normally and glanced around at the group.

"Most," Micah said, then quietly added, "One man tried to engage me in passing, but he has intimidated others that I care for deeply and needs stopping sooner rather than later." Micah smiled at Farrington as if they were having a jovial conversation.

Micah saw Ezekiel stepping over to join them, but Sir Benedict approached and clapped Micah firmly on his back and offered him a glass of madeira.

"Thank you," he answered and took the offered glass from a footman. Ezekiel did likewise, but only tentatively sipped the liquid as he preferred his warm cup of tea on an evening.

A bell sounded and Lady Adams moved to the centre of the room. Two footmen stood either side of the door waiting.

"What a lovely gathering you all make," she said as she graciously looked around the room.

From Micah's perspective they appeared a mismatched group, with Miss Donaldson at the centre wearing a gold silk gown of the finest quality that shone like the sun. Her hair was curled and set to perfection with a delicate finely twisted gold tiara upon her head, contrasting beautifully with her russet brown hair.

"Dinner will be served 'a la russe'," Lady Adams said and was rewarded when her guests nodded their approval. Mr. Skaggs raised his glass.

"I must apologise for the imbalance of the table, it is not quite de riguer, we are a little short on female company as Lady Farrington was indisposed and Mr. Skaggs is enjoying his bachelor life!" she simpered, but Micah had to look away and caught an equally scornful glint in Farrington's eye. Skaggs winked and interrupted his hostess.

"Not for much longer, Lady Adams," he declared and raised his glass again.

His hostess was gracious enough to giggle politely. "Please Lieutenant Arrow, would you escort Miss Donaldson to the table, I am blessed with you two young people, so you will sit at my right hand and Reverend and Mrs. Arrow to my left. Lord Farrington, please take your seat to the right of Sir Adams and dear Lord and Lady Speers to my husband's left. Come, let us eat!" She turned and on cue both footmen opened the doors wide.

The table was laid out ready for soup. Micah could see his mother's gaze flying over the delicate porcelain and crystal reflecting the flickering light from the candles down the centre of the table.

The butler moved Sir Benedict's chair back as a footman did similarly for his wife at the other end of the table. Once the host and hostess were seated each took their own.

Micah was next to Miss Donaldson and opposite his father. His mother's pride oozed at him across the table as she stared, beguiled at Miss Donaldson. She seemed less impressed by the bulk of Mr. Skaggs who sat next to her, separating her from Lord Farrington.

"You look beautiful, Miss Donaldson," Micah said, before they began savouring the hare soup off solid silver spoons, served in the finest porcelain dishes.

"Why thank you, sir," Miss Donaldson said. "Have you settled to country life again after your adventures overseas?" she asked, her face a picture of attentiveness. Micah held in the sigh as the game began and each of them appeared to be captivated by the other.

He knew his father was monitoring his conversation as was his mother. Glancing at the menu card held in the porcelain shell shaped holders placed between their places, he could see that this dinner was going to be a drawn-out trial of patience and digestion, the difference in his parent's expressions being that his father looked sceptical, whereas Lady Adams and his mother seemed totally convinced by their performance.

Occasionally the politely blank expression of Lord Farrington met his eyes, but Micah tried to ignore Jethro Skaggs and his endless boasts. The man ran tanneries in Leeds and York. He had houses and tenants. Ruth nodded whenever he spoke to her but was becoming more flustered as she desperately wanted to engage in conversation with Lady Adams and listen in to Micah and Miss Donaldson's exchanges.

Soup, game pie, roast meat, apple compote… one course and small glass of wine finished, and another began. The two footmen worked quickly and efficiently. The butler rinsed the stemmed wine glasses, and they were refilled with the next course's accompaniment. Ruth was becoming flush of face but would not insult her hostess by turning it away. As the courses passed by, less of her glass was emptied.

Once the tablecloth was changed and fresh dishes laid out for the desserts Micah felt the end was in sight. Ezekiel chatted with Lady Adams about the charitable work she was engaged with at the alms-houses. Farrington and Speers talked of fishing, whilst Skaggs interrupted seeking to impress as his uncle had a boat that went out of Whitby and his cousin had cobles at Ebton. Micah caught Farrington's eyes, both looked away, so there was the connection. These could easily be used to ferry in contraband.

After a brief pause, once the final course was finished, the door was opened, and Lady Adams invited the ladies to join her in the withdrawing room for tea and some sweetmeats.

"Micah, I hope you enjoyed your dinner," Sir Benedict asked, as the ladies retired, leaving the menfolk to enjoy a gentlemanly conversation over their port.

"Very much so, sir." Micah felt a warm glow from too much food, although the wine had been only moderately sipped. Skaggs was cerise of cheek, his waistcoat, stretched across his girth, looked fit to burst.

"You have done wonders with the restoration of the Hall," Micah commented, it was a shame that it was empty for a while, so I hear," Micah said only taking a cursory sip of his exceptionally fine port. He had been fortunate to be able to taste many fine wines in Oporto as well as this particular drink that the English loved so much. "I missed all the excitement of events at Bagby Hall." Micah was merely making conversation but there was a cool exchange of looks between Farrington and Speers.

Lord Speers nodded. "Indeed, you have given the Hall a new lease of life – I had occasion to visit it a couple of years ago and consider it much improved."

Thurley Manor was a Jacobean manor house that had been restored to its now splendid pastel colours with ornate Wedgewood design plasterwork on the ceiling and around its large white marble fireplace.

Lord Farrington remained silent. Sipping his port and watching, listening whilst both Micah and he were fully aware that Sir Benedict had not paid for, or orchestrated, Thurley Manor's transition from the neglected state of Bagby Hall and its murky past.

"Yes, we are pleased with it," Sir Benedict said and emptied his glass, filling it up immediately himself as the footmen and butler had been dismissed. "It shall come alive in August when the grouse shooting begins on the moorland. I shall be holding parties, dinners and balls. You must all join us." He smiled at Micah. Skaggs muttered something about it being marvellous. His father's consternation that for some reason, unbeknownst to him, his son was much in favour with these gentlemen was evident by his expression. Micah hoped that his recent good fortune would not be revealed by them. He had tried to tell Imogen and had been interrupted by Pickles and then outranked in importance by Mary and her apparent fear of bogs! When he returned home, he had tried to speak with his parents but his mother was becoming frantic about coming to their dinner and so he had given up on that attempt also.

"That would be something to look forward to," Mr. Skaggs said straightaway, but Micah chose not to answer for he had had enough of shooting and killing man or beast. The notion of enjoying it purely for sport and not to fill hungry bellies meant he was at odds with these people. Killing purely for killing's sake seemed to be an affront to God's beautiful creatures. However, he would not offend his host by saying so openly to him.

"Mr. Skaggs, you have also moved into the area recently. Was that for the love of grouse shoots also?" Micah asked innocently. He stifled his contempt at the man.

Ezekiel was happily sipping the excellent port and taking all that was said in, casually watching Lord Farrington observe the other guests, a man of few words. Speers talked of parish matters, which showed how involved he was with this community he seemed to love and yet was destined to leave.

"Perhaps. However, I also like the races, and the area is blessed with some good bloodstock and tracks." He was addressing them, but his eyes were on Sir Benedict as he spoke. There was a strange air between them. Micah wondered if he worshipped his patron, for in his alcohol fuelled vision, he looked as if he hung on every word or whim of the gentleman.

"Ah, you are a breeder of Thoroughbreds perhaps?" Micah asked.

Skaggs laughed at the notion. Inside he scoffed at the notion, he could not breed a donkey, unlike the shrewd Miss Donaldson. "No, Arrow, I like betting upon them, not raising and training them. I am a man who sees and takes an opportunity, turning it into something worth having." He drank, content that his somewhat poetic answer had apparently impressed Micah.

"You speak intriguingly in riddles, sir," Micah said, and watched the man's moustache twitch. He was clearly humoured by Micah's interest and attention.

"You see, to make the most of life's opportunities you have to look beyond what is there to something that could be, using the natural resources God gave us." Mr. Skaggs tapped the side of his nose and winked at Ezekiel who smiled politely back. "You need a keen eye for an opportunity and the commitment to strike."

Micah pretended to be fascinated as the man then patted his bulging stomach. The idea of him touching Imogen made Micah's gut churn.

"What is it about Dibbledale that you seek to change?" Micah sat forward slightly to appear engaged with his words. After the previous hours of fawning over Miss Donaldson Micah felt like he should join the local players for surely, he would do well in the theatre! He just hoped that Speers did not take this gullible vision of him as Micah's true nature.

"Ah, the enthusiasm of the young!" Skaggs said. "Just as it should be," he added seemingly happy that Micah was taking the bait. He glanced at Sir Benedict and winked. Micah struggled to keep up his façade.

"The fast-flowing river is a power source to be harnessed for the good of all who are entitled. It cuts through the woodland and Dibbledale." Mr. Skaggs laughed. "We can use it to our good, and it will provide work for the villagers."

"You mean fishing? That will provide them work?" Micah appeared bemused, and sat back in his chair sipping his port, realising that the rumours were true. This man was going to try and alter, or even destroy, Micah's home. He needed to visit Bishop Denton as soon as possible and bargain with the man.

"The villagers are already gainfully employed. We have some rare talent amongst them," Reverend Arrow pointed out.

"A blacksmith, a laundry, a bakery and even talk of a witch, I hear." Skaggs laughed, his mouth gaining momentum, but Micah and the reverend exchanged quick glances.

It was Lord Speers who spoke out. "Old wives' tales. Loose tongues spread menace."

"There is no such person living in my parish, I can assure you of that," Reverend Arrow said emphatically before Micah could respond.

"Well, tittle-tattle, but as Miss Donaldson and your good wife, Reverend, were engrossed in the topic, it is something that could be used to our advantage. Distract the locals, but it may not come to that, whilst we see to the important matters in hand. However, my concern is that we harness the power of that water."

"Is it?" Micah asked.

Sir Benedict intervened. "I fish for opportunity. If, collectively, investors buy the land, develop it, use local labour, we can make this backwater thrive. We have the expertise and most of the capital. However, we would like another partner to come in with us; a man of vision who is investing in his own future too. A local man who had his eyes opened by travel. One who has a life to live before him."

"Who do you hope to engage in your venture?" Micah was looking so convincingly curious that his father was no longer paying attention to his port or Lord Farrington and was avidly watching his son.

"Someone young who has vision and the money to invest," Sir Benedict replied.

"I mean, with no disrespect to either of you gentlemen, why do you need another investor when you both are successful, with your own wealth?" Reverend

Arrow's voice filled with genuine curiosity, seemed to surprise the gentlemen.

Mr. Skaggs smiled, but Sir Benedict coloured, before he answered. "The renovations are ongoing. I am already thinking of investing in the future of Thurley Manor and its estate. There are many tenants on the land. Mr. Skaggs has businesses elsewhere and so his expertise would need to be given here too, and someone would run the company… Someone with a personal stake in its success. Someone we trust and can see taking the business into the next decade."

"Well, should we hear of someone who has the money to spare and an eye to invest we will send them your way, but I think the population of Dibbledale does not offer such people up readily," the reverend answered. "In my opinion, they are happy as they are."

Both men were looking at Micah. They smiled at him, but neither said more in front of his father about their business plans. "Their happiness is not important, their livelihoods are," Jethro Skaggs explained.

"Perhaps happiness goes hand in hand with wellbeing," the doctor said.

"Ah, perhaps," Sir Benedict cut in. "We shall continue the conversation at another time." He turned to Micah. "Let us talk of a more convivial topic. Were you impressed with my niece, Micah?" Sir Benedict asked.

"She is a beautiful lady, sir. What man could not notice such fine looks and grace? She has the makings of an accomplished hostess." Micah smiled pleasantly but inside his stomach was turning in knots. He was very aware that she and his own mother had, perhaps inadvertently, linked Mary Underwood with the word 'witch' and that would never sit well in a small, God-fearing community. Scaremongering could lead to threats. Was this why she had run off in fear to the moor road? All through greed, ignorance and fear. Besides, Miss Donaldson was a selfish minx. He did not envy the man who settled for her. Such a cunning and manipulative lady would do well in society, but not here, she was far too vibrant, insincere and obvious.

"I want you to know that I would see her happily married. I shall not barter her in the Season in London, letting her hand be offered to the highest bidder, if you pardon my bluntness. You are a fine young man, Lieutenant Arrow, who has served his country well, and are from a good, moral family and I would be happy for you to pay an interest in her, if you wish to do so." He smiled contentedly at Micah who froze momentarily.

Micah was not expecting such an open invitation. But it confirmed to the fact that the man knew more about his personal affairs than he should do.

Lord Farrington was leaning casually against the back of a winged chair warming himself by the open fire… listening. Speers sat on the window seat quietly observing his fellow guests.

Reverend Arrow calmly finished his port and set the crystal glass down on the table. "Lord Farrington, have you any interest in this business opportunity?"

"My dear man, I dote on my young wife and daughter. I have no more ambition than to grow old gracefully indulged by their presence. I have no need to invest in my or their future, so I shall leave it to the younger and more eager generation."

Ezekiel nodded his acceptance of this and regarded his host. "And you, Lord Speers?"

"I am afraid my future will shortly be elsewhere as I have an estate to return to. So, I too shall decline."

Ezekiel nodded. "Well, that is uncommonly generous of you, Sir Benedict. However, Micah has just returned to us, and the lady is unquestionably grand, yet we are humble people. Flattering as this invitation is, it is more than slightly surprising, and beyond Micah's grasp, I fear." His father was not intending to deride Micah in their eyes, but merely stating the truth as he understood it.

"Not at all! Catch her eye, Micah. Win her heart. You could do much worse and, if you will excuse my frankness, you may never get such an opportunity as this again. Many a man would snap my hand off for such a blessing from me." Sir Benedict was being bold and if Micah had not known he had an ulterior motive, he would have been overcome with pride at his flattery.

"I am certain they would," Micah said. "Perhaps I may ride with Miss Donaldson tomorrow. She did say how much she enjoys it."

"Yes, yes, fine idea! Now more port, sirs, before we re-join the women and our conversation is stilted to the tittle-tattle of their gossipy tongues," Sir Benedict said, chuckling as he filled each of the gentlemen's glasses.

Reverend Arrow, Micah knew, could not wait for them to regroup, and then escape. Ruth would be berated for her idle gossip and Micah would have to find the right words to explain their generous offer to the vicar's son. They were certainly in the knowledge of his change in circumstance, but perhaps did not care where his funds came from, or how. Micah could no longer wait for the appropriate time; they had forced his hand and the hour of disclosure was now upon him.

Lord Farrington caught his eye and subtly nodded to Micah as if reading his thoughts.

By the time they managed to leave it was too late in the evening for any discussion about the gossip of Ruth Arrow, who had imbibed too much wine and swayed slightly as she was unused to it.

Ezekiel was noticeably quiet the whole way home whilst Ruth prattled on about dresses, hair, food, finery... Once they alighted from the coach that Sir Benedict had sent them home in, Ezekiel stood stock still and looked at Micah and his wife. "I will check on Wilfred and then work late in my study." He stepped away from them.

"Ezekiel," Ruth said.

"We shall speak tomorrow morning, all of us. Go to bed now. It is always better not to sleep on angry words. We will talk calmly at breakfast."

His determined stride took him quickly up the stairs.

"Whatever is the matter with your father, Micah?" Ruth was perplexed. She obviously thought her evening had been delightful. The idea of Micah and Lady Donaldson walking out was more than she could ever have imagined.

"In the morning, Mother," Micah said, and he too retired, or in his case, escaped, leaving Ruth to wonder at the menfolk in her life and what had occurred in their evening that she had missed.

Chapter 30

Breakfast was later than usual in the Arrow household as Ruth, feeling slightly unwell, did not join her husband until the hour had passed nine. Ezekiel rose at six every morning, going to his study for an hour of quiet reflection over his Bible and prayer, before he began his parish duties. He took them seriously and had put off the option of having a curate to do his bidding, but as he aged, it was something he now considered.

Imogen arrived hoping to see Betsy first, as like all maids, she was an early riser. Then she could slip into the vicarage and see her father having brought some coddled eggs that Mary had made for him. He was talking of returning to the cottage today and both thought it would be a good thing. Despite Imogen's best efforts, Mary just did not do well when Wilfred was not there. She looked more lost daily.

A smiling Micah greeted her as she appeared from the kitchen passage into the hallway.

"Good morning, Imogen," Micah said brightly.

Imogen was pleased to see that he did not appear at all perturbed by her sudden appearance in his home.

"Good morning, Micah, I was just bringing…"

"Go ahead, Imogen, I understand."

Imogen nodded and carefully carried the covered bowl before her as she ascended the stairs.

Micah watched her go, realising that his mother was standing in the dining room's doorway.

"Really, Micah…" she began, and her words ran on. Ruth's mood this morning was short. He ignored her protests about their food being more than adequate for the blacksmith, and anyway Mr. Underwood would be home soon enough before he ate them out of house and home. Such exaggeration Micah thought, but he did not wish to rebuke her as he had enough to explain this morning.

Micah entered the dining room where his father waited for them both. He needed to break his own fast before he addressed the matter of divesting himself of his secrets.

Ruth followed Micah in. "This has to stop! That man is fit enough to go and go he must! I will not have the Underwoods traipsing into this house at all hours as if it was a common lodging house. I will…"

"You will sit down, eat and be silent, woman! But first let us give thanks to the Lord that we have such food upon our table to eat! Although at this hour of the day it may well be lukewarm!" Ezekiel took his position at the head of the table. Micah sat down to his right and a truly shaken Ruth slid into her chair to his left side.

He had never admonished his wife in such a way before, neither in private nor public. Her already pale countenance from the excesses of the evening before faded further.

Once the maid had brought in their food and returned to the kitchen, Ezekiel put a hand up to silence Ruth before she had a chance to protest further.

"Woman, one more word and I will have a scold's bridle placed on your head or perhaps you would prefer a public ducking stool." Ezekiel stared at his wife, who looked like she had seen a ghost, or was fading as one.

Micah stared at him not knowing his father was capable of such harsh words. Scold's bridles, historically, were used to silence gossips and harridans, hardly an image that would apply to his frail mother. Micah knew that the reference would pierce her heart like a knife.

His father continued, breaking the shocked silence. "Well, isn't that what you want? For us to revert to a bygone time when witches were stoned, ducked or burnt? Innocent or guilty? That's the kind of trouble that gossips stir with loose words. Ignorance begats fear, and fear begats cruel sin."

Ruth's colour suddenly flushed her cheeks, her bottom lip trembled, but his father's features did not soften.

"I never said anything of the sort," she said, but could not look at her husband's face; instead her eyes were downcast.

"Before this day is out you will go to the home of Mary Underwood and take her a gift. Some baking, perhaps. You will break bread with her. You will admire her lovely herb garden and assure her that Wilfred will be well and will shortly return. You might even offer to buy some herbs. I have heard they are excellent. Before the week is out you will also go into the village with your new friend and be seen behaving in a sociable and accepting manner. Visit Mrs. Emily Weeks perhaps, and see how Imogen fares?" Ezekiel began to eat.

"I will not!" Ruth responded angrily.

"You will, or I will send you to Lindisfarne to spend a month in a retreat so that you can repent of your wicked tongue and the way it spread malicious words to people who have reason to stir up trouble for the Underwoods, our neighbours, making it easier for those who want to destroy their land to do so. They are folk who wish to live peacefully, Mrs. Arrow! As do I." Ezekiel took a drink and then added, "I am proud to call them my friends."

Ruth's eyes watered. "Micah..."

Micah relented, he hated to see his mother so upset. "Father, you have filled mother with such fear, it is unlike you. Can we step back from this confrontation? I agree with you, Mother needs to be seen befriending Mary Underwood, who is a harmless, kindly woman. But she cannot be terrified into doing it. That will only create a bigger divide between them for it will not be heartfelt, and Mrs. Underwood will know it as she is a sensitive soul."

"And I am not?" Ruth asked quietly.

Micah addressed his mother, "Mrs. Underwood is no more than a woman who understands her plants. Imogen is important to me. They are hard-working, good people. So please, think before you speak carelessly, your words can be repeated by vicious tongues and dropped into superstitious ears." Micah saw approval in Ezekiel's eyes.

"Ruth, you can apologise to me now and God later, for the malicious thoughts you have carried, and then make amends with the woman you wronged." Ezekiel stared at her, his attitude relenting only a little. "I hope that you have just sampled a small amount of the fear you caused her. Can you imagine what it would be like to live in dread of the villagers turning upon you? And by someone people will speak only the truth!"

Ruth blinked and looked from one to the other. "I am sorry. I may have made an ill-thought-out jest at her expense." She looked sheepishly at them both.

"Indeed!" Ezekiel said. "But you will do what I have asked, starting today. Micah, you must speak with Imogen and ask her when her father wants to go home. I do not want him to think we will cast him out."

"Yes, Father," Micah replied and smiled down at the food upon his plate, ready to cut into his bacon. He loved both his parents deeply.

Ezekiel took a deep breath and placed his palms either side of his place setting as he finally took his seat. "Now, Micah, whilst you eat you can tell me what secret you hold from me that would lead to the extraordinary scenes of last night." His father nodded at Micah, giving him the opening to explain. His attention did not waver from his son and Ruth was now regarding Micah with an even more puzzled expression.

Micah swallowed, emptied his hands, and took a deep breath. "Very well, Father. I did try to find the opportunity to tell you what has weighed heavily upon my heart since I returned."

"Did you?" His father's words were heavily laden with sarcasm.

Micah flinched for he knew that he had not tried at all. He just wanted to have things as they were. Time to recover and confirm his thoughts.

"How hard it must have been not to insist we give you an hour of our precious time to listen to what our son is so burdened with. You must accept our apologies for being so self-indulgent."

Micah took in a slow breath. His father was rarely so riled. "The fault is mine, Father. I needed time to assimilate the circumstances I have found myself in."

"Spit it out, son, before your mother faints with all the suspense." Ezekiel stared as if bracing himself for some awful or unpalatable truth.

Micah stated simply, "I am now a rich man, Father."

Ruth stared wide-eyed at him. "What? How?"

"But not a word of it to anyone, Mother!" Micah's plea tumbled rapidly from his lips.

Ruth dropped her fork in amazement. "How so?" she asked.

"Because, whilst in Portugal, I married…"

Imogen skipped down the stairs, light of heart that her father was eating well, looked rested, and was keen to be up and return to his family. Once home they would all be able to come up with a plan to remove the threat of Skaggs. She had gone on ahead of him as Imogen thought it was polite to inform Mrs. Arrow that her father was leaving today and thank her once more for their hospitality and the trouble, they had put her to.

She heard voices coming from the dining room and so approached the doorway cautiously in case they had another visitor. Who knew with a man of the cloth, they were there to serve the congregation, weren't they? Although some did their vocation better than others. Pausing, just outside the doorway, to straighten her dress, and tuck a few stray locks behind her ears, Imogen heard Micah speak the most incredible words…

"Because, whilst in Portugal, I married…"

Imogen stepped back away from the doorway, her brain freezing at hearing such a declaration. Everything around her felt unreal. She stumbled slightly and propped herself up by the door. It opened wide and she felt the air freshen her face. Imogen took off down the path to the lychgate. There she stopped and bent double to breathe, breathe deeply and clear her mind, but one word resonated until her head throbbed. Married!

Of course, he would have been, he was tall of frame, muscular, handsome, kind and had he not said that he wanted them to be… friends? He had never said more. But she had not foreseen this coming. Micah was supposed to be hers, but that apparently was no more than her wishes, not a vision of her future.

Imogen had to get away from them. She needed the freedom of the woodland, the calm of the trees, clean air that she could breathe in, and the sound of the fast-flowing stream to mask her sobs. For a brief time in her life, she had dared to dream that someone who she adored, a soul mate, had returned to her. Imogen had believed her own instincts, not the leaves that had randomly been placed in a teacup.

How foolish she was. Oh, Micah had cast a long shadow right enough, but it now hung over her like a dark cloud. Mary had got it all wrong too. They had merely seen what they wanted to. Now, how would she be saved from marrying Jethro Skaggs? Unless they all moved away?

Chapter 31

"Explain yourself, Micah." Ezekiel sipped his tea and listened intently.

"Because, whilst I was stationed in Portugal, I married." Micah wanted to put their minds at rest, but his words had shaken his mother further and he thought she may collapse. "Take a sip of tea, Mother," he said and paused whilst she did. Ruth looked like she was going to swoon, so Micah waited.

When she nodded to let him know that she had composed herself again, he continued.

Micah glanced around and thought he heard Betsy at the open doorway but when he investigated there was no one there. Cautious of being overheard, he closed the door firmly.

"When were you going to tell me this?" Ezekiel asked; his face looked more confused, rather than shocked, unlike Ruth.

"Who is she? Where is she?" she asked. "Is she... foreign?" His mother had twisted on the chair to face him; he had her complete attention.

He returned to the table and sat down again.

"She is not anywhere, Mother, not anymore." Micah rubbed his hand through his hair, surprised that the emotions welled within him. "You see, tragically, she died."

"Micah! Tell us the story and speak plainly. Enough of this drama and suspense." His father crossed his arms, sitting back in the chair ready to listen thoughtfully to his son's words.

Micah sighed and cleared his throat, before carefully beginning his tale.

"When under cover in Spain, I saved the life of a man and his daughter from an enemy attack. It was a significant risk as I was behind enemy lines. It was not my mission to step in-between the enemy and any target they set upon, but to report back about their positions. But I could not just ride away and leave them to perish."

"A good man could not turn the other cheek and watch innocence be killed, Micah," his father concurred. "You acted honourably, that I do not doubt."

"You could have been killed!" Ruth said.

"Mother, anyone could be killed in war." Micah shrugged. "The carriage was attacked. The De Silva's were helpless and within it. I had no idea who they were or that they were wealthy. Carolina was beautiful and, as I later found out, pregnant." Micah saw the concern turn to disapproval on his mother's face.

Ruth gasped, but his father encouraged him. "Go on, tell the complete tale."

"I took them back to near where I was staying. In our relatively brief time together, I learned that Carolina had been attacked when the family home had been ransacked. Her father, Senor De Silva, had lost his son and wife. His daughter was all he had left. The baby, the result of the attack, would soon be obvious, and that would bring shame upon her. After all they had endured, they did not deserve that, so I offered to marry her. I gave her my name and the child would be guaranteed to have a father's name. The old man was happy to have been saved and said he would honour our union by having his will drawn up to leave means down to me when he passed. I had no idea that the man was seriously wealthy. He died nearly a year ago. Phillipe was as good as his word. He left the banking side of his business to his brother, who is immensely rich and glad to have been free of the burden of a sister who could have birthed an illegitimate baby. Phillippe left his other assets to me."

"You agreed to be a husband to a woman who was already with child... who was the father? What was this fallen woman like?" Ruth's face showed her distaste for the situation he described.

Ezekiel looked at the ceiling briefly. Ruth clearly had not understood the woman had been raped in an attack and Micah had stepped in to protect her from further rejection and abuse.

"Micah, I know you are not a man who would leave a wife and child alone in a country ravished by war, so what happened?" Ezekiel asked, leaning forward intently.

"She died, Father, in childbirth. The baby too." Micah clenched his lips together. He had imagined that in time he could fall in love with both mother and child. The war was near over, he had seen so much sadness, that if this could bring new life and joy to Carolina, then why not? Imogen was bound to have found someone whilst he was away and so his young infatuation had been lost to him, or so he had reasoned. They had never openly declared their interest in each other before he had left.

"I am sorry, Micah, you lost both," Ezekiel said quietly, stood and came to his son's side. He placed a hand on Micah's shoulder.

"But you still are the heir to this man's money?" Ruth asked, her eyes alert.

"Yes, Mother, I am. Lord Farrington helped me immensely. I would not have known where to begin, but Oscar is a man of law, papers and languages. He has been a true blessing to me, Father, and he suspects…"

"How do you know a lord, Micah?" Ruth asked.

"I served under him. My duties involved going behind enemy lines, to seek out information, mapping and reporting, and to train people to do likewise. I was honoured to serve him dutifully," Micah explained.

His mother gasped. "You spied behind enemy lines! You could have lost everything!" she declared.

"War demands we do things that normally we would never imagine ourselves able to." Micah looked at his father. "Lord Farrington suspects that Sir Benedict Adams has somehow come to know of my fiscal good fortune. I can only assume through someone with a loose tongue amongst the legal people that I have been dealing with in Northallerton. Someone must have shared information with him, which is why suddenly a vicar's son is eligible to court a fine lady from the southern counties." He shook his head.

"But, Micah, you could still court Miss Donaldson. She could open doors for you... I saw how you two really struck a chord last evening." Ruth's tongue and mind were running away with her again as she smiled at him not realising that the two were playing a game. "They must know that you are eligible now."

"Mother! I married once to come to the aid of a woman who had been left in an unpleasant situation through no fault of her own. I will not settle on a marriage of convenience to suit anyone else's purpose again, or to open doors that were not previously open to me before."

"But Micah!" Ruth said.

"But nothing! I will marry for love and when I am ready. Not a word of this to anyone, Mother, or I will walk out of the house, and you will not see me again."

Ruth pursed her lips.

There was a silence whilst his news was absorbed.

"Father, will you ride to Gorebeck with me tomorrow? I would like to speak to Bishop Denton. Lord Farrington is arranging an introduction."

"Of course! We will need to discuss your plans before we get there. His Grace does not appreciate any time wasters. Meanwhile, Ruth, make our guest feel welcome. Visit Mary Underwood and make sure you are generous with your comments. I have parish matters to attend to today, so I am free for you, Micah, tomorrow."

Ruth stood up and forced a smile onto her face. "Of course, Ezekiel. I will make all well."

Micah added to his father's instruction, "Mother, I am becoming very fond of Miss Imogen Underwood. I would not like her to be scared off by idle gossip. If you want me to remain in Dibbledale and have the joy of seeing any future grandchildren grow and flourish in the parish, then please show you can make peace now."

"Come, Micah, enough talk." Ezekiel turned as Micah left the room.

"Ruth, return to me that sweet woman I married and stop this nonsense over Mary Underwood. I want Micah to live here. We need him. If you do not build this bridge and walk across it willingly it will not only be your son who you will lose contact with."

As Ezekiel left, Ruth stared at the empty doorway, the thought of grandchildren to come filling her home with noise and joy made her smile genuinely alongside her husband's voiced memory and the thought of Micah's good fortune. She ignored the threats for she could see a more engaging future. No matter what folly Micah had done by marrying this foreigner, God had set him free right now. She ate a hearty breakfast and planned her day.

Chapter 32

Micah rode to Thurley Manor as arranged to meet Miss Donaldson. His heart was not in this rendezvous, but to catch them out he had to seem interested until he could secure the land himself.

The lady was already dressed in her riding attire and practically bolted past him as the footman opened the door. She was either eager to leave her present company, or to join his.

"Come, Lieutenant Arrow, let us ride," her words sounded like an order as she descended the stairs to the mounting block where Matthew, the stable hand, was holding her saddled horse.

Micah who did not really wish to share pleasantries with Sir Benedict or any of the guests who may have stayed the night, happily remounted his horse. A few moments later the lady sitting elegantly on her side saddle cantered down the tree lined drive. Micah saw they were being watched from the study window by Sir Benedict and Jethro Skaggs. He let his horse have its head and joined Miss Donaldson. They did not slow until they were outside of the estate grounds and beyond sight of prying eyes. Once in the shelter of the ancient woodland on the outskirts of Dibbledale, they stopped and dismounted letting their horses rest and drink from the river.

"You have a fine seat, Miss Donaldson," he said and laughed at her glare.

"Yours is competent too." She checked whether there was any way they were being observed. She apparently wanted to treat him as if she were his equal in the game.

"What to do now? Do we stay out long enough for their curiosity to be sated, or ride straight back?" Micah asked.

"We return shortly. They will not expect it to take me long to have your measure and to begin my seduction of your wits," she said without blush or hesitation.

"Really, they have such a high opinion of me." Micah raised a brow.

"They have a much higher opinion of me, Arrow." Her words were curt. "Skaggs has a boat arriving Friday week, which will bring in some tobacco in the form of a hidden brick in the bottom of the boat. It will have a false bottom. Brandy kegs will be anchored off the headland of Stangcliffe near a place called Ebton. His nephew will collect them on his way back in and bring them to the tap room of the on Inn on the moor road. Do what you wish with this information."

"How do you know all this, Miss Donaldson?" Micah asked, intrigued at the detail of her knowledge.

"Because they discussed it between them when I was reading in the library. Doctor Speers and Lord Farrington were playing bridge with Lady Lydia and my aunt. No matter, if they knew I was there they cared not, because they think I have too much to lose to inform on them. If they did not see me sitting in the chair in the bay of the window, then they are even more stupid than I credited them to be. Either way, they underestimate me. Did you know that Lydia Speers knew the fallen Bagbys?" She shrugged when he did not respond. "If I do as they wish, my life will be as a puppet to them. I would rather take my chances on my own than that."

"You really hate them, don't you?" Micah commented.

She stood in front of him and touched his cheek with her gloved finger. She lingered a moment her eyes staring into his, but Micah felt nothing, yet when he touched Imogen, his senses took flight. This woman left him cold, like her heart.

"Skaggs wants to claim and tame your little friend and they would have me bleed you dry for their own ends. Micah Arrow, you have as much reason as I do to hate these men. So, together let us bring them down."

She laughed as he watched her remount.

He stepped to the side of her horse and stroked its neck. She sent a chill through him, not of excitement, but of uncertainty. He could never trust such a calculating person; she would sell him out if it suited her purpose. He had not met a lady who was so sure of herself, but he would not have her read his thoughts. Her weakness was her over confidence.

"You are correct, I do hate them, but what is your mission here today?"

"I shall report back like a dutiful and indebted niece that you are interested in their scheme. You want to be accepted in Society. You have accepted my invitation to go to Harrogate when we travel there in three weeks' time and are coming around to possibly looking at their plans in finer detail. You had never thought that you would be in a position to own land yourself but feel awed by the idea." She stroked his hair, slowly letting it fall back, "It really is beautiful," then laughed as he stepped away.

"I am not a dog, a puppet, or a horse, miss," he said and remounted his own horse ready to return to the Hall. "I will escort you to the gates and watch you ride down the driveway to safety but give my excuses as I am needed at home to help my father with parish business."

They walked their horses back along the road. "You know I might have considered you if my hand were not being forced. You are attractive, Micah Arrow. I think we could have rubbed along well."

"Do you never cease, lady?" Micah snapped.

Miss Donaldson stopped her horse and faced him, obviously surprised at his brusque manner and comment. "What can have offended you? I flattered you, Arrow!" she snapped.

"No, Miss Donaldson, you flatter yourself. You toy with people. You are so used to being envied and preened that you believe yourself to be the prize everyman seeks. However, I do not. You are accomplished with horses, etiquette and have social bearing, yet you cannot comprehend that not all men's hearts, or loins, beat to the same drum!"

She laughed and looked up at the sky. "I hope you make your little friend very happy and have lots of little babies." She kicked her horse onwards and Micah followed.

Once at the gates of Thurley Manor he sat and watched her ride brazenly back to deliver a basket full of lies to her uncle. He rode away.

Imogen had ambled aimlessly, lost in thought, along the riverbank mesmerised by the water's flow. Opposite her, two riders appeared and walked their horses down to the water's edge. Imogen recognised Micah instantly, followed by that woman. She ducked back behind a bank of undergrowth and watched.

Whatever they were saying humoured the lady. Imogen saw her approach him, finger Micah's jawline obviously savouring the moment. Did she have any idea that Micah was a married man? Did she care? Worse still whilst seated on her horse she openly fumbled Micah's hair. Still, he did not instantly back away.

Imogen stared at Micah. What was he doing? How many women did he want to capture the hearts of?

Watching Miss Donaldson's eloquent detachment, she wondered if he was having difficulty in finding that particular organ in this lady!

She turned and headed back into the woodland. Imogen did not want to see anymore. Enough was enough! She had her own problems to sort out. Once her head was clear of this girlish infatuation, she would see her way out of their current situation with Mr. Jethro Skaggs... somehow. Every time she tried to view her future her mind became muddled. As soon as Micah filled her vision, her senses were overwhelmed with longing. Yet, he looked so fine with that Miss Donaldson! She brushed tears off her cheeks. 'No good crying over things that can't be changed' – she could hear her mother's voice as though she was there.

Imogen took her time to return to the cottage. If her mama had not been involved in settling Wilfred in, who was trying hard to convince his wife that he was feeling fine and had just needed a rest, they might have realised that she had been upset.

She hugged her papa and then helped to make a dinner whilst Mary talked to her husband. She tried hard to push the image of Miss Donaldson touching Micah's golden hair out of her mind until she saw her father do that to her mother's.

"Right!" Mary stood up; her old confidence returned. "We eat and then sleep. Tomorrow is another day. We shall all talk then."

Mary looked straight at her daughter and Imogen realised that Mary had been aware of her upset. Imogen nodded and ate her food, her small family reunited.

Chapter 33

Micah had received a note sent from Lord Farrington to say he had fixed an appointment with Bishop Denton for noon at the bishop's home, Netherton House, on the outskirts of Gorebeck.

"Father, can we leave now for Gorebeck?" Micah was anxious as so much depended on this meeting going well. He entered the study only to be disappointed as it was empty.

"Mother, where is Father?" Micah asked, as she met him by the door.

"He had to go to Beckton, there has been a farm accident. I am not sure where exactly, and someone he knows died."

Micah did not press for details because his father would have spared Ruth any gore and time was passing by.

"Please tell him I will be meeting Bishop Denton at noon. If he can, please ask him to meet me there. If not, I will understand."

"Oh, Micah, first Lords and now Bishops, how your fortunes are changing," she said brightly.

Micah patted her shoulder as he left. Now was not the time to address his mother's priorities again.

He decided to go through Dibbledale and head up to take the road across Gorebeck Moor to the town.

As he crossed the small stone bridge, he saw Mrs. Weeks and Imogen parting as they left the house. He rode towards her, just a few minutes of seeing that spirited face was all he needed to set him up for this meeting. Micah would reassure Imogen that all would be well. He had no time to explain to her now, but after talking to his parents he must now reveal his true circumstances to Imogen.

"Miss Underwood," he hailed her as he approached.

To his surprise she did not turn. He had expected to see that lovely hair flick around her face as it lit up, eyes bright as they always were whenever they met, but instead she did not even stop. He rode slightly past her and halted.

"Imogen," he said to her as she walked alongside with apparently little intention of acknowledging his presence. Something was clearly wrong, reluctant eyes met his, but they looked angry not eager.

"Mr. Arrow," she replied and took a step forward.

"I would like to rendezvous with you later today," he said quickly to catch her attention. "There are things we need to talk about that I need to explain to you... quite urgently."

Imogen stopped. "Are there, Mr. Arrow? Well perhaps if you get off your high horse you can tell me now and be done with it. Save you returning later as you are such a busy man." Her waspish words stung.

"What has happened, Imogen?" he asked. "Why are you being so provocative. It is unlike you and does not suit you at all."

Imogen defiantly faced him. "Tell me what it is that is so urgent for me to know and be done with it... say it out here in the street!" she snapped back.

"I... I can't... not now... but later." Micah looked around but the few people that were in sight were not within earshot and were paying them little heed.

"Then perhaps not at all! Good day, Mr. Arrow," she said and walked into the general store leaving a perplexed Micah to continue his most important journey alone and bemused.

He stared at the door momentarily and considered bursting in and demanding to know what the hell had got into her. Had Skaggs returned with more threats? Would she do this to send Micah away so that she could fall in with the letch's plan and save her parents' – no that was not Imogen. She would fight her way out of trouble, but why be prickly with him? So far today was not going at all to plan.

Micah had made many perilous journeys on his own, but this one carried the future of a village with it, so he must not fail them. Micah brought the horse half circle and headed out of Dibbledale without looking back. He hoped his fortune would change when he saw Bishop Denton. Then later he would find Miss Imogen Underwood and learn what had spiked that character.

Chapter 34

On retirement Bishop Denton had returned to his hometown and taken possession of the family home from his elder cousin, Ignatius, following his death. Netherton House had a ramshackle appearance from its stacked brick chimneys to the archway that led into an inner courtyard. Micah felt he was stepping back into a time of knights and serfs.

He was admitted through large oak doors and stood on centuries old stone-flagged flooring. The footman took his hat and coat and asked him to wait on the bishop's pleasure, in the entrance hall.

Micah tried to force Imogen's cool greeting from his mind and instead stared at bold black artificial eyes that peered at him from a large stag head mounted above a stone empty fireplace. Miss Donaldson came to mind, and he shook his head slightly to clear the images. The suits of armour to either side were faceless yet menacing. Warfare had moved on, war was still pain and loss and not to be glorified, although many did.

Stone stairs climbed up at either side of this hall to the landing above. He could be overlooked at either side from a narrow minstrel's gallery. The flags which adorned the wall looked sad and neglected.

"His Reverence will see you now." The footman showed him the way. Micah followed looking more closely at the fine yellow and black livery the man wore and realised that it too had been mended and was well used.

Micah was instantly hit by a wall of fusty warmth as he entered the room.

"Lieutenant Arrow, Your Reverence." The footman stepped aside after giving a slight bow to the diminutive figure waiting for them and left.

Micah was facing a short, slightly stooped man wearing a lavish, loosely fitting, wool banyan. The bishop seemed lost within it, as he stood with his back to a log fire that generated heat from its ancient iron grate.

"Approach, Arrow, and tell me what this business is that Oscar has been twittering in my ear about!" He shook his head. "All I want is to have some peace, yet people still pester."

Micah did as he was bid. Crossing a slightly threadbare rug, he was amazed that there were only two tapestry covered wing chairs by the fire and one low table, with a glass, a decanter, a small prayer book and a monocle upon it. The rest of the room was draped in tapestries but was sparse of furniture. Ideal for a small banquet, but hardly a commodious reception room.

"Bishop Denton, I would like to thank you…" Micah began, fighting to sound confident, but having an ill-feeling about this meeting.

"Yes, yes, get on with it man! I have not got all day. At my age one never knows…" He looked up.

Micah glanced up and noted the Yorkshire roses in the plasterwork overhead.

"Yes, my pardon, I would like to talk to you about the purchase of woodland that stretches from the Bagby Estate to the river in Dibbledale." There he had got to his point straight away.

"You're behind the times, man! Bagbys! Bagbys! God rest his perverted soul. Do you know how much one must pay for decent cognac now?" The man opened his hands wide.

He walked over to a decanter which was on the table and poured himself a drink.

"I would like to buy the land, sir, and request you do not consider any other offer, as I can and will best them." Micah liked the truth within his words.

The bishop stared at him.

"You get to the point; I like that, Arrow... I know that name, don't I?" He scratched his grey hair and looked to be deep in thought.

"My father is the vicar in Dibbledale." Micah met his eyes as the man assessed him afresh.

"Aye, you would be his son. I can see it. He once presented himself as young man at my desk and pleaded the case of the heretic priest, Thomas Fletcher, the man who took my daughter from me and brought shame to us all. I can see that you inherit your father's outspoken traits."

"Sir..." Micah was taken aback by the venom within his words.

"Reverence," he snapped.

"Your Reverence, I cannot influence or change the past as it is not humanly possible, but I am here to plead my case for the future. There are men who seek to purchase your land and will destroy its beauty and the lives of the villagers as they set it to become a manufactory of animal skins for the making of leather goods. A tannery would destroy the village, but I have plans that would see it thrive and help veterans of the war at the same time..." Micah's passion began to show.

The bishop's right palm was raised to stop Micah who had to still his tongue.

"Let me ask you a question, young man," Bishop Denton began.

Micah nodded.

"Am I selling this land? Is it up for sale? I will save you the effort of answering. No!" Bishop Denton asked, folding his arms gathering the ample fabric into his stooped body. He shuffled to one of the chairs and closed his eyes.

Micah came forward at once. "Bishop, should I fetch Doctor Speers?" he asked thinking the man might be about to collapse like Wilfred had.

The bishop's eyes shot open as he glared into Micah's. "Never mention that man's name in my presence again. Now go! Is that it? Fletcher's daughter wants the land she has no right to lest I deem it so. This is underhand, I sense subterfuge and I will not be party to it."

"No, on my word of honour, she has nothing to do with this," Micah said.

"Go!"

"But, sir, the land…" Micah began, but the bishop rang a small bell on the table and the footman instantly re-appeared.

"It is my land, and I will do with it what I wish. Now, go, your audience is ended." The bishop stood up and walked to a door at the opposite end of the room as the footman ushered Micah outside.

The sun shone on Micah's face, but as he felt the warmth of it on his skin, a cold feeling swept through him. How badly could he have handled this? To top it all the old man remembered Ezekiel from his younger days and then Micah had mentioned Speers. He shook his head at the folly he had made of the meeting. Now Dibbledale was doomed. How else could Sir Benedict and Skaggs be stopped if they were able to convince the old man to sell?

Micah imagined the bishop just might do so to spite his imagined conspiracy. He gritted his teeth. What had he done?

Chapter 35

Imogen sat for a while in silent fury, which she was struggling to abate. Micah had acted as though nothing had occurred at all! Pickles had met her as she faded into the woodland, unable to forget what she had witnessed. He rubbed his head against her arm until she relented and fussed him, scratching behind his ear. It was as though the animal knew she needed comfort, or nature's calm as her mother would say. She would not cry! Micah was married, he openly flirted with Miss Donaldson, and had claimed to be her friend. Now he acted as though nothing was amiss! Imogen was annoyed with herself for believing in her golden-haired knight in shining armour.

Mary's insistence that he was destined to shadow her life, had turned a younger girl's infatuation into a woman's hope of a lifelong soulmate. Seeing Pickles' devoted eyes released the hurt that her heart felt.

The minute she had overheard those words from Micah's mouth: "Whilst in Portugal, I married…" her chest had tightened. There was no denying it, she had fallen in love with him all over again. Before he left Dibbledale, to fight a far-away war that seemed to have no end, she had watched him whenever he was nearby. His fine looks, sense of humour, warm smile and confident walk had drawn her attention to him like a bee to nectar. But when he winked at her it was those eyes, so warm and welcoming, that had stirred up her emotions. Once he left, she decided her infatuation must end; a young maid dreaming of what could never be, and those thoughts back then had been correct.

Imogen shook her head, for it seemed she was still no better than that infatuated girl.

When she finally returned to the cottage the last person she expected to see there was Mrs. Ruth Arrow. The lady was approaching carrying a small basket looped over her arm, its contents carefully covered with a pretty square of gingham cloth.

"Did Papa forget something, Mrs. Arrow?" Imogen asked. For she could not imagine any other reason why the woman would arrive at their threshold carrying what looked like a gift. Perhaps she was there to gloat about her son's wife.

To say Mrs. Arrow looked wary would have been an understatement.

"No, Imogen. You look… pretty today. That dress really brings out the lovely vibrant colour of your hair. I have always admired it." Ruth's awkward words stopped. Next, she looked at Mary's plants admiring the herb garden outside the cottage. It was beautifully tended. "How marvellous. Betty does not have green fingers. I should send her over for some lessons. Or I could invite Mrs. Underwood to share some of her plant knowledge with the girl. Perhaps stay for tea." The nervous voice dribbled to a stop.

You could dirty those hands of yours yourself, Imogen thought but then decided she was being unfair. A vicar's wife is not expected to dig around in the dirt, even if she were good at stirring it up! Imogen knew her anger was with Micah and so tried to soften her heart to the woman who was doing her best to make polite conversation. Although Imogen could not fathom why. "And you are well?" Imogen asked. She sent Pickles off to his outside bed in the open outhouse. It was his place when they wanted him from under their feet in the cottage.

"Yes, nothing is wrong. In fact, this day is better than… well, it's a good one!" She looked around her as if seeing the woodland for the first time. "It is beautiful here," she admitted. "Look, Imogen, I brought a fresh loaf of Parkin for you all to share as a coming home celebration for your father," she said. "There are also two jars of blackcurrant jam and one of honey. Your father works so hard… for us all really… I mean, we all need a blacksmith from time to time, don't we?" Her hands were shaking slightly, words were beginning to ramble and tremor, but Imogen was so taken aback her mouth opened, yet no sound came out.

"That is very generous of you," Mary said, as she appeared in the doorway of the cottage causing Ruth to flinch momentarily. Imogen's mother cast a quick, questioning look over at Imogen. "Would you like to come in and have some tea with us?" Mary added.

"That would be lovely," Ruth said. Her smile was fixed.

"Come on then," Mary said, and welcomed them both inside. "Step over my threshold, we don't bite, Mrs. Arrow, and I guarantee the only thing you will catch here is your breath." Mary chuckled as the woman cautiously entered.

"Oh, I never thought that!" Ruth followed Mary into the cottage brushing the yellow flowered jasmine as it framed the low doorway.

Perhaps Ruth was relieved that Micah was already married and could not become involved with her, Imogen thought, but then why visit them unless to gloat? Imogen did not think Mrs. Arrow would bother to dirty her shoes coming into the wild woods and facing Mary just to do that - something was very odd. Had she been drinking the forest fruit liqueur Betty enjoyed making for her puddings, or had she accidently partaken of the magic mushrooms that her mother had told Imogen about. Perhaps she had mixed them up with the safe ones? Imogen tried not to smile as the likelihood was fanciful. Imogen was bemused but would not miss seeing these two women being cordial with each other for all the world. Micah's betrayal of her trust was set aside for the moment.

"This is a lot more homely than I realised it would be." Ruth's eyes took in the details of their home, genuinely surprised it seemed. Her words were breathy, but she was clearly trying hard to be social as she looked around the cottage with all its homemade décor: quilting on the cushions, dried lavender hanging from the beams to give a faintly fresh smell and the oval clip rug by the open hearth. Their table had a simply made, prettily embroidered tablecloth over it. Mary's delicate hand had easily turned to such needlework and crafts. Window shutters displayed birds' engravings on them, each delicately balanced on a branch, which was Imogen's doing. Three wooden dug out chairs were positioned by the fire, each had foxes etched into their backs and cushions on their seats that were made of a deep red plush curtain material. These had been crafted by all. Every detail that Ruth took in showed a much-loved home, that obviously had gifted people living within it.

"You have certainly turned whatever is to hand to make some beautiful adornments. Even the coat hooks are carved from antlers. Quite ingenious," Ruth admitted.

"Mrs. Arrow," Mary said, as they sat at the table, whilst Imogen saw to preparing their tea. "Please do not take offence at my question, but are you well? Has something.... happened? You do not seem to be quite yourself..." Mary glanced at Imogen.

Ruth sighed. "Oh dear! I am not particularly good at

this, am I? Well, it is simply that something has happened, and it made me realise I have perhaps been judgemental. I mean about you. I mean you growing plants and me rattling on about, well… things I know little about, nor should I…" Ruth was becoming flustered, her cheeks colouring. Her eyes darted from mother to daughter.

Mary placed a hand over the woman's as it trembled; she looked like she may well run away.

"Take a breath, breathe easy for you are with friends. Believe me on that, for I have never wished you ill." Mary slipped into a more familiar, comforting form of speech to the lady, as if they truly were friends.

Ruth's eyes took focus on a wooden carved cross, which was placed above the doorway into the cottage, as she had momentarily looked to the door as if thinking of beating a hasty retreat.

"I see that I really have made some unbelievably bad assumptions… Mrs. Underwood. I am so sorry." She swallowed. "When I was a girl, my grandmother used to tell me such tales about, well, a scary lady that lived some time ago called Mother Shipton, a seer. She lived in the woods and lived off the things she grew, killed, or 'magicked'. I think a cave was mentioned and she turned things to stone," Ruth explained and shuddered. "That was in a place near Knaresborough, which as you know is not so far away. I had nightmares about her for years…" Ruth blinked back tears as if reliving the fear that had been instilled in her as a young girl. "Mother said if I misbehaved Mother Shipton's ghost would come back to haunt me. Silly really, what we believe as children and the cruel things that are said to us."

Imogen was amazed at the similarities between these two quite different women; they both had harboured deep seated horrors from their childhoods, created by others.

One had good reason from an actual horrendous event that changed her life's path, the other had folk tales used as a weapon against her to ensure her obedience.

"We all have fears. Some stay with us for life and fester and grow. However, they can cause so much pain and stop us knowing the truth. So, tell us, what has brought you here today?"

Imogen knew her mother would want to change the subject for they had once visited Mother Shipton's cave and Mary had been intrigued by the folklore thereabouts. Imogen thought it ironic how one was so afraid of what the other found fascinating. Perspective, she reasoned, skewed all.

Ruth smiled – a child-like smile, which was quite beguiling as she looked at Imogen. "Well, Micah brought us quite remarkable news. But, more importantly, it is my news that I want to share because I will bring harmony to Dibbledale and we will be harmonious, won't we?" She looked at the two confused faces for their goodwill and agreement. "Ezekiel thinks he can secure the cottage for you as he has spoken up as your reference to the current owner."

Imogen spoke, "Thank you, we shall move to the village for Papa's sake, won't we, Mama?" Imogen seized the opportunity to sort this issue once and for all, there was no backtracking to be allowed for Mary.

"Yes, I have given my word," Mary said.

Imogen then turned to Ruth and was quite bold in her next question, "Is Micah bringing his wife here?"

"People who eavesdrop do not always hear what they want to, you know," Ruth admonished, and Imogen thought that she was still very much the preacher's wife.

Mary's head shot around as her eyes met Imogen's moist ones, but Ruth laughed at her. "Oh, of course he isn't." Then realisation dawned. "It was you I heard at the door! Not Betsy, she was still baking! Ah, well, dear you know what they say about listening at doorways, you don't

"I only lingered a moment by your door before interrupting your meal because I was going to thank you for your hospitality before leaving, but as I approached, I heard clearly what Micah owned up to." Imogen did not wish to put the previous bad blood back between them, but she was not prepared to be rebuked for accidently learning the truth.

"Oh, then I apologise again for misjudging you. I shall have to address that trait. However, if you had lingered longer, you would have learned that indeed he has no wife, she died." Ruth became flustered again. "It was not exactly a love match; he married to preserve the honour of a fallen woman in challenging times. He really is a good man, just like Mr. Arrow. Anyway, neither the lady nor the child survived. All is sorted. Poor girl. Never mind."

"He lost them both!" Mary said and shook her head. "Shame," she added.

"For her, yes, but Imogen he likes you, and clearly you reciprocate, I have seen that twinkle in your eyes when he is near," she said and raised an eyebrow towards Mary who sat back in her chair and laughed.

"Oh, Ruth Arrow, you are quite something. I detect the shade of a romantic heart lingers still! Who would have thought it? Let us drink to our collective future in Dibbledale," Mary said.

Imogen watched these two women, so recently adversaries, sitting together and tentatively deciding upon their and apparently her future, yet she knew that the very land they were on could be stolen away from under them, even if her hope had just been partially restored. He had not led her on to believe he was free when in fact he was married, or lied to her, and so they could still be friends. Her instincts had been true, it was her ears and mind that had misled her. Why had he married a 'fallen' woman though? There was obviously more to the situation than Ruth had shared or knew.

"Why did he wait so long to tell you?" Mary asked.

"His father-in-law was well to do and of course that means Micah also is, as he inherited. But please do not say a word about it. He may want to tell Imogen the details of that himself.

"You mean he has wealth?" Mary asked and Ruth nodded, her delight almost palpable. "That changes things a lot, doesn't it?" Mary looked at Imogen and smiled. "He will be a man to reckon with and I do not think Mr. Skaggs realises. His reckoning is coming!" Mary added, but quickly changed the subject as Ruth was beginning to look bemused.

"Thank you for your lovely gifts, Mrs. Arrow," Mary said.

Instantly Ruth's face broke into a smile. She had achieved what she set out to do. "Well, I must be returning as duty calls. You can drop the basket back when you have time to Betsy. Oh, I nearly forgot, could I buy a bunch of your herbs, Mrs. Underwood?"

"You may have them. What do you need?" Mary asked, but as she saw Ruth's blank face, Mary suggested, "Perhaps I could pick you a selection and Imogen could pop them over to Betsy later."

"Excellent!" Ruth said as she left.

Mary and Imogen stood in the doorway and watched her walk back uncertainly towards Church Lane.

"Your shadow man is rich, Imogen," Mary said.

"He is not mine, Mama, or why has he not shared this news with this simple village girl?"

"Aye, well that remains to be explained. Now I'll look after your pa, you follow her, 'cos that woman is liable to get lost in the woods if someone doesn't go with her."

Imogen realised that if she went with Ruth, she was certain to see Micah and although still angry with him she could not resist that opportunity, so did as she was bid.

Chapter 36

Micah rode slowly back, stopping on the open moor road to look at the vast expanse as if he would be struck by divine intervention and have an epiphany. He smiled at the sight of the approaching rider through his defeat. It seemed he had been sent his father, as an earthly representative. "How to tell you I have failed abysmally?" he muttered quietly.

"Micah, I am so sorry. I was delayed. There had been a shooting over in Beckton Dale."

"A shooting?" Micah was shocked. "Mother said it was an accident." Micah wondered how she could have got it so wrong.

"The captain of the yeomanry sent for me. I spared your mother the details, but it seems that he had been rounding up some unsavoury characters who have been taking in contraband. There was a kerfuffle and, long story short. they shot a man dead in Beckton who should only have been injured as he ran from a suspicious meeting. Doctor Speers saw to him, but the man would not stop bleeding. Looks as though he will not make the day out." Ezekiel glanced at the sky above and sighed. "It was Mr. Jethro Skaggs."

"I would not wish that on any man," Micah said, trying to stifle a feeling of relief. "I failed to secure the land, Father. The plans are already drawn out. Sir Benedict could hire someone else."

"There will be a way to stop him, you will see, Micah," he came close to his son, "have faith."

"I do, but the meeting went badly," he added sadly.

After a short silence Ezekiel began a new topic. "Did you love her? This lady who you lost." His father was riding alongside him. It was a pastime they had enjoyed from him being a young boy right up to before he went to war. Micah's grandfather had been a Dean and Ezekiel had never been poor, but he chose to live in a small parish, in touch with his community rather than at a distance. His dedication clear, his worldly possessions simple.

"No, Father, I cannot claim to have been in love with her. I was lonely, she was grateful, and I would have treated the child as my own. Stupidly I presumed that Imogen would have wed and have babies of her own by now. However, it appears that neither was to be for me." Micah stared ahead.

"Do you feel any guilt for inheriting the money?" Ezekiel asked.

"No, for I had no idea of the size of the inheritance I was to be blessed with before he died. Nor did it save her life. So, the least I can do now is to put it to effective use." Micah looked at Ezekiel who nodded.

"By saving Dibbledale?" his father asked.

"My dream is to help some of the injured soldiers who have returned from the war, if I can, and have them trained in some craft or skill. I cannot help them all, but locally there is a way that I believe I can assist some and that is dream enough for me. Dibbledale is unspoilt. It has all that is needed for many crafts. I would make Dibbledale synonymous with craftsmanship and quality. Use existing skills and teach others. Use the waterpower for a flour mill, buy arable land so that families can use it to grow their own food for themselves and the village; we can send any excess to the market. We will have a communal dairy herd, use wool to make high quality products for the wealthy. Buy in tanned leather from York and…"

"I can see you have many good and honourable ideas. It is an admirable dream, but can you make it happen?"

"Yes, if Bishop Denton had sold to me, I could have guaranteed its future use for generations to come."

"I am so proud of you, Micah," Ezekiel said. "You are my only child, but I could not have asked God for a more caring one. I am going to Thurley Manor now as I must impart the news regarding Mr. Skaggs to Sir Benedict. The man made me promise."

"Then I shall accompany you," Micah said.

"Very well," Ezekiel said. "Micah, the detail in any plan is so important for that is where the devil is, and you need God to be there. If you start too many ideas off all at once, you may see your dream doomed to fail. Plan your stages, make a firm root at the centre, and grow it from there."

"You are quite correct, and the fire of the forge will be where my plan begins. Thank you for your support, Father. I may well need a steady hand to steer my enthusiasm. Besides, I think the church needs some work doing on it also," he said and smiled as he saw his father do likewise.

"What of Miss Underwood?" Ezekiel queried.

"Let us deal with the immediate problem now," he replied as they approached Thurley Manor, then I can bring good news to her door, if she will douse her own fire and hear me out. Part of my dream is to ensure that Imogen will be at my side."

Chapter 37

The two men rode in companionable silence as they entered the drive to Thurley Manor, reining in behind a coach.

"Lord Farrington's," Micah said, as he nodded to the crest on the door.

"I wonder why his lordship is calling?" Ezekiel said as he slid down effortlessly from his saddle.

Micah shrugged. "We shall see," he replied.

Ezekiel approached the footman who greeted them politely. "Could you tell Sir Benedict that Reverend Mr. Arrow has some urgent news he wishes to impart to him? Please pass on my apologies if my arrival has clashed with guests, but this matter is important."

The footman showed them into the hallway where they waited to be summoned.

Micah's attention was taken by the excited voice of Miss Donaldson that drifted out of the morning room. A man appeared in the open doorway, curious to see who had arrived.

"Julian! Where are you wandering off to?" Miss Donaldson appeared at his side. "Ah! Reverend and Mr. Arrow, how lovely of you both to call. Please come in and meet my brother, my mother should be down again within the hour!"

"We would love to, Miss Donaldson, but I am afraid I must speak with Sir Benedict as soon as possible. However, Micah, please go ahead." Micah's father patted his back, so Micah joined the other guests keen to discover what Farrington was doing there.

"Arrow, join us," Lord Farrington said, as Micah appeared within the room.

Ezekiel was ushered into Sir Benedict's study. The door closed.

Micah reflected that Miss Donaldson's smile was genuine and infectious, she had what her heart desired. Her pathway back to her beloved estate, the life she was born to was suddenly clear. It seemed that another pawn in Sir Benedict's power game had been removed.

"Lord Farrington managed to pull a few strings and help Julian's return along by a few weeks. Mother is resting upstairs. She is so happy to be back in England and for us all to be reunited." Miss Donaldson stepped close and momentarily rested her hand on his arm. "I am so sorry to disappoint you, but you will understand. Now, excuse me, gentlemen, I must make sure that she does not need anything." She swept out of the room; a good deal lighter in spirit than when Micah had last seen her.

"Again, I give you my thanks, Farrington," Julian said. "I can't wait to return to normal life. It has been a dammed deal too long since we were a family." With a polite nod to Lord Farrington and Micah, Julian followed his sister.

Micah walked over to Lord Farrington. "You organised this?"

"There is more than one way of bringing a man down, Arrow," he said quietly. "In chess you remove the pieces the King and Queen rely on until you have the key pieces where you want them."

Micah raised an eyebrow.

"He depended on Skaggs to implement his scheme – the man's contacts, his knowledge of tanneries could be brought in but that would take time. He depended on Miss

Donaldson to entice you out of your fortune; he now must hand her and the funds back that Julian Donaldson placed with him to look after her. In short, he now is a much poorer man and as his accounts are in a weakened state, he shall not be able keep leasing Thurley Manor. Trouble shall be vacated from this place once more. Call the place tainted if you will, it is how the people behave within its walls that determine it and their fate."

"Were you involved in Skaggs'... downfall?" Micah asked softly.

"I was miles away. Someone tipped off the yeomanry that there was a meeting of smugglers happening right under their noses." He sipped his port and smiled. "Good stock this."

"So, who does own this manor?" Micah was curious.

"Why, I do, Lieutenant. I recently purchased it as an investment for future generations and with it the tract of woodland that goes from it to Dibbledale. I have ordered the blasted man traps removed too. There has been much work done to make the Manor pleasant enough to live in. I shall look for a tenant or sell it on."

Micah considered this news as an idea dawned. "It is a fine place. Just needs to be loved and used for good."

"You are a dreamer at heart, Arrow. Brave but your head is governed by honour, duty and love."

Micah ignored this comment. He had been a good soldier. "But the bishop would not sell that land to me. I went to see him like you said. He nearly threw me out."

Farrington laughed... "He can be difficult. Denton explained to me that he could not sell to you or anyone because he had set it up to secure a loan from his cousin, so, on further investigation I discovered it had been left in the hands of his solicitors. You arrived before I did and well, you had already ploughed in, before I could calm his mind and get to the bottom of it. Age does peculiar things to people. His Grace was once so astute. His cousin, a barrister in York, now maintains Netherton for him. He can reside there as long as he needs to, with a small, dedicated staff. However, I was going to break this news to you once I had dealt with my 'tenant'." He chuckled, as Micah stared blankly at him.

"Would you rent the estate to me… or sell it, at a profit? It could be the centre that I dreamed of making, my home and a hub of skills." Micah wondered if he had asked one favour too far, but Lord Farrington already owned property and had a home of his own.

He considered, and said, "Excellent idea, we shall talk later."

"How can I ever repay you?" Micah asked.

"You saved my life, man. It is a debt now repaid."

"It never needed repaying, sir. It was my honour and duty. I have exciting times ahead of me, no small part of that is due to you."

Lord Farrington cocked his head to listen. Sir Benedict's voice could be heard in the vestibule. "Put the past behind us." He waved Micah away to join his father.

"Reverend Arrow this is a damnable business," Sir Benedict was saying. He looked downcast and anxious. His previous bombastic presence had left him. "Jethro must have been caught in the crossfire; I'll be bound. Still, some men are born with luck, others not so." He glanced up at his graceful wife as she descended the stairs. Her smile seemed more genuine than when Micah had seen her at the dinner.

"Have you heard our good news, gentlemen?" she asked, and her husband looked sheepishly up at her as she stopped two steps up from the hallway.

"And what would that be?" Ezekiel asked. "We could certainly do with some," he added.

"We are returning with Beatrice and her mother to Wiltshire. We shall be one big happy family. You must excuse me; I have guests to see to and much to arrange." She finished her descent and made her way into the drawing room.

Sir Benedict shrugged. "We leave at the end of the week. Sorry, lad, you will have to fumble your own way through society. It won't be easy; they do not like new money. Try your luck in the new cities of manufacture in the west."

"No, he won't. He has me to guide him if needed," Lord Farrington said from behind the Arrows.

Sir Benedict stood straighter and stared back. "Your hand is in this somehow, Farrington, don't think I am unaware of that. One day some of your meddling will come back to haunt you!" Sir Benedict snapped. "Go, back to your lair, man, and leave me to lick my wounds."

Ezekiel stood forward between the two men who faced each other, Lord Farrington composed as always.

"Take your boy and leave a man to enjoy his last few days in his own home," he said and slammed the door of the study shut behind him as he retreated.

"Come, gentlemen, our welcome here has passed by," Ezekiel said as the three made their way outside.

Micah stopped and looked back at the Manor from the bottom of the steps up to the front door.

Lord Farrington ascended the step into his carriage. "What shall you call it, Arrow?" he asked after lowering the window.

"The answer to a prayer," Micah laughed. "I do not know, we shall have to see."

The three went on their way. Where to begin to explain all this to Imogen?

Wilfred, Mary and Pickles had eventually joined Imogen and Ruth as they made their way back to the vicarage. Wilfred had wanted to see this transformation with his own eyes.

Imogen heard their horses before she saw them and instantly announced, "Micah and his father return!"

Ruth's head shot around as she squinted at the two blurred figures just coming into sight along the lane. "My you have such good eyesight, Imogen!"

Mary nudged Imogen in her side and shook her head. Imogen mouthed a silent 'sorry' to her mother, delighted that she now spoke openly to Ruth Arrow.

Micah dismounted quickly and entered the church grounds making straight for Imogen. He hesitated momentarily until Imogen's eyes met his. Micah stepped forward and swept her up into his arms before acknowledging his mother. Once Imogen's feet were back on firm ground, he kept one arm around her waist as he glanced from Mary to Ruth.

"This is indeed a day for miracles!" Reverend Arrow declared.

"Do not blaspheme, Ezekiel," Ruth chided. "Don't they look a handsome couple."

Mary, speechless, nodded, her eyes laughing.

"Bloody hell!" Wilfred said, as he leaned against the church gate, proudly wearing a clean freshly ironed, starched shirt, which showed under his tweed waistcoat and breeches.

Mary hugged him close.

"Sorry! I mean what a lovely sight," he said, and winked at Ruth who blushed.

"Why don't we take a walk to the village, and we will tell Mrs. Weeks and all of you the good news, that Dibbledale is saved and then we can plan our future together privately." Micah said as he looked down into Imogen's eyes. "Wilfred, I would have you meet Jamie and agree a start date for Dan."

Wilfred nodded but Micah realised his exuberant welcome had not been returned by Imogen.

"You go on, we shall catch up," Micah said and waited before he spoke again to Imogen who, with arms folded, stared at him.

"Why so angry with me, Imogen?" he asked as Ezekiel shepherded the rest of the group to discreetly move away towards the village.

"You were married, widowed, befriended me, and then flirted with Miss Donaldson, yet you claim to have your destiny entwined with mine. What am I to believe?" she rallied.

"Yes, I was. I thought of you many times but was certain you would have been snapped up whilst I was away. We had not exchanged words promising each other anything. She needed a father for her baby, and I needed someone to care for and, I hoped, would in time, love. I had been at war, seen horrendous things, but Carolina died in childbirth. Miss Donaldson merely toyed to her own ends, I had no interest in her, but she made it quite plain she preferred her horses to the attention and commitment of a man. I wished her well. I did not prefer or desire her in the least."

He leaned into the gate, the sun on his back as the light lowered.

"And your wealth? When were you going to trust me with that knowledge?" she asked.

"When it was truly mine, for until Lord Farrington finalised the arrangements, I did not dare believe my plans could be realised." Micah detailed how Dibbledale would be a centre of craft excellence and help the wounded regain their lives. He leaned over her and asked, "Will you forgive me for not sharing all with you earlier. I never intended to hurt you. I just wanted everything to be arranged before I raised our hopes. But never doubt me, Imogen, you stole my heart years ago. War created an insurmountable barrier to my intention to court you back then. But there is nothing now to stand in our way."

"I knew you could do it. I didn't doubt you!" she said, her tone softening.

"Really?" he whispered.

"Really!" she whispered back.

"Not even when you heard me declare that I married a woman in Portugal?" he added.

"How did you know it was me?" Imogen asked.

"You think you are the only one who has gifts, Imogen? I worked it out after you dismissed me in the village. Yet you and I had a meeting of our spirits before I left this land, and we were drawn back to each other as soon as I returned. Now, I would make all our dreams come true. He looked back at the church and then into her wide-open beautiful eyes. "Marry me, be at my side as we build a community that can breathe fresh air, heal the wounds that are not visible to the eye for men who have suffered long, and create a place that children can grow healthy within?" He drew her into his embrace, and openly kissed her.

"Micah!" Ezekiel's voice shouted back to them as he had hung back and let the ladies and Wilfred walk on ahead.

Micah laughed but it had broken their moment of intimacy.

That moment had begun to stretch out, both completely lost in each other as the intensity of feelings deepened. Imogen felt so alive, so happy and driven that she had forgotten where they were. She could have happily taken him into the woods there and then and given her all to him, and he to her.

Micah pulled his head away, his eyes sparkling with joy.

"Yes, Father," he said, his smile so wide.

"You will be married in church. I would be happy to officiate," he offered. "Sooner rather than later, my son!"

"That would be delightful, but he has not asked me yet, sir," Imogen said.

"Yes, Imogen, he just did, and you just accepted." Ezekiel returned to Ruth.

Imogen stared up at Micah who was still smiling. "Did you?"

"Don't you know, Imogen?"

She winked at him. "Did you understand my answer, then?" she asked.

"Definitely and your desire will be fulfilled very soon. Thurley Manor will be our home and it too will be used for the good of those who return. Your mother will have the biggest garden she could ever wish for and people to share her knowledge with. Your father can use some of the outbuildings for his trade and apprenticeship school. You will have anything you need to make your jewellery shine and I will have everything I dreamed of and more, with you." He laughed at her shocked expression.

"How?" she said.

Taking a step away, Micah rapidly explained his thinking and what Thurley Manor meant for his plans.

"It will be the beating heart of Dibbledale's resurgence. We shall talk as we walk, but I am glad you do not see everything, my little wood nymph, or there would be no surprises, and I aim to give you plenty of them from this day forth."

Imogen moved up to him and they embraced, their world comprising of them totally lost in the moment of bliss.

Together they began to walk towards the village.

When they caught the others up, Imogen kissed Micah's cheek, then ran to her father and gave him a big hug.

"All will be well, Father, Micah has seen to it!" she exclaimed.

"Aye, lass, I never had a shadow of doubt that he would, but every shadow needs light to form it, and you, girl, are his beacon!"

Imogen stared at him as he and Mary exchanged knowing looks.

"Go to your man, Imogen, and I shall look after mine." Mary looked to Micah who opened his arms for Imogen to join him.

A Note to the Reader

Thank you so much for reading Secrets. I hope you enjoyed it.

Secrets is book 2 in the Friends and Foes trilogy. The first book being Betrayal. Both books could be read as stand-alone novels, but references are made to the action in the preceding book. There are recurring characters within the books whose past would be useful to know.

This book is set in 1816. The Peninsular Wars had finally come to an end and society was facing soldiers hoping to return to their previous lives, but machines were increasingly being used and agricultural workers found there was no longer a demand for their employment. The growing cities found families squeezed into tiny accommodation, often shared, with little work and disease and hunger were prevalent. Injured soldiers struggled to work or support their families and had to turn to begging or/and crime.

Society had not forgotten the effects of the French Revolution and mutterings of unrest among the 'common folk' were met with great unease and very little understanding! The Jacobite threat was still in people's memories and Ireland was a hotbed of sedition and unrest. All of this made people like Lord Oscar Farrington, trusted and wily, experienced men, invaluable to the authorities as a source of information and control.

Book 3 will follow Lord Oscar Farrington and his family's lives a little further. I hope to meet you there in

'Silent Revenge'. If you would like to learn a little more about his lordship, and information about the setting and times, then please visit my website: www.valerieholmesauthor.com

Lastly, I always enjoy discovering my readers thoughts so please post a review on Amazon about your experiences with this book. They are hugely helpful and much appreciated!

Thanks,

Valerie